The Magnificent Agony

A Love Story

BARBARA ANN BARRETT

THE MAGNIFICENT AGONY
A LOVE STORY

iUniverse books may be ordered through booksellers or by contacting:

iUniverse
1663 Liberty Drive
Bloomington, IN 47403
www.iuniverse.com
1-800-Authors (1-800-288-4677)

ISBN: 978-1-4917-5732-1 (sc)
ISBN: 978-1-4917-5734-5 (hc)
ISBN: 978-1-4917-5733-8 (e)

Library of Congress Control Number: 2014922703

Printed in the United States of America.

iUniverse rev. date: 01/16/2015

To my husband
for encouraging me
You are simply my best moment
my happiest laughter
my most tranquil sleep
You are my everything, my all—
You will always have my hand to hold
Always ...

And for all those who
Loved her ...

Contents

THE FIRST VISIT

One 3
Two 8
Three 20

THE COMMODORE'S BALL

Four 29
Five 34
Six 39
Seven 51

THE INQUISITION

Eight 57
Nine 66

THE MORNING AFTER

Ten 75

Eleven 89
Twelve 99

THE AGONY AND THE ECSTASY

Thirteen 107
Fourteen 111
Fifteen 113
Sixteen 118

THE THIRD VISIT

Seventeen 123
Eighteen 133
Nineteen 136

THE INTERROGATION

Twenty 149
Twenty One 159
Twenty Two 162
Twenty Three 179

THE PHONE CALL

Twenty Four 193

THE CONFRONTATION

Twenty Five 203

THE ARRANGEMENT

Twenty Six 215
Twenty Seven 225
Twenty Eight 230
Twenty Nine 235

THE MÉNAGE À TROIS, PLUS ONE

Thirty 239

Thiry One 247

Thiry Two 251

Thirty Three 257

Thirty Four 262

Thrity Five 265

Thirty Six 273

THE PILATES CLASS

Thirty Seven 279

Thirty Eight 287

Thirty Nine 289

THE SECOND CHANCE

Fourty 297

Fourty One 306

Fourty Two 310

Fourty Three 315

THE GOOD LIFE

Fourty Four 321

Fourty Five 326

The First Visit

One

everly Edwards backed her Pacifica station wagon out of the driveway of the big gray and white Cape Cod that sat high atop Ridgecrest Drive and headed down the hill toward the village. The large two-story house that overlooked the bay and the mile-long spit that separated it from the ocean was on California's beautiful Central Coast almost exactly halfway between Los Angeles and San Francisco. The climate was moderate year-round, with just the right amount of rain and fog to break the monotony of the otherwise year-round perfect weather.

As an amateur chef de cuisine—a title loosely derived after completing a weeklong course at the famous Le Cordon Bleu Institute in Paris—Beverly loved to cook. Not only was it her hobby but also her passion, and she had recently discovered a new recipe for "triple death by chocolate" brownies that she intended to try out on Davenports. She and Jack had made a host of new friends since moving to the small town several years ago, but none was closer than or as intimate as Susan and Ted Davenport.

She followed the winding road that led down the hill and

provided fabulous views of towering Morro Rock, from which the small fishing village took its name, and the expanse of ocean beyond. Depending on the season, there were frequent sightings of deer, and quail and an occasional flock of wild turkeys. The narrow roadway was nearly deserted this time of day until she turned off onto Main Street where the Davenports had a comfortable home on a wide corner lot. The place was on a quiet, tree-lined street just two blocks up from the beach and situated in one of the cozier parts of town.

"Hello! Anybody home?" Beverly entered through the garden gate and had called out after knocking on the kitchen door and letting herself in as she usually did. She heard a TV on somewhere inside.

"Come in, come in! Who is it?"

She heard Ted's baritone voice and looked around. "Hi, it's me. I brought over some goodies. Where are you?" she said and sat the plastic container of freshly baked brownies she had prepared for them on the granite countertop.

"Ah, the People's Choice! In here, my dear! Come in, come in. Sue's stepped out. She'll be back."

Ted's spirits lifted and he felt a slight edge of excitement when Beverly entered the room. She was wearing designer jeans and a dark velour sweatshirt that clung to a figure that caused men to stare at her wherever she went, and women to glare enviously, instantly on guard, disliking her immediately. At five-feet ten, she was taller than most women, had a slender figure, and weighed not much more than she had in high school. She had large expressive eyes that were as dark as roasted chestnuts. Her features were soft and feminine with a straight Roman nose and she often wore a mysterious Mona Lisa-like smile that made you wonder what she was thinking. Her silky hair fell in soft swirls just above her shoulders and was the color of burnt-honey with subtle highlights running through it. Her perfect makeup completed the classy image and Ted knew she liked the way it all went together. Beverly knew from the way he undressed her with his eyes that he liked it too.

Beverly smiled briefly at the compliment when she found him on the sofa in the living room watching the sports channel. He was in his usual cotton sweats, complete with the UC Berkeley logo where he had been the head swimming coach until his recent retirement. He had a thick mane of silver hair, iceberg-blue eyes, and the lithe physique of a serious swimmer and a former Olympic champion.

"Where's Sue?" Beverly asked brightly as she entered the large tastefully furnished room. Susan possessed an outrageous personality that had attracted Beverly from the moment they met and she had quickly become the big sister Bev never had. The room was filled with expensive antiques from the upscale shop Susan had opened when she retired from the movie business, ending her Hollywood career after winning an Oscar for best supporting actress for her last film that had garnered no fewer than four Academy Awards that year. She was past the age of being offered the leading roll in her next film and decided to quit gracefully—when she was on top.

"Sue's out. She'll be back later. Off to the club for a meeting of the dance committee and bridge afterward, I think she said. The Commodore's Ball is coming up." He did not get up but patted the cushion next to him. "I hope you and Jack are still going. Sue's reserved a table for us."

"I think I've talked him into it," Bev said with a doleful look. With Susan gone, she did not intend to stay, but sat down briefly. Ted leaned over with his usual peck on the cheek.

Ted had never hidden the fact that he thought Beverly gorgeous or that he was attracted to her. He had even confessed that he had hopelessly fallen in love with her. And he often displayed his affection in the form of a full-body hug when the opportunity presented itself, an occasional kiss on the lips if she failed turn her head in time and a rare pat on the fanny when Susan was out of the room. But she had never been offended by his display of affection, and since he was at least twenty years her senior, she suspected that his age had something to do with it. Still, she smiled inwardly when the look on his face said differently, that there might be more on his mind than benign fatherly affection.

"How are you and Jack getting along these days, my dear?" Ted gave her shoulder a friendly pat and reached across her with the remote control to turn off the TV, his forearm lightly brushing the swell of her breast as he did. "You two still having problems?"

Beverly felt a slight tingling where he was touching her and then a pang of guilt when she hesitated too long before shifting her weight, causing him to withdraw his arm. Lately, however, she was not so sure if her guilty conscience was because she was a married woman, or if it was because Susan was her best friend.

"Not much change," she said after a moment. "Actually, sometimes I think he cares more about work than he does me." She had casually mentioned the problems she'd been having with Jack in the past, but not recently and glanced at him. "Has Susan said anything to you about Jack and me?" The two women shared everything. But she hoped her personal life was still just between the two of them.

"Not much, actually," Ted said. There was no guile in his handsome face, but there never was. He was as easy to read as an open book. "Only that you haven't been getting along for a while and it hasn't gotten any better the last I heard. I just wondered if that meant ..."

She looked up again when he hesitated. "Meant what?"

"You know, meant that you weren't sleeping together." He grinned awkwardly now that he had stepped across that unseen line that formed the boundary between friendship and something more.

They held each other's gaze for a moment while Beverly decided how to answer. "Yes, we still sleep in the same bed," she said finally, deciding to be honest and tell it like it is, but not elaborate and to tell him that was about all they had been doing in bed lately. Their love life had not been all that great lately and she was happy to see that Susan had apparently not discussed that part of her personal life with him.

Ted's smile held as he casually rested a hand on her knee and gave it a gentle squeeze. "I wish there was something I could do to help. It must be hard for you. I don't like to you see you unhappy, my dear. You know I've been secretly in love with you from the first time we met." His look was one of friendly concern, but there was also something more.

Beverly had always felt comfortable with Ted and liked being with him, but they had rarely been alone together. And this wasn't the first time he'd said he was in love with her. Still, the shadow of a smile crept into her face with the obvious double meaning. She'd bet he wished there was something he could do for her, she thought, and decided to test his playfulness with a little of her own.

"I could tell Jack how friendly you've been lately. Or I should say *overly* friendly." Just in case the veiled threat and what was showing in her face wasn't enough, she removed his hand from her leg. "And he carries a gun, remember?"

In the past, she had mentioned Ted's affectionate behavior to Susan, who said she thought his age might be catching up with him since he had shown little or no interest in sex lately. In fact, she had confessed, it had been more like living with her brother than her husband for nearly a year. But Bev wondered if something hadn't changed all that. She noticed lately that when he gave her one of his affectionate hugs, there was definitely something very firm between them.

"I just wish there was something I could do to help, that's all," Ted said in his own defense and smiled at the threat. "But I don't see any reason to say anything to Jack, my dear."

Two

One night Beverly had mentioned Ted's growing affection to Jack when they had returned home from one of their three-martini dinners where she had caught him ogling the young woman who had waited on them.

It had taken a full fifteen minutes for her to fully relate the details of how Ted sometimes kissed her on the mouth instead of on her cheek as he usually did. She told him about the hungry looks he gave her if Susan happened to step out of the room, how he occasionally touched her leg or brushed against her breast, and the intimate way he spoke to her if they were alone for a few moments.

Jack had listened quietly to the account, knowing that three martinis was her absolute limit, and wondered if it was the gin that was causing her to be so chatty. But he had noticed her glaring at him at dinner as he watched the waitress clear their table, and wondered if Ted wasn't retribution for his bad table manners.

When she finished her story he said, "Ted's always had a thing for you. But it sounds like you might be leading him on by putting up with his hanky-panky. Or have you all the sudden taken an interest in Ted Davenport?"

Bev had just given him a blank look that did not really say how she felt. "Well, how about it, which is it?" he asked more seriously. "Are you all the sudden attracted to him? From what you've just said, you apparently don't mind him copping a feel once in a while." But there was no denying that the thought of what she had just told him was beginning to aggravate him.

"What if I was?" she said. The three martinis she'd had for dinner were making it easy to be honest and she paused just long enough to make him think she might be serious. "Not that I've actually thought about him—like that," she added, trying to blunt her honesty. "But he's certainly attractive." She knew her answer would not escape the curious mind and suspicious nature of the ex-cop turned PI she was married to. In fact, she was counting on it.

"I'm sure you mean for an older guy." Jack had no idea how old Ted was, only that he was definitely too old for Bev.

She bristled when he put words in her mouth. It was one of the things she had come to resent most about him lately. "That's *not* what I meant at all," she corrected him sternly. "If you want the truth, I think Ted is ..." She paused, purposely fueling the fires of suspicion in him again, adding to his discomfort.

"Think he's what?"

"Sexy, if you really want to know. Very sexy, in fact. And I think the feeling's mutual. He calls me 'The People's Choice,' and said he's in love with me." The seeds of doubt she had been sowing since starting the conversation were bringing to show up in his face.

Jack was sitting on his side of the bed and half turned to face her when he saw that she was staring at him. "Maybe he just wants to get in your knickers," he said, his irritation no longer confined to just his expression but showing up in his voice now as well.

She could tell he was beginning to wonder why she had even brought up Ted Davenport in the first place. Actually, the idea had come to her at dinner when she caught him leering at their young waitress, who had failed to use the customary "Bunny Dip" when she cleared away his place setting. The view down her low-cut blouse was matched only by the oily look on her otherwise pretty face when she saw him gaping at her; making it obvious the gesture was on purpose and not simply a breach of etiquette. Bev had shot them an icy glare they were both too busy to notice. Her story about Ted's escalating affection was simply payback time.

"I'm sure that's exactly what was on his mind," Bev said answering his question, certain that it would further agitate him.

"And what makes you so sure?"

She could only imagine the havoc his over-active imagination was causing him at that moment. Then, in retaliation for his voyeuristic table manners, she said, "He's a man, that's what. And it's exactly what you think about whenever a woman happens to show a little cleavage."

The frown on his face deepened at her suggestion that all men were lechers—all the time, anyway. "First of all, cleavage doesn't just happen on its own, Bev. It's on purpose, by God. And of course that's what we have on our mind. Because it's exactly what women want us to think when your boobs are hanging out all over the place."

"That's not only a sexist thing to say, Jack, but it's chauvinistic as well." Then, less defensively, she said, "Why do men make such a big thing over boobs?"

"How the hell should I know?"

"Well, don't tell me that's not exactly what you were thinking tonight when you were looking down that little tart's blouse at dinner. You were practically drooling all over her while she made goo-goo eyes at you the whole time."

An attack of male guilt flashed over him. "What I was actually thinking about was whether or not I should thank her or just add a little something extra to the tip," he said stiffly. "And, just in case you hadn't noticed, she was a little young." He tried to make eye contact with her but she wouldn't look at him. "Any guy beyond high school would probably get twenty years in the slammer for just thinking about something like that," he groused back, sounding like a cop again.

"Tits is tits," she clucked at him flippantly, dismissing his explanation and her poor English at the same time, still miffed, no matter what he said.

"So, is that what you think we have on our mind all the time?"

"If you mean *sex*, yes. That's exactly what I think. We can tell what's on your mind when you get that dumb look on your face." Beverly shrugged, as if it really did not matter what she thought; men were men, they were all that way when it came to the opposite sex, and that's just how it was.

Jack shook his head. He wasn't about to win a battle that had been raging since Eve ate the Apple. And since he had already been accused of being a sexist, he decided to take a more direct approach. "So, does that mean you want to fuck Ted Davenport?"

Beverly twitched inwardly and looked directly at him now with a defiant expression, knowing he was trying to shock her. It wasn't exactly what she expected, but she wasn't shocked either and decided to retaliate.

"What if I said, yes?" she shot back, just as flippantly as he had given. Then a more provocative thought popped into her head. "Ted's enough to make any woman curious."

"Like how—?"

"Like … well, like big." She suppressed a vengeful grin.

Jack knew she was playing with his mind now but bristled just the same. "Would you like to tell me how the hell you know that? I hope to Christ he hasn't been waving it around the room at you. Has he?"

She dared not crack the smile that was lurking just below the sober look on her face and aimed directly at his wounded ego. "As a matter of fact, he didn't have to. Susan told me. She says he's hung like a mule. And—" She purposely demurred, as if she had caught herself just in the nick of time, sure that it would add to his frustration.

"And *what,* for God's sake?" His voice rose, challenging, when she did not finish.

Beverly donned the half smile she often gave him when she wanted him to think she knew more than she really did. "And … well, sometimes it's obvious," she said finally. "You can see it. Down there." Her look said she was giving up a major secret normally shared only between women. His brow arched questioningly, his green eyes flashed, shooting daggers at her. "He has this, this bulge—sometimes."

"Jesus H. Christ, Bev!" he protested. "That's obscene! The man is old enough to be your goddamned father, and he's parading around with a … like that, in front of his wife's best friend? For God's sake! That's going too far. Not only that, but apparently you've been staring at his goddamned crotch to boot."

It was a weak attack, but she realized it was probably the best he could come up with about Ted on such short notice. In the years they had been friends, Jack never had a reason to dislike him—until now.

"I just said it's hard not to notice when … that happens, when he gets like that." The ghost of a smile lingered on her face, the reason for it all too obvious. "And what does his age have to do with anything?" Her expression turned impish, meant to aggravate him even more, and was doing a good job of it from the look of him.

"Does this happen just around you? Or does he show off in front of all your friends—that women's social club you belong to?"

"How should I know? What a silly question. Does it really matter?" she said, as if *she* wasn't reason enough to cause such a display.

"Maybe it does," he answered testily. "So, what we're talking about here is this old guy, with a big schlong, that apparently turns you on. Is that it?"

"Which one?"

"For Christ's sake, Bev, knock it off and give me a break. Any one of them, damn it. All of them!"

Beverly inwardly braced herself, took a breath, and stood her ground. "To be honest, probably all of those." When she saw that he was about to snap at her again, she cut him off. "I've already said I think Ted is handsome ... well endowed, and he says he's in love with me. His age only makes it all a little more interesting as far as I'm concerned."

"Good God, why? He's—"

"I know—a little older," she said, cutting him off again. "But that's the whole point. I think a lot of women are attracted to older men." She hinted at a fantasy he apparently never thought she'd had before. "In the first place, there's a certain mystique about an older man. And, they're probably very creative, and patient and gentle. They know how to treat a woman. And in Ted's case, there's the other thing I mentioned. I suppose if you were to compare, it's probably a form of penis envy. But it's certainly a real plus—for a woman, anyway." She paused to give him an accusatory look. "I guess you could say all that's a pretty good turn-on."

When Jack muttered something under his breath that she could not understand, only that it sounded like an obscenity of some sort, she glared back at the sour look he was giving her with one of her own.

"So, what's this leading up to? Why are you telling me all of this?" he said, finally.

Bev was glad that he had not asked some of the questions any woman would have thought of, such as what she intended to do about Ted or how far she was prepared to let him go, since she really didn't know the answers herself. But the way Ted had been acting lately, her intuition warned her it was only a matter of time until the situation became more serious. Either she had to stop seeing the Davenports altogether, or ...?

The alternative caused a flash of doubt to creep over Bev. When it passed, she said, "I really don't think Ted would do anything stupid, if that's what you mean." However, she could not think of a reason why he should believe anything she said after the way she was goading him. "I'm sure he wouldn't hurt Susan like that."

"I'm not sure he could, or that it would even matter after all the sleeping around she's done." When Bev just shrugged, he said, "What about the other part?"

"You mean ..." She could not stop the tiny grin in time, the one that told him exactly what she was thinking. "Well, that would interest any girl with two hormones to rub together." She saw the look in his eyes as they flicked over her. "Of course, I've never had that much to compare it to," she said provocatively, even though she had never felt deprived, always considered Jack as above average. But in her limited experience, she wasn't even sure what *average* was. "Does it bother you, Jack, knowing that Ted says he's in love with me? Does it make you jealous?" She looked up at him innocently now, but not without a streak of guilt that caused a chink in her armor over some of the thoughts she'd been having about Ted Davenport lately.

"What if I was jealous?" he asked slowly. "Only natural when some guy's been waving his willy around in front of his wife." But his expression said it was more than that. "I wonder if we're both playing around with the truth a little, Bev." Jack paused and then added, "If you have sex with him—that is, *if* you could—would you tell me about it?"

"If I *could*? Huh! Listen to you!" she huffed at him, her voice kicking up several decibels, eyes riveted now, as if she hadn't already had such doubts on her own. Men weren't the only ones with an ego.

"Okay, okay!" he conceded, not wanting to argue, and decided from her reaction that all the talk about the size of Ted's privates was probably more wishful thinking than anything else. "If you do—or have—or what the hell ever?"

"So, which one are we talking about?"

"Damn it, Bev, come on. What do you mean 'which one'? Any of them. Before or after." She was really starting to get to him now.

Once again, Beverly purposely considered the question too long, making him even more suspicious, before she said, "I don't know. I'd have to think about it." She saw his brow knit, accusing her without saying a word. "Certainly, not before. That would be like asking permission. Maybe afterward. It all depends."

"Depends on what—?" His voice rose for the umpteenth time since she started on him. He still wasn't sure where this whole thing was going.

"—On what you consider having sex is," she said, fortified by the martinis that were still making her a little dizzy.

"Oh, that's great! Now you're beginning to sound like a certain president we used to have," he scoffed.

"And *you're* beginning to sound like a cop again," she shot back, firmly holding her ground. He was trying to bully her—again, but it wasn't working this time.

"All right—all right, I give up," he said, holding up his hands. "But it's definitely having sex if you sleep with him, right?"

"Duh," she taunted and covered her mouth to stifle a hiccup that tasted like Tangueray. She made a bitter face.

"And, unlike a certain unnamed politician, I think a blowjob is also having sex."

"Also agreed."

From his expression, it was plain that he had expected an argument out of her when he said, "So, what's left?"

"Oh, for God's sake, Jack, I don't know how you were a police detective for so long, let alone a private eye. I can think of all sorts of things, all the way from mutual masturbation, to fondling and groping, to just plain talking dirty."

He looked at her, an exasperated expression plastered all over him this time. "All right, okay, all those things. The question is, if

you did any of them with Ted—or anybody else for that matter—
would you tell me about it?"

She pretended to think about it, not really knowing what she
would do, but enjoying his discomfort. After all, this was payback
time. "Would you?" she said finally, answering his question with
one of her own as he often did to her. He gave her a look. "I don't
really know," she continued. "It depends on which one of them you're
talking about and how many martinis I've had when you ask me."
She knew the answer would irk him, and was surprised that smoke
was not pouring out of his nostrils by this time.

Jack said, "So what about Susan? She's supposed to be your best
friend, for God's sake. And you're talking about climbing in the sack
with her husband."

"And we've discussed that ... sort of ... just not in those exact
terms. My God, you make it sound so—almost evil." She grimaced
and shook her head. "But I'm not sure Sue would mind all that
much," she said, as casually as possible for what she was implying.
Bev forced herself to calm down while trying to decide how much
more punishment she intended to mete out. But she was delighted
with her decision to discuss Ted's behavior with him.

"Actually, I'm really not worried about you running off with
Ted Davenport," Jack said during a short lull, suspecting now
that she was avenging his behavior at dinner that evening. "So
it wouldn't be the end of the world if you wanted to sleep with
him—or have."

It was obvious that the last part was an attempt at rescuing his
ego, but she knew better. She suspected by this time he had a knot in
his stomach that was probably sloshing around in the pool of acid his
dinner had turned into, and he was trying to keep it from showing.
But Beverly wondered if perhaps she had gone too far and decided
to soften her approach.

"Just so there's no mistake, I think you should know that I really
don't want to sleep with Ted Davenport, though I think he'd jump

at the chance," she said honestly. "I know Susan doesn't do it with him anymore."

"I hope to God *she* told you that and not *him*," he said, his frustration obvious.

"Please ..." She looked annoyed. "Susan, of course—"

"Did she really say that?" He could not believe how women gossiped—about everything. "And it's beginning to sound like you're feeling sorry for the guy, which is hardly a good reason to jump in the sack with him."

"Maybe it's the motherly instinct women have." Beverly knew she was rationalizing now and possibly riling him up even more in the process. "We mostly just talk about things. But in Susan's case, I guess she pretty much did whatever it took. My God, it got her Best Supporting Actress."

"If you can believe the woman, she screwed every swinging dick in Hollywood to get it," he said flatly, though it was no skin off his nose. In the past when they had been out together, Susan had hinted at some of her philandering, and he wondered why Ted had stayed with her all of these years if even half of them were true.

"But she's never tried to hide it, not from me, anyway. And, of course, Ted knows about it, what she's done, and it doesn't seem to bother him too terribly. She left him once. Ran off for almost a year with the co-stare in one of her movies."

"Love is a Many Splendored Thing,*"* he added, having already heard the story. It was the only one of the dozens of movies Susan had made that he could remember seeing, and the supporting role she'd played wasn't exactly *starring* in it, but she had won an Oscar for it and he didn't quibble.

Beverly nodded. "The point is, Tom didn't divorce her. He took her back. Not many men would do that for a woman—even a movie star." Her tone made it clear that the reference to Ted's devotion was aimed squarely at him. She looked at her husband curiously now as another thought popped into her head. "What do you think of Susan, by the way? Does she appeal to you—I mean like that? Even a little?"

The change in her expression matched the gravity of her question. She was asking him to admit that he was a healthy, male who harbored a few surreal thoughts from time to time about other women, which of course he was, and did. "Like what?" he hedged, not so much in self-defense as in being unsure of exactly what she was fishing for.

"You know very well like what. Like *that*. You've said before you thought Susan was attractive. I think it was her big boobs you were talking about."

"She does have a set of knockers, that's for sure. But like that? I mean ... sexually?"

"Come on, Jack, we've even talked about a threesome before. Several times, in fact," she said seriously. "It was one of the reasons we decided to leave LA."

She was referring to the New Years Eve party several years ago when they'd had way too much to drink and actually had sex in the same room with her brother and a client of his and their wives, who hinted at their willingness to make it a more permanent arrangement.

"So come on, I've told you about Ted. I was just wondering if you ever thought about Susan like that. Would you like to sleep with her?"

"You would ... with Ted?"

"I asked first."

Her checkmate caused a slight grin to show up in the corner of his mouth. "The last I recall, we decided against that sort of thing. In fact, if I remember correctly, the last time it came up you said if you ever found a man *or a woman* you were interested in, you'd let me know."

She wondered if that wasn't exactly what she was doing. Instead, she said, "That's because you were always talking about another woman. So, hypothetically, if we were to invite someone, Susan is very sexy. I wouldn't be surprised if you were attracted to her. And I suppose I shouldn't tell you this, but she said she thinks you're very handsome—gorgeous, I think was the word she used. So come on, be honest. Would you like to sleep with her?"

Unable to mask his surprise, he said, "She really talked about me like that, about having sex?"

"Not in so many words, only that she wouldn't say no to spending the night with you. But I don't think she has any plans to seduce you right away."

Jack grinned openly. "Susan is a beautiful woman, no doubt about it. I'm just not sure what we'd do with Ted during all this," he said, halfway answering her question.

She noticed, and a strange look came over her. "Something to think about," she answered slowly and wondered if perhaps the four of them might have more in common than she realized.

Three

everly's breath caught when Ted suddenly turned toward her and kissed her on the mouth, taking her by complete surprise. Her body tensed, but she did not pull away.

After a moment his lips parted, the tip of his tongue touching hers, and then cautiously went deeper. He took in her sweet breath, the warm scent of Chanel, and the taste of her saliva mixed with lipstick that caused a surge in him below his waist.

Beverly instantly felt the stab of excitement like an electric shock as his soft lips covered hers and his thick tongue slipped halfway down her throat. She felt his heat and the scent of Irish Spring, as if he had just stepped out of the shower. When he began to probe deeper, she nearly gagged in spite of the wave of anticipation that fluttered through her like a sheet of summer lightening.

She finally pulled back to catch her breath and stared into his glacier-blue eyes, her surprise obvious. She remembered Susan had once said it was a girl's prerogative to be naughty occasionally, and wondered if she would still feel the same way if she were here and knew what they were doing.

"How are you going to explain my lipstick all over your face when your wife walks in?"

Ted tried to mask his guilt with a crooked smile. He shifted his weight to accommodate the growing presence in his groin and licked his lips, the flavor of her intoxicating him even more. "She won't be home for hours." His heart was pounding. They had never gone this far and his mind began to fog with excitement and anticipation as he managed to fish a handkerchief out of his pocket. "Those bridge games go on for hours."

Beverly took the hanky from him, dabbed at the smudges on his square, handsome face until he was reasonably presentable again, and noticed how clear and unblemished his complexion was. "I wouldn't put this in the wash if I were you." She handed the stained hanky back to him. "We don't wear the same lipstick."

Ted shrugged and grinned sheepishly. He could feel her heat where they were touching, her heart beating nearly as fast as his, the swell of her breast pressed against his arm.

"You know we're acting like a couple of high school kids with a severe case of hormones, don't you? And Susan would kill both of us if she walked in right now, not to mention what Jack might do."

"I don't know about Jack," Ted said huskily, his breathing already shallow and irregular, "but Susan probably wouldn't say much. She said you've talked about us before—you and me, and she wasn't upset."

They had talked, and Beverly wondered just how much Susan actually told him. "What we talked about is *you*, and how friendly you've been lately. And I also mentioned it to Jack."

Ted twitched. "What did you tell Jack? We haven't done anything wrong—not really." His voice suddenly changed.

"Well, maybe you not think it's anything. But if you ever pinch me on the butt again ..." Beverly let the threat hang in the air while she settled back on the couch, patted her hair back into place, and tried to calm down. She knew she should get up and leave, but the excitement twirling around inside of her was bothering her in a strange way, leaving her to wonder how far he intended to go with this.

"And …?" Ted asked hopefully. "He wasn't upset?"

Beverly shook her head, wondering if she had misread him, why he was being so chatty after running his tongue all the way down her throat. "Sue and Jack aren't worried about us running off together, if that's what you mean." She found the idle conversation was making it a little easier for her to breathe, but also distracting. "Sue asked if I needed her to say something to you. I told her that I could handle it. And *you*." Beverly donned her Mona Lisa smile now, leaving him to wonder what else she was thinking. "And Jack says you're old enough to be my father, whatever that's supposed to mean."

He held her gaze for a moment. "Do you feel that way? You know I'm in love with you, Bev." His eyes twinkled at her with a mixture of hope and foreboding now that she had brought up the difference in their ages, something they had never discussed before and he had tactfully avoided until now.

Her own gaze was steady, unwavering. "What do you think— do I?"

He thought for a moment. "I guess that depends on how you feel—about me. Does it bother you that I'm … a little older?" The easy smile he was wearing vanished, but his eyes were still dancing with the emotional bridge they had just crossed. They had kissed before, but never like this, and never when they were alone.

"What bothers me is that we are both married," she said firmly, but her voice hinted at something else. "But, no, not really." She took in a deeper breath to help calm the jitters that had come over her. "I've never thought of it like that. I don't even know how old you are." She hesitated, struggling for a more appropriate answer, but there wasn't one. They had never discussed age in the past, but she knew it bothered him. And since the night when she talked to Jack about him, she had caught herself thinking more about it—and about *him*.

He moved closer, their lips mere inches from touching. "Then tell me how do you feel about an older man who is married to your best friend and happens to have fallen very much in love with you?" he said, barely breathing as he gazed into her large brown eyes, waiting for the answer they both knew would determine what happened next.

Beverly pulled back until she could focus on him and saw the uneasiness in his face. "I feel … I think you're … well, actually, a very interesting man who happens to be a little older, is all," she said, but knew it was a lot more than that, not really what she wanted to say, certainly not what she was feeling.

It was a stupid time for a grin, but he couldn't help himself. He had just asked her to go to bed with him, in so many words, and she thought he was *interesting*. "Is that it?" he said evenly. "You think I'm … interesting? Nothing else—?" He moved close enough to set off an electric spark between them. His hand settled on her upper thigh, feeling her heat.

"Well, I, if you must know …" She tried to breathe normally, but it was impossible. "I—I suppose you're, ah, rather handsome—for a father figure," she said nervously, trying to make light of what they were doing, leaving open the escape hatch she might need as they waded ever deeper into uncharted waters.

Beverly held his gaze, her heartbeat kicking up another notch, hardly believing the thoughts flashing through her mind. My God, her mind was in a whirl. She was not only a married woman, but he was her best friend's husband. She wasn't supposed to feel this way, not like this. But she had no control over the effect he was having on her.

"If you think I'm handsome, does that mean you also think I'm sexy—for a father figure?" He inched even closer, their bodies touching now.

There was no doubt what he meant. Did he appeal to her, at his age, that way? Good God! What was she thinking? But the truth startled her. She took a breathless moment to collect herself. "I ... I guess so, maybe. What if I did?" she said, leaving the question unanswered, but not really. She had seen the look on him before. He was undressing her with his eyes now, stripping her bare, piece by piece, but never after a kiss like that. She wondered if she was wearing the same look.

She was sure of it.

It was all the answer Ted needed and he kissed her again. Her lips parting first this time as she kissed him back. When his tongue went deeper than before, her head began to spin, her mind in a twirl.

Then Beverly froze.

Her heart skipped several beats when his hand slipped under her velour top and cupped one of her breast. She didn't know what she expected, but this wasn't it, and she clutched at his arm.

But it was a weak effort. She knew exactly what to expect. She squirmed as he caressed her through the lacy bra she was wearing, her nipples hardening under his touch. She pressed her nails into his arm now, the only protest she could manage, at first hoping he would stop, then hoping he wouldn't, or that Susan did not walk in and put an end to it.

Blocking both Susan and Jack from her mind and ignoring the alarm bells going off in her head, she curled an arm around his neck, stifling the gagging reflex deep down in her throat. His tongue was long and thick and filled her completely.

Suddenly, she went completely rigid.

Ted had moved his hand down over the bare flesh of her stomach, thumbed open the top button of her jeans, and slid the zipper all the way down. The first vestiges of panic overtook her, clouding her mind, making it impossible to think clearly. But it was more than fear that paralyzed her. What she felt building deep inside of her was as frightening as it was thrilling.

Then she stopped breathing altogether as he continued over the swell of her belly, fingers searching, probing, exploring, until he found what he was looking for. Time stood still and her heart began to beat wildly, and then seemed to stop altogether. Without thinking, she recoiled violently, gasping for air when he tried to force her down onto her back. She clutched his neck, trying to remain upright; knowing what would happen if she didn't. Then her breath ratcheted in her throat when he entered her. She tried to pull back, to push him away, but the emotional storm streaking through her prevented any escape, only surrender, as her hips uncontrollably arched upward to meet him.

Beverly had no idea how long she had laid limp in his arms, breathing heavily, when he finally withdrew his hand and placed it over the top of hers, guiding her down into his groin.

"Oh—my—God, Teddy …" Beverly gasped when she settled over the mass. She clutched it in both hands, as if to make sure it was real, roughly moving over him and glancing down at the same time to confirm what her senses had already told her was true. She pushed back at the trailing veil of fog her intense climax had left behind and was still clouding her mind, just as the throbbing enormity that stretched from his crotch nearly to his knee erupted beneath her marauding hands and kneading fingers.

A new respect for Susan suddenly came over her.

The
Commodore's Ball

Four

It was past six o'clock, and Beverly still was not ready.

When Jack entered the bathroom with Maggie Mae hot on his heels, he found Bev fresh out of the shower wrapped in a velour robe and seated at her dressing table amid the various tubes and jars of makeup that were forever a mystery to him.

He gave Maggs an affectionate pat, careful not to get her hair on his black, satin-striped trousers. "Dinner's at seven," he announced dryly, as if she may have forgotten the party she had spent nearly the entire day getting ready for. "If we hurry we can still make dessert." However, the way she had been acting lately, it came as no surprise when she ignored him.

Beverly had thought seriously of not going. It would be the first time the four of them had been out together since she and Ted started seeing each other. She did not like to think of Ted as an affair; it somehow made her feel unclean. She knew from the butterflies that had been flying around in her stomach all day that the evening would be more than difficult, at least until the martinis she intended to have kicked in. And she could not deny that the stress of keeping her secret from Jack and Susan had taken its toll, making her bitchy and hard to live with. She had seriously considered just accepting the consequences and telling Susan everything. After lunch earlier in the day while they were at the salon having their hair and nails done, would have been the perfect time. However, the butterflies had easily talked her out of it.

Annoyed that he was already fully dressed and standing there watching her, Beverly applied the final touches of the soft apricot blush she had chosen for the evening, stood up, and then leaned into the large magnifying mirror to make a tiny correction to her eyeliner before she said, "Give me a minute while I get dressed. And I wish you'd stop staring at me."

Jack looked away into the side mirror to adjust his black satin tie, which matched his vest. "That means we'll miss dessert, right?"

Glaring daggers, Beverly brushed past him, stormed into the large walk-in closet they shared that spanned the full width of the master bedroom, and slammed the louvered door hard enough to rattle the full-length mirror attached to the inside of it. She stood in front of it fuming for a moment, trying to calm down and collect her thoughts, before tugging at the belt of her robe. She caught her full reflection in her Victoria's Secret black-lace panties and matching bra and quickly checked for any telltale signs of cellulite. As usual, she liked what she saw. Her body was firm and tanned from top to bottom, and she discarded any earlier thoughts of wearing panty hose.

She slipped the new party gown she had bought just for the occasion over her head, being careful not to muss her hair. The clinging full-length dress was slit on the left side from hip to floor and revealed the entire length of one long, shapely leg. Then, a wicked thought popped into her head and she pulled out of the lacy panties, tossing them on the shelf. She had done this for Jack in the past and wondered if it was a turn-on for all men or if it was just one of his personal fantasies. Tonight, it was an overt act of defiance that she did not intend to mention to him.

Beverly tried to reach the zipper at the back of her dress, felt a stab of pain in her left shoulder, and reluctantly gave up. Entering the bedroom, she found Jack had put on his dinner jacket and was standing in front of the mirror arranging a burgundy silk pocket square in his breast pocket when she crossed the room and turned her back to him.

"Do you mind?"

He glanced at her over his shoulder at the patronizing tone, then turned to oblige. "Shoulder still bothering you?" he asked, remembering an earlier complaint and ogled her new gown for the first time, immediately noticing the strategic parts of her it was designed *not* to cover. She had been sullen and not very talkative lately, and when she shrugged off his comment, he changed the subject, trying a different approach.

"I'm surprised the price of this little number fit on your credit card." The expensive dress reeked of class and was beyond gorgeous—a black silk chiffon original that sounded like Rice Krispies when she moved in it, liberally dashed with sequins and rhinestones that could have just as well been dollar signs for what it probably cost.

Beverly knew it wasn't the money. It was just too revealing for his taste—but all of the right places for hers. "Business must be slow," she said sarcastically when he began to fiddle with the zipper, tossing a bored frown at him over her shoulder. He sometimes questioned the outrageous price tag that often went with her shopping sprees, especially the expensive things he could not write off as a business expense, but he never denied her. He could afford it.

Jack eyed the label before finishing the zip-up. "Dior," he said under his breath, expecting nothing less. His tone indicated that he had revised his original estimate and confirmed his suspicions of why she and Susan had driven all the way to San Francisco last week after their recent shopping trip to Santa Barbara a few weeks before. "I'll probably have to work overtime for this one."

"You haven't worked since you were a cop," she said dryly, dodging his meaning. It was common knowledge around town that he ran a successful PI business devoted mostly to a variety of Hollywood clients and she had never had to worry about price.

"Lucky for you," he sniped back.

"And screw you back, Jack," she said testily.

"A cop's pay used to be good enough for you."

"Right, and then I grew up." Her sarcasm proved that she was cruising for a fight. Even before she had started seeing Ted Davenport she had begun to resent him, the way he never seemed to have the time to do things together anymore, the business trips to LA or Vegas that kept him away for days on end while she sat at home alone or had lunch with the girls just for something to do. Now, not only did she feel trapped, but she was obliged to watch everything she said or did to keep from giving away the secret life she was leading when he was gone. Mostly, she resented the guilty conscience she was forced to haul around lately like so much excess baggage that was beginning to wear her down, and the foul temper it caused her to have at times.

Yeah, right, she thought more honestly. Like Ted was Jack's fault. On the other hand—? Maybe he was, she told herself.

Simple logic, however, told her that blaming it all on Jack was the easy way out. She knew, after all the excuses and self-denigration she had put herself through, that in the end it was of her own making. Still, not being able to see Ted had only served to frustrate her to the point of distraction. He had awakened something in her she had not felt in years, while at the same time prevented her from making love with Jack, since she couldn't think of a single way to hide the physical changes Ted had caused in her.

Beverly needed desperately to vent her problems, to get the leaden burden of guilt off her chest. Certainly, she couldn't confide in any of the girls in the Women Social Club she belonged to. She adored each and every one of them, but the caliber of such gossip was just to big to hold back. It would be all over town in a matter of hours. She wondered what Susan would say if she knew she had slept with her husband. She wasn't sure how she would react. Or, from some of the intimate things she had shared with her about Ted, if she would even care.

Five

The hotel was the biggest in town and sprawled over twenty acres of prime real estate with over a hundred rooms, a huge conference center, and a spacious ballroom in the main building adjoining a four-star restaurant. The entire complex was surrounded by lush green meadows and painted in a shocking hot pink. The excellent food and service and the uniquely decorated theme guestrooms—the urinal in the men's toilet, for example, sported a rock-studded waterfall that cascaded down one entire wall from floor to ceiling that made it difficult to concentrate on what you were supposed to be doing there—all added to the resort's charm and popularity.

The large ballroom was gorgeously decorated and packed with members of the yacht club and their guests for the annual Commodore's Ball. Bright bouquets of spring flowers and elegant candelabra graced each of the linen-covered tables. Men in tuxedos and women in elegant ball gowns crowded the dance floor and swayed to the mellow, sentimental music of the full twenty-piece orchestra.

By eleven thirty, dinner was long over, dessert cleared away, and Beverly was working on her third 007 of the evening—a double shot of Tangueray gin, one of vodka, a splash of dry vermouth, two large olives, with shaker ice on the side. She lightly shook her head to settle her perfectly coiffed hair around her shoulders, took the last sip of her drink, which was mostly ice water by now, and looked out over the crowded dance floor. Forever in charge, Susan had naturally insisted on boy-girl seating, putting Jack on her right, Ted to her left, and Susan across from her.

"Can I get you another drink, my dear?" Ted smiled, leaning toward Bev, the tone of his voice casual as he nonchalantly glanced down into the ample cleavage she was showing tonight, the naked image of her already etched in his memory.

Ted glanced at his wife, who was busily chatting with Jack. Her dress was outrageous in a fiery red, puffy taffeta, low-cut and saucy, exposing the fleshy tops of her very large breasts. Tons of bling and silver-sequined slippers completed her ensemble. He thought her strawberry-blonde hair was lovely if a bit too long for her age. He would never tell her that. But that was Susan, still playing the part of the movie queen, still turning heads of both men and women.

"That was my third, and I'm not responsible for my actions after two," Beverly replied, smiling through the effects of the martinis she'd already had that evening. At the moment, she was feeling no pain. Tomorrow would be another story.

"All the more reason for another, my dear," Ted said with a rakish grin. He had already signaled to the overly attentive waiter, who had earlier pocketed the sizable tip he had given him, and seemed to come from out of nowhere, placing a fresh martini in front of her. After the waiter had departed, Ted's fingers casually brushed her leg under the table where the slit in her gown exposed the long expanse of her thigh. When she did not react, he gingerly continued until he had confirmed what he had suspected after their first dance of the evening.

"Umm, I just noticed, my dear, I don't think you're wearing panties this evening," he said in a hushed voice, careful not to attract attention from across the table.

Beverly blocked his hand from its intended destination with her own. She glanced at Jack, but he was still engaged in chatter with Susan. Cautiously, she put down an impulse to scold Ted for the trespass. However, while the gin and vodka mixture had relaxed her, it had also dangerously raised her level of confidence and common sense told her that could mean trouble if she wasn't careful.

Chin in hand, her elbow on the able, Beverly turned slightly toward Ted. "I'm glad you didn't find someone else's hand—up there," she said, not needing to explain further or daring to use any names for fear of arousing attention. "What would you have done then?"

A grin instantly creased his face. "I guess I'd have to excuse myself and go to the restroom," he replied with a subdued chuckle, as if they were exchanging some pleasantry. "Does he, ah, that is, check you out like that, under the table?" Ted spoke in a guarded tone, his lips barely forming the words, twiddling his fingers as he did. Neither dared to look across the table, not sure of what was showing in their faces.

She returned his look in kind. Her eyelids were becoming heavy as she brushed his knee with her own. "He says it drives him crazy. Is that true?"

"So this was just for me?" The tips of his hidden fingers made it clear what he was referring to.

Surprised, she barely nodded and slightly shifted her weight to prevent any further intrusion. "Is it true?" she quietly insisted.

"I think that's putting it a bit mildly, my dear," he said with a noncommittal smile. Then, since he was already in the neighborhood, he lightly pinched the soft flesh of her inner thigh where he judged the little tattoo she had of a pussycat should be, knowing she hated that, but it was in retaliation for her moving out of range.

Beverly felt the tiny jolt of electricity, but kept it from her face. She hated to be pinched yet managed to smile sweetly at him through clenched teeth after swallowing the yelp that had nearly come leaping out of her on its own. "If you do that again, Teddy, I promise to pee all over your hand."

He grinned with satisfaction this time. "And ruin that beautiful dress? I don't think so. And I bet you wouldn't do that to ... ah ... you-know-who." He said casually, as if they were discussing the weather.

"Well—" She gave him back an inert smile. "It's your hand up my dress this evening, not ... umm ... his."

"You are being very naughty tonight," he whispered, his silent yearning showing on his face as well as somewhere else. His tone of voice said one thing, but his look another.

"Your wife says being naughty is a girl's prerogative."

"She's certainly proved that more than once," he groaned. Tonight he had purposely worn one of his old athletic supporters he had kept from his coaching days for just such an occasion, and was already putting it to good use. He had found early on in life that if he could keep what was often a cause of embarrassment for him at a young and impressionable age rained in, it wasn't as likely to get out of hand.

"I wish we could go somewhere," he said quietly, unable to completely hide the strain he was under. "You're so beautiful. I need you tonight."

"There's always a quickie in the car," she teased in a hush, knowing full well that Ted did not lend himself well to such frivolities, yet pleased with the way she affected him.

"And you-know-who has a gun, remember?"

"I'm not sure he cares enough to use it."

Ted tried to mask his surprise. He had thick white eyebrows, and they clicked up with the revelation. "And what do you propose we do with the other, ah ... you-know-who during all this? Let her drive while we make out in the backseat?" His grin was casual and pleasant, as if they were chatting about one of her new recipes.

"Invite her back?" Beverly teased again, batting her perfect cosmetically enhanced lashes at him. She took another sip of her fresh 007 when she noticed that Jack was staring at her from across the table while Susan jabbered on as if he were listening to her. She wondered if he was reading her mind, if what she was feeling was showing in her face, or if it was just her guilty conscience.

Ted caught the dangerous glances that flashed between them and immediately got up from the table. "Want to dance, Bev?" he said, coming to her rescue. Then he purposely looked over at Jack and Susan, who were both staring at them now, his face a blank chalkboard. "Care to join us, you two? Good music."

It was an oldie out of the sixties. Susan got up and automatically reached for Jack's hand. "I just love that song, don't you, darling?" she said, a little tipsy, showing the effects of one-too-many wines.

Six

everly took a sip of her drink and almost knocked over a water glass as she unsteadily got to her feet and followed Jack and Susan toward the dance floor, with Ted close behind. Her gown snapped, crackled, and popped with the provocative swaying of her hips, causing heads—that had just seconds before been fixated on Susan—to snap back as she passed, the women pretending not to notice, the men with approving smiles.

Beverly turned to face Ted when they reached the edge of the crowded dance floor and came together, their bodies perfectly matched. She lightly ran her fingers through the thick mop of silver hair at the back of his head before settling onto his shoulders to keep from falling off the four-inch stilettos she was wearing. Ted held her by the waist to steady her. When she had regained her balance, his hands settled lower on the curvy swell of her hips not to be noticed as they swayed to the satin strains of the music.

With their lips lightly touching, Beverly curled her arms around Ted's neck, their bodies clinging all the way down. Glassy-eyed, she pressed her hips into him and could feel the growing presence of him through the thin fabric of her evening gown as if she were already naked.

"Have you been sleeping with Jack since we, ah ...?" His voice trailed off as he checked the crowd around them, relieved to see Jack and Susan some distance away. Susan's arms were comfortably tucked around his neck, and he was politely holding her off by the waist.

"Would you be jealous if I was?" In her heels, she was slightly taller than Ted and lightly touched the tip of his nose with her own just as the music ended.

The band immediately struck up again and they began to sway once more to the romantic music. "Very much so," he said. "But you *are* married to the guy after all. And I guess there's not much I can do about that. But I have to admit that I've been feeling a little possessive lately. I know he's your husband, but since we ..." He nudged his lower body into her, letting the undeniable presence there, trussed as it was, finish the sentence for him.

"Since we *what*—?" she teased, feeling naughty and nudged him back when he did not finish, knowing exactly what he meant. The alcohol had lowered her defenses, and was making her tipsy.

"You know what I mean. When ..." he stammered, but again did not finish. He knew everyone had been staring at them since they left the table; the lucky-beyond-belief old fart with the tall, gorgeous woman who was dripping sex all over him. She was stunning in her provocative gown that did not begin to cover all of the strategic parts of her willowy figure, and the way they had been clinging to each other was enough to raise the most staid of brows.

Bev toyed with the ruffle on the front of his formal evening shirt, noticing that she had gotten a tiny smudge of lipstick on it. "Are you talking about the last time you screwed me silly," she said, loud enough to be heard over the music and nearly stumbled. Other nearby couples had cleared a small circle around them and many of them were glaring now. "Is that what you're talking about?" She stifled a hiccup and held on to him to maintain her balance.

Ted stiffened when heads turned to gape at them, once again, the men smiling, the women gasping for breath. "You never cease to amaze me, puss," he said with an embarrassed grin.

"That was better than ..." She hiccupped this time, the taste of gin strong, her eyes fluttering dreamily, "... than the first time you fu—"

Ted was ready for her this time. He instantly pulled her hard against him, causing a swoosh of breath out of her before she could finish and made a fast, tight twirl away from the glaring eyes. Clutching at him, her eyes dizzily flickered open again as a wave of nausea gripped her.

"I just meant that I'm jealous as hell that you're sleeping with Jack—married or not, that's all," he said when they had once again settled back into swaying rhythmically with the music.

Impulsively, she pushed back to glare at him and shook her head. "I can't actually *sleep* with him," she said, forgetting what she had been about to say before he nearly caused her throw up. "I don't dare. He could tell you'd been there. He knows how you are. I told him what Susan said about you," she murmured, her voice trailing off, lost in the smooth strains coming from the orchestra. What he was pressing into her thighs was making her knees weak. She knew if they kept this up, he would definitely have to carry her back to the table.

Ted's brow knitted. "There's that much difference? That he'd notice?"

She peeked at him through the drowsy slits her eyes had become. "That you'd been there?" she said and saw the doubt on his face. "Oh yeah, you bet. You still don't have any idea what it takes for a girl to sleep with you, do you?" There was no resentment in her voice, only the painful truth, laced with a certain degree of pride that only another woman would understand.

"Well, I thought I did," he murmured, looking into her half-open eyes. "How can you be sure? About that, I mean, if you're not sleeping with him. There isn't someone else, is there?"

"Now you're being silly. You know very well there isn't. You're my only guy, all any girl could possibly want or handle." She nestled into him a little closer, if that was possible, feeling his warmth and strength beneath his dinner jacket—and farther down. "I have no idea how Susan managed to find time for anyone else when she had you. Besides, I knew I was in trouble when I couldn't get out of bed for three days. And ... well, I tested it. But not the way you think," she said with a small frown.

Ted smiled, her answer piquing his interest. "You just said you weren't sleeping with Jack—or anyone else. So, how did you do that?" He expertly maneuvered her through the crowd and noticed that a few couples were still staring at them. He smiled.

Beverly was tempted to tell him about the gag birthday gift meant to keep her company when Jack was out of town that she kept in her lingerie drawer; it was so big that she and Jack had both laughed, knowing it would never be put into service. However, out of curiosity while she was recuperating, she had tried again and was shocked at the results.

"Trust me, he would just know," she said sleepily, brushing him off. In the condition she was in, there was no way she could explain such a delicate matter.

"I bet he's not too happy about being cut off like that, especially if he's still in love with you." He looked into her sleepy face just as a new thought came to him. "Do you think it's possible to love two people at the same time?"

"Mmm ... that's too confusing to even think about right now," she purred sleepily, liking the way their bodies fit together and nudging her hips into him again, using him as a pacifier against the urge she felt building up her, and getting stronger by the minute.

He felt her against him and pushed back. "I suppose that means you haven't said anything to him about us."

Beverly opened her eyes wider this time to glare at him. "For God's sake, Teddy, I can't imagine you even thinking such a thing."

It was the possibility of Jack finding out about them that had been causing her sleepless nights, a loss of appetite, and making her bitchy in general. The only good part was that she had lost three pounds in the process.

"You said he didn't think I was a threat. I thought if he wasn't worried about me we might get to see each other more, that's all," Ted said, trying to add a thread of reason to an unreasonable situation.

"He doesn't think you're a threat because he's never seen you in the shower," she breathed in his ear and rested her head on his shoulder, the naked memory of him flashing through her foggy mind. She closed her eyes again, his body heat wafting a faint scent of cologne. In her gin-induced euphoria, a pang of guilt went off in her, threatening to spoil the high she was on, and she pulled Ted in even closer for moral support. "But I have been thinking about telling Susan ..." Her voice trailed off as she waited for his reaction, but she already knew what it would be.

He tried to push her back to see if she was serious, but she held him tightly. "Why in the world would you do that?" he said finally, his voice up a notch.

When Beverly's head finally came up, her gaze had already turned serious. "I guess I just need to get this whole business off my chest, to talk to someone about it, and she's my best friend. The trouble is, I'm sleeping with her husband." When he grunted, she went on. "You just said if Jack knew we might be able to see each other more often. Why not Sue? She might even want to join in." Bev almost giggled at the silly thought. "She wouldn't feel left out that way, or that I was trying to take you away from her."

"And are you? Trying to take me away? Is that what's worrying you?" They glided past another couple he recognized from the yacht club that was glaring at them. Ted smiled deferentially before the crowd swallowed them up as they moved away.

"Some, I guess, but I would never hurt Susan like that." She made a face and stifled a Tangueray-tainted hiccup with the back of her hand. "Besides, she's still in love with you, and I know you love her back. And I'm … well, I guess I just fall somewhere in between."

"And you think if she finds out about us it isn't going to hurt her?" he challenged, since he had been worrying about the same thing.

She pouted at the accusation. "And you can go straight to hell, Ted Davenport, for all I care right now," she said and tried to pull back from him just as the flash of a camera went off nearby startling her, and she clutched at him to maintain her balance.

When she recovered, Ted said, "You really don't think Jack might be up for something like that, do you?" he asked at the rather bizarre thought that had just occurred to him.

"Like what?"

He did not try to hide the lecherous grin that had worked its way into his face. "Hell, I don't know like what. I guess it's called wife swapping."

"Good God, no! He would never agree to anything like that. And for once, I'm not sure I don't agree with him. Who could do that? Watch while your wife or husband made love with someone else?"

Just then, they bumped elbows with another couple who had encroached on the small circle others had cleared around them. Ted smiled his apologies and guided her away. "Well, hopefully, you'd be too busy to notice. Would that bother you, seeing Jack and Sue like that? Even being in the same room—you and me—with them—in the same bed even?"

Considering the scenario, Beverly said, "I guess the good part is we could all keep an eye on each other that way."

"Well, let me know before you ask Jack, please. I want to be somewhere else when you do," he said, half-meaning it. "Do you think he would be interested in Susan?" The afterthought suddenly dawning on him.

Beverly had briefly considered the possibility before. Now that he brought it up, she found it strangely intriguing. "Susan's a beauty. What man in his right mind wouldn't be interested? Would you care if he was?" she asked, still slightly uneasy with her own feelings.

He hesitated, but only briefly. "I guess not." He had dealt with similar issues during Susan's entire movie career, which had been a good part of their married life, and he had either accepted the fact or risked losing her. "It wouldn't be the first time she's slept with someone else. But the way you girls talk, I suppose you know that."

"We talked about it a little, some of the stories," Beverly said and nodded with a suppressed grin, wondering if she really had slept with some of the most famous men in Hollywood as she claimed. She could feel Ted hard against her, and pressed her hips back into him, just because it felt good.

"Like what?" he asked, looking down into her cleavage, surprised at how much her new dress revealed, especially from his vantage point.

Beverly shook her head. "Uh-uh! Oh, no you don't, buster. That's strictly girl talk. Ladies' secrets." Susan had always been open and frank with her, but she had no idea what or how much she may have confessed to him, and she did not intend to tread on such dangerous ground.

Ted wanted to pursue the matter but knew by her tone that it was useless and let it pass. That part of their life was in the past, they had dealt with it and it no longer mattered. "Have you and Jack ever done anything like that, with another couple, I mean?"

"Only talk. Like most married couples," she admitted, but was caught off guard by his question and hesitated to mention why she and Jack had decided to leave LA. Bev knew the wild tale about the New Years Eve party they'd attended several years ago would titillate him, and she'd had far too much to drink tonight to handle the Pandora's Box it was sure to open. "But not seriously," Bev continued. "You have? You'd be quite a challenge for any girl. I'm sure Susan would have a hard time finding you a bed partner."

The grin on his face gave him away before he answered. "Well, yes, I suppose we have thought about it. But, like you, not seriously. Mostly talk. There was one couple some years ago we were pretty friendly with, but nothing ever came of it. Susan used to flirt with the guy something terrible, tease the pants off him. And his wife wasn't bad looking. But I think Susan was afraid she'd lead me astray and I might like it. Has she ever mentioned anything about Jack? That she might like to …?"

"You mean *screw* him—?"

Ted's brow arched sharply and he looked around to see a sour-faced, rather round, middle-aged woman he recognized in a frumpy gown with large garish flowers all over it who looked like a cross between Margret Meade and Julia Child. She had a cell phone in her hand and had obviously overheard them since she was glaring their way. It was the commodore's wife this time, which all but guaranteed their conversation was bound to get back to Susan by tomorrow at the very latest, and the rest of the gossips in town shortly thereafter.

"Not in so many words," Bev went on when he had looked away and didn't answer, unaware that she had been overheard. "Only that she thought he was handsome, which I suppose he is. But I get the feeling she wouldn't mind. She's told you she would?" Beverly was surprised at the slight pang of jealousy that went with the thought.

"Once, I think. Said she wondered what it would be like." He could feel her heat all the way down where their bodies came together as they swayed to the music.

"Has Susan said anything about me?"

He looked at her. "She said she thinks you're very tasty, whatever that means."

Beverly thought she knew exactly what it meant.

"And I probably shouldn't tell you this—but you're younger than she is, of course. Oh, and that you have a great ass." He grinned at this. "I think she might be a little jealous." Ted kissed her lightly, the tip of his tongue flicking hers. She licked at him in return. "You're not thinking of sleeping with her too, are you?" But he had to admit that the idea intrigued him as his fingers traced the outline of her spine from top to bottom, feeling her squirm under his touch, and looked down at the top of her breasts that she was pressing into him.

"Not yet," Beverly said sleepily. "I'm still working on her husband. Maybe later." Her eyes closed again, nothing showing in her face that wasn't caused by the way he was grinding his hips into her.

"Have you ever been with another woman?" Ted asked, suddenly unsure of what her answer might be.

"No, but maybe the right one just hasn't come along," she said, more to titillate him than anything else. She knew men liked that sort of erotica. Personally, she had always been ambivalent when it came to sex between two women, while the thought of two men together caused her to shudder.

After a beat, Ted said, "As long as we're fessing up, has Susan said anything to you about me?"

"Only that the thing you're trying to push all the way through my new dress belongs on a mule." She nudged her hips into his again to make her point.

A childish grin crept across his face as he reciprocated. "So, what's the verdict, my dear? Do you think I belong in a barn or in bed?"

"The verdict, my darling, is that I haven't been able to think of anything else for the past few weeks." She kissed him wetly on the mouth, his probing tongue causing a tingle all the way down to where her panties ought to be, and she realized for the first time that her estrangement from Jack had a face.

And it belonged to Ted Davenport.

Susan clung to Jack as they slowly moved to the rhythm of the soft music, an old standard out of the sixties. Since she had rather long legs and was wearing the four-inch stiletto heels that she and Beverly had agreed on that afternoon, her hips fit almost perfectly into his. Pressed against his six-foot frame, she still had to look up to see his face when she felt him tense.

"Anyone I know, darling?" She untangled herself and noticed the serious frown he was wearing.

Jack realized they had not spoken three words since leaving the table when she broke his concentration. He glanced down at her. He was a full head taller and could see well down into her cleavage that was artfully but barely contained in her low-cut gown. It was a pleasant view, but was having little effect on him at the moment.

"Sorry," he said, preoccupied. "I was looking around for Bev and Ted."

Susan was not able to see them from her lower vantage point and did not really care, but apparently, he did. "Is Ted being a little too friendly with Bev this evening, darling? I noticed them at the table, acting way too casual for what they were probably talking about. But you know he adores her."

"She mentioned it a couple of times. I just wasn't sure the feeling was mutual until now," Jack said. He had located them cuddle dancing a short distance away just as Beverly tilted her head and kissed him, too long and too hard not to mean something else. And, from the way they were trying to suck the breath out of each other, it certainly wasn't the first time. Susan strained to follow his gaze and saw how the other couples had cleared a circle around them as best they could to watch the spectacle. A flash went off here and there, lighting them up. But they hardly noticed.

"My goodness," Susan said, "I wonder if it isn't time to take those two lovebirds home."

Beverly's head was spinning from the intense embrace that had lasted far too long, and they caught a glimpse of Jack and Susan staring at them from halfway across the ballroom when they finally came up for air just as the music ended.

"Don't look now, puss, but I think we've been busted," he said when they parted, lightly clapping their approval for the orchestra. "We're both going to be answering a few questions when we get home tonight." He smiled at his next thought. "If Susan finds out about us, she's going to shit firecrackers. What about Jack?"

Beverly glanced around again and found Susan and Jack glaring at them from their table now. "He carries a gun, remember? But I don't think he'll use it."

With the damage already done, they kissed again. Their audience now included the bandleader who had noticed them at the center of the small clearing the other couples had formed around them, and was grinning openly in their direction as the music ended to light applause.

"Thank you. Thank you very much, ladies and gentlemen," he said into the mike. "And let's hear it for our happy couple here in the middle of the floor!" He began to applaud energetically in their direction. The band members took up the beat followed by the audience and the drummer began a long drumroll.

By the time Beverly and Ted had worked their way back to the table—to the amplified *tap-tap-tap* of drumsticks against the rim of the drum with each step she took, spiked heels clicking, hips swaying—Jack had already retrieved her coat, had a sour look on his face and abruptly said good night for the both of them.

"You still want to do lunch tomorrow, darling?" Susan asked stiffly, reminding her of the date they had made earlier in the day, before leaning over to give her a peck on the cheek and whispered in her ear. "We need to talk, darling."

"Ummm," Beverly groaned under her breath, her eyes hooded and her head swimming. Unsteady on her feet, she was feeling abandoned, knew she was in trouble, and in no condition to resist.

"I'll take that as a yes," Susan said in a hushed tone and then lowered her voice even more. "You're going to have your hands full when you get home, darling. He suspects something. You were very naughty out there."

With her mind in a whirl, hardly able to keep her eyes open and Susan's warning ringing in her ear, Beverly coolly took her coat with a haughty glare, refusing his grudging offer of help and started toward the exit to the resounding crescendo of a drumroll. Dragging the expensive fur behind her in one hand and without bothering to turn around, she raised her other hand high over her head and twiddled her fingers in the air as the entire room erupted in applause behind her.

Jack took her by the arm and she stifled the urge to angrily pull away from him, turn around, and bow to the round of enthusiastic applause she was getting from an admiring audience. However, in her condition she knew she would probably fall flat on her face and spoil the bawdy image she had created, one she was sure she would need to deal with when they got home.

Staring after them with an envious smile, Susan shook her head. She muttered something Ted could not hear over the cacophony that was still going on as the beginning strains of "The Stripper" was struck up in honor of Beverly's departure. Ted leaned toward her and cupped a hand to his ear. "What was that, honey?"

They were still at their table when Susan turned toward him and raised her voice over the din. "I said, 'That's my girl!' Did you see how she bump-bump-bumped that big ass of hers in perfect timing with the base drum, like it was rehearsed." Then, the wry smile she was wearing abruptly faded into a sallow scowl and her cold gray eyes pierced him like a pair of deadly ceremonial daggers.

"And don't you dare call me honey again, you low-grade sonofabitch!"

Seven

I t was after 1:00 a.m. by the time Beverly put her head back and closed her eyes as Jack drove smartly out of the hotel's sweeping driveway with a chirp of rubber as the wide, high-performance tires gripped the dew-slicked pavement. He was driving the same way he felt, and the powerful sedan responded in kind.

There was only one other car on the road at that time of the morning. The blue and red lights on the police cruiser headed in the opposite direction promptly came on as it made a quick U-turn. Jack had slowed to just ten over the speed limit by the time the cruiser fell in behind them. He had committed what street cops called a head-in-ass violation—nothing serious, but at that time of the morning, that was all it took.

Jack knew the drill: license, registration, and an apologetic smile to the disapproving glare he was about to get.

"Better buckle up before we get pinched," Jack said as he slowly pulled over to the curb and came to a complete stop. Beverly glared at him but did not move. Jack opened the center console and retrieved the worn leather badge case that contained his retired police ID and PI creds, driver's license, and the CCW for the model 92, 9mm Beretta he always carried, and he slowly got out of the car with his hands where the officer could plainly see them.

With an effort, Beverly adjusted the rearview mirror, watched as Jack proffered the faded-leather case, and saw the flash of gold as he flipped it open, exposing his retirement badge under the beam of the officer's flashlight. The city cop relaxed the hand that had been resting on the butt of the Glock .45 holstered on his belt. They talked briefly, both men smiling as if they had been classmates somewhere, and shook hands before Jack got back into the car a few minutes later.

"No ticket—?" she asked, as if she didn't know.

"The guy's just doing his job. A car peeling out of a driveway at one in the morning tends to make the local *gendarmes* a little curious is all." He turned the key and the powerful 550 horsepower, 5 liter V8 purred to life with a throaty hum. Jack buckled up and slipped the J-shift into the drive slot. After readjusting the mirror and checking for traffic behind them, he eased back out onto the deserted roadway.

"If you hadn't badged him you'd still be back there walking a straight line, or trying to," she said peevishly and put her head back again to ease the beginnings of a very bad headache that was already setting in.

"I haven't had anything to drink in two hours. I'd blow maybe a .03 or I wouldn't have peeled out of the driveway like that." A blood-alcohol level of .08 was the legal limit in California. "No need to risk my license." When she did not reply, he glanced over at her. Her head was back, eyes closed, a blank expression on her face. "Or I might not be able to pay for that new dress Ted was trying to climb into with you tonight."

She ignored the challenge, and him. Her head was now swirling in time with her stomach. The flashing warning light on the dash came on again. "You going to buckle up? The light's blinking again."

"Then I suggest you turn the damn thing off," she snapped

without looking at him. They drove on in silence for a few blocks before she opened her eyes. "You better pull over, open a window, something. No, stop! I'm going to be sick."

Jack pulled to the curb, got out into the cool early-morning air, went around the car, and opened the passenger door for her. "Try not to get any on the car, will you?"

"Fuck you!" she snapped, glaring up at him. Then, with a retching gush, deposited the gin and the few bites of dinner still in her stomach into the gutter. She kept heaving until there was nothing more to come up.

When she finished, Jack held out his silk pocket square to her. She took it and wiped the residue from her mouth. "Feel better?" he asked. She was as pale as a ghost, drawn, and looked awful.

With her eyes closed against the nausea that was still threatening her, Beverly did not see the grin plastered across his face when she leaned back into the car. If she had, she would have spit the F-word at him again.

"Take me home, Jack ... please."

The Inquisition

Eight

It was nearly 2:00 o'clock on a chilly morning when Ted and Susan entered the house through the side garden. She was tired after the long day and doing her best to control the anger that had been steadily building in her since before they left the party. Beverly, who was still very much on her mind, appeared to have a natural-borne talent for theatrics and her dramatic exit this evening had both surprised her and caused a pang of professional envy to flare up in her.

With the early morning chill in the air, Susan had donned a warm flannel nightgown before climbing into bed after she had finished with her toiletries. Ted was wearing a faded blue and gold T-shirt containing the UC Berkley logo and sweatpants when he came in from the bathroom to sit on his side of the bed. She knew he was expecting her to begin the inevitable inquisition and was doing his best not to show it.

She let him wait.

In spite of her pique, she liked the way his back was ramrod straight and the way the thick silver hair at the nape of his neck came down just over his collar, giving him that healthy, sexy look she adored in a man. She had always thought he was ruggedly handsome, and she would kill for his complexion. His skin was smooth and unblemished, not showing the ill effects of sun and chlorine or the swimming pools he had spent half his life in. Then there was his special attribute about him that most women only dreamed of but very few could tolerate and would probably never experience. Still, after tonight, she wondered if there wasn't someone else who was doing just that.

"By the way, did you call the cable guy about something, Sue?" Ted asked after he had settled onto the bed and began to fiddle with his alarm clock. She had not said so much as a word to him all of the way home. He knew she was angry, since she seldom used profanity. The curse she had hurled at him still rang in his ear, and he was doing his best to act as if nothing had happened. He knew he could not win with her. He never had. Long ago he had decided that you either you took Susan the way she was or not at all.

Susan was waiting to bring up something a lot more interesting than the cable guy. "I don't remember," she replied coolly, breaking their long silence. "No, I don't think so." She pretended to concentrate on the movie magazine she had been mindlessly thumbing through while she waited for him to come to bed. She put it aside now and worked to keep the anger from her voice. "Is something wrong with the TV?"

"I forgot to mention he was here the other day while you were out and about. Couldn't find anything wrong though. Said everything was working just fine."

"Well, that's a good thing." Then, feeling like she might throw up and determined to get the whole thing over with, she took a deep breath and plunged ahead. "You and Bev were quite a sight tonight," she began, her speech stilted in spite of her efforts.

"We were just having a little fun, hun ... ah ... Sue," Ted answered, a stupid grin creasing his face instead of the denial he knew from experience would be useless when she got like this. He continued to fiddle with the alarm setting on the bedside clock for his early golf game and purposely avoided looking at her.

Ted had never been good at lying. It wasn't his style, and Susan knew it perfectly well. She also knew she could cow him with merely the harshness of her voice, and had done so many times over the years. But never over anything as serious as tonight.

"I know you've been flirting with Bev a lot lately when you think I'm not looking. We've talked about it. And, by the way, if you ever pinch her on the butt again, she'll probably give you a good smack. She hates that."

"Thanks ... er, for the, ah ... the heads-up," he said hesitantly, guilt written all over him. He didn't know what else to say. But he knew how the two women talked and wondered what else Bev may have told her.

"Of course tonight went way beyond flirting," she said icily. The guilty look that came flooding over him confirmed her worst suspicions as she let the tension hang between them like a leaden brick for a moment. She would pull every single detail out of him if it took all night. "Everyone at the party was watching. And I don't think Jack appreciated all the looks you were getting any more than I did. Not to mention that your hands were all over her ass, or that you had that fat tongue of yours all the way down her throat half the night. It was rather disgusting, if you want to know."

"You have to admit that we—I mean, Bev—got a pretty good hand when they left," he said sheepishly.

"Don't you start with me, you snake in the grass," she warned, accepting his shrug as all of the argument she was likely to get out of him under the circumstances, and pressed on. "So, there's no need to beat around the bush over this. I want to know what's going on with you two, how long you've been carrying on, and how far it's gone." Her glare was icy. "And don't you even think of lying to me."

Ted blanched and swallowed hard. He had not been sure what

to expect, but it certainly wasn't a full frontal assault like this. He wondered how much she suspected and how much she actually knew. "Has Bev said something?" he croaked, stalling, giving his churning brain a chance to catch up. "I know you girls like to talk."

"Not about what I saw tonight, we haven't," she said hotly. "Flirting is one thing, but trying to screw her with your clothes on is quite another. Especially in front of the entire freaking yacht club. And did you see the look on that witch's face, the commodore's wife? By tomorrow the talk will be all over town." In spite of all her efforts, she was unable to hide the vitriol that was showing up in her voice.

"I—I don't know what to say, except I don't think her dress was anywhere near as nice as yours, honey."

"I already told you not to *honey* me again, you philandering bastard," she hissed at him like a hooded cobra ready to strike. "And I'll tell you exactly what you *can* say. How about starting with the *where, when,* and exactly *how long* you've been screwing around with Beverly Edwards? And if you even think about lying to me, you, you jerk, I'll know. And I'll be in Jack's office so freaking fast tomorrow morning it'll make your head spin. Not only that—"

"I know, I know, he's got a gun!" Ted finished for her. What he wasn't sure of was if the threat was real or if it was just because she was slightly north of pissed off at him. Still, the threat of retribution put any thought of lying to her completely out of the question. And the crack about the gun, especially since it was the second time he'd heard it tonight, was the clincher. It suddenly dawned on him that carrying on with an ex-cop's wife could actually be dangerous.

Ted cleared his throat and tried to think, but the dark scowl staring back at him from across the big king-sized bed was making it almost impossible. Then in a weak effort to blunt the attack, he said, "Did Bev ever show you the little tattoo she has—?"

Susan fixed him with a suspicious stare. "I hope it's not on her ass."

"No-no," he shrugged like a scolded child, "... but close. It's on her, that is, the inside of her thigh, next to … er … well, it's a little pussycat."

"Is that why you've been calling her 'puss' lately, or is that just love talk for *pussy?*" she demanded sarcastically.

"Pussy*cat*, maybe … I guess," he offered timidly.

"You lousy bastard," she said in a disgusted tone, and made a clucking sound in answer to the stupid look that had washed over him. Her scowl deepened and she looked away.

"So, where should … uh, do you want me to start, hon … I mean, Sue?" Ted gulped in a breath in an attempt to steady his nerves and collect his thoughts for what he was about to tell her, only slightly fortified by the fact that it wasn't anything she hadn't done to him before—in spades.

Jesus Almighty Christ! Susan thought. The poor bastard was actually about to confess! She had already made up her mind that something serious was going on between them, but found herself smoldering just the same, her heart rate kicking up a notch. All he had to do was deny, deny, deny. There was no way to prove a thing. And Bev was certainly not about to admit to anything as underhanded as having an affair with her husband. My God, it was almost impossible to believe that she was even capable of such a thing. She was a much bigger woman than she was, but not *that* big. And, since there was virtually no one else to confirm or deny his story, why would he be so stupid? But she knew the answer.

Because he was a man, that's why.

It bothered Susan that she had always able to read him like that, especially now. She felt her heart begin to thump in her chest like a trip-hammer as the green-eyed monster reared its ugly head. She came down from the mountain of her fury and took a deep breath, forcing herself to calm down until she was able to bring her emotions under control again. Then she put on her matronly stage face that said, "There's no need to be afraid, darling, you can tell Mother everything," and took several deep breaths and waited until her heart stopped thumping enough that she could trust her voice.

"Why not … why don't we just start with tonight?"

Ted looked confused. "But that's not where it started, dear, er, I mean, honey, er, Sue," he corrected her timidly.

The harsh look she was wearing softened with the tactical error she had just made. "Of course, dear, I know that," she said, quickly recovering from her faux pas. "Everyone at the party could see that." She silently chided the bad habit she had of leading him around by the nose most of the time. However, she had never scolded him for something this serious before. But then, the lousy bastard had never cheated on her before, either.

"I was just trying to help you get started, to get your thoughts together so you don't leave anything out. Actually, I hate to admit it, but the two of you were rather cute out there together, acting like you were all alone. And the band certainly loved it. Of course, Bev's exit was the real showstopper." She felt another tinge of professional jealousy, but hurried on. "And I want you to know that I'm not mad at you now that I've had a little time to think about it. Just surprised that you would do something like that is all … with my best friend."

"She's younger, too." Ted swallowed hard when he saw her silently flare up behind the mask she was wearing, but bravely continued. "Well, I've been thinking. I didn't do anything you haven't done to me before, lots of times. And I never got mad."

"Ted Davenport! You can just stop that this minute!" she scolded, her voice notched up to command status, a sharp edge to it again. "Don't you *dare* start with me about the few mistakes I made in the past. We've been through all that over and over, and I've told you it will never happen again. I've apologized for what I had to do for my career, and you accepted it. Now, that's the end of it."

"Sorry," he said, his head hanging, shoulders slumped with guilt, as if the entire shame was his. But he wanted to laugh at what she considered to be a *few mistakes*. By her own admission, there were so many *mistakes* that she could not remember them all.

Susan took a moment to calm down. "Why don't you just start at the beginning and get this over with so we can both get some sleep tonight, what little night there is left." At this hour of the morning, her eleven-thirty luncheon date with Beverly was beginning to sound more like an early call; one of the pitfalls of the movie business that she had always managed to avoid unless the director was gay or a complete cretin. And the luncheon date with Bev was one she did not intend to miss.

Ted settled himself to the task, ordered his thoughts, and in less than a hour—in spite of Susan's constant interruptions for the intimate details—related the entire affair he'd been having with Beverly Edwards over the past several weeks, leaving nothing out—all three times they had been together.

"Three times—?" She eyed him suspiciously, one brow arched high, her gaze piercing. Knowing him as she did, in earlier times it had been three times a day.

"I swear, Sue." He held up a hand. "Between you and Jack, it was hard enough to find the time for even that."

Susan made a nasty face, shook her head, and waved a hand in his face, all at the same time. "All right, all right, go on. What happened then?" She would wait to make up her mind after she'd heard the whole story—and talked to Beverly Edwards.

When he assured her that was all there was to tell, Susan sighed, letting all of her breath out as she continued to turn over his confession in her mind. She found that, while she was surprised that Bev was sleeping him, she was even more surprised that she *could,* and oddly wondered which one of them was responsible for the sick feeling she had in the pit of her stomach that made her feel like throwing up. But she already knew the answer.

You lousy bastard! Susan thought, vengefully.
Both of you!

Ted idly listened to the soft sound of Susan's breathing. She had fallen into a fitful sleep just before dawn and finally settled down into a deeper, more relaxed slumber. He had never seen her in such a state, but he could not blame her. Bev was her best friend and he had never given her cause to wonder in the past, in spite of her own philandering. She had to be feeling hurt and betrayed.

He knew the feeling well enough, though he had never confronted any of her paramours. He had no idea how many there had been over the years, and she claimed not to remember. She never offered anymore, and he had never asked. Then one night she had told him that she loved him and that she had done some things to further her career that she wasn't proud of. Not long after that, she had gone off to Africa with another man.

For almost a year she had written, declaring her love for him, promising to come home soon, until one day she had. Her Hollywood career had come to an end and she was home for good. God, how he remembered the weeks that followed, hardly getting out of bed except to eat. Then the supply of food had run low. There were quick showers, the necessary toiletries, then falling back into bed, only to drive each other to exhaustion all over again. The days that followed had been long, tumultuous, filled with fits of anger and stormy sex, until an exhausted acceptance had finally settled over them. Most of all, there was the promise that it was over. His movie star was home to stay.

Now, lying beside her watching her sleep, he felt a surge deep in his loins, a hunger he thought long dead. Susan was lying on her side with her back to him, and Ted softly touched her shoulder, not wanting to wake her, just to feel her warmth.

Susan stirred lightly, barely coming awake, and surprisingly felt him pressing her from behind. She turned onto her back and saw him staring at her through the gloom, his features soft, wanting her.

After a moment when she had mostly recovered from the troubled dream-like state she had been in, she silently touched his face, coaxing him over her, his presence huge and familiar, undeniable.

Ted nestled onto her, his torso wedged between her thighs, and began to firmly press himself into her. When there was almost no progress, he pushed harder with only minimal success. "What's going on, honey? You're you so tight," he breathed heavily into the crux of her neck.

Susan's breath caught in her throat with the force and urgency of his efforts. She adjusted her hips for better access, and felt him go deeper. When he finally settled all the way into her, she sighed with a small shiver of excitement and whispered in his ear, "Susan's a little snugly, darling, because you haven't fucked her in almost a year."

Nine

$\mathcal{J}$ack let his big St. Bernard back in the house when she had finished her business, sniffed around the yard for any possible intruders since she was last out, had lapped up half a bucket of water and he had wiped down her slobbery chops with the shop towel he kept by the back door.

When he had locked up and set the alarm, he went to the bar and poured himself a nightcap before the two of them headed upstairs for the night. He thought he heard Bev in the bathroom as he hung his dinner jacket over the polished-brass valet, stripped off his tie and studs, and tossed his shirt on the seat with his trousers, ready for the cleaners. By the time he had slipped into his PJs he was feeling the effects of the long evening and some of the disturbing questions that had been clouding his mind all evening, along with a few unpleasant conclusions he'd been forced to accept.

Before Jack came up the stairs, Beverly had closed herself off in the closet, not wanting to face him and to be alone with her misery. She was exhausted and weak from the effects of the four double martinis she'd had over the course of the evening, and she struggled to crawl out of her evening dress and into a nightgown just as another wave of nausea swept over her and she hurried back into the bathroom. She sprawled on all fours in front of the toilet as she threw up green, foul-tasting bile, which was all that was left in her stomach, and was overcome by the worst case of dry heaves she had ever experienced. After rinsing with mouthwash, some of which she accidentally swallowed and was threatening to make her sick all over again, she went back into the bedroom where she found Jack nursing his nightcap and Maggie Mae patiently waiting for them to come to bed.

Beverly looked pale and drained as he watched her cross in front of the fireplace to her side of the bed and thought she probably felt about the same way she looked, which was god-awful. He waited until she sat down with her back toward him before breaking the silence.

"You want to tell me what's been going on with you and Ted?"

She cringed inwardly but did not turn around, and did her best to ignore him. She did not dare look at him, afraid of what was showing on her face. Between fits of alcohol-induced nausea, Beverly had been dreading the inevitable interrogation she knew was coming, the same that Susan had warned her about. Not that she needed to be warned—she was married to an ex-cop, for God's sake. It seemed that half of her married life had been one long interrogation.

After giving her a minute, he tried again. "I think we need to talk about this. Obviously, what went on with you and Ted tonight wasn't the first time." He took a sip from the snifter of cognac he had poured from the heavy crystal decanter in the bar and brought upstairs with him. He swirled the glass in his hand, warming the aged amber liquid, its pungent aroma helping to clear his head. "I'm surprised someone didn't tell you to go get a room."

"Do you have to play cop right now?" she snapped. "I'm really not up for it, jack." Her voice was so icy it felt like the temperature in the room dropped several degrees.

"Then what if I just play husband and wonder what the hell's going on between my wife and another man playing grab-ass with her all night?" Jack tried to control his tone and doing his best to do the same with his temper. But the anger that had been building in him since watching the two of them on the dance floor—not to mention the hanky-panky he observed at the table and suspected what was going on under it—had already molded his otherwise handsome features into a mask of despair. "I don't think I'm being unreasonable here. You two put on one hell of a show for everyone."

Angrily, Beverly spun around at the accusation, setting off a sharp pain in her head that showed up in her voice as well. "What's that supposed to mean? We were dancing. So what?"

"I think everyone at the party could see the '*So what,*' part. Ted's hands were all over your butt, and you were literally hanging on him. Not to mention the bump-and-grind act you were both putting on."

"That's not true!" she snapped even more angrily, but she knew that it probably was. With her head aching as if it were being squeezed in a giant vise, it was hard to think, let alone remember exactly what they had done. Another wave of nausea flooded over her, held down only with sheer willpower.

"Well, whether you like it or not, it was pretty obvious to everyone else," he said, as evenly as he could manage under the circumstances. "Any fool could see you were both very comfortable mauling each other out there."

"What is it I actually did, Jack? What do you want from me?" Her voice spiked in anger. "You know, why don't you just come right out and accuse me of fucking him. Isn't that where you're going with all this cop crap of yours, what you really mean? What cops do all the time? Accuse someone without proof? God knows, I really didn't think you'd even care what I did. You said you weren't worried about Ted, that he's too old for me, wasn't a threat. Better still, why don't we just get a divorce and be done with it? In fact, I *want* a divorce!" She paused to suck in a deep breath to keep from being sick again.

Maggie Mae whimpered at the outburst, jumped off the bed and headed downstairs in a scramble as if someone had stepped on her tail. Jack looked after her, his mind reeling at the tacit admission he'd just provoked from her and was still ringing in his ear: *"I didn't think you'd even care."* The misstep was exactly what an experienced interrogator could expect from a hassled witness—or in this case, a suspect. But there was no satisfaction in his prowess as a detective, only sorrow.

"I thought Susan was supposed to be your best friend," Jack said, his tone resigned, and he waited for her to lash out again, but she just glared at him. "As for a divorce, I've told you before, Bev, and I'll say it again, I love you, or I wouldn't give a rat's ass what you did with Ted. But if there's any divorcing to be done, you're going to have to do it, kid." He took a gulp of brandy this time, thankful for the distraction of the burning it caused in his throat and all the way down.

Beverly took a deep breath, forced herself to calm down, and with a huge effort lowered her voice. "Frankly, I really didn't think you'd give a damn what I did with Ted, or anyone else," she said, realizing the misstep she'd just made, caused in equal parts by her anger and the alcoholic state she was in. This was exactly what Susan had warned her about. Her stomach turned over for the umpteenth time.

When it settled again, she said, "You said you didn't think Ted was a threat. I'm just not sure if you meant to *you* or to *me*." Then she added in a smaller voice, "So, why the interrogation? Is it because another man's interested in me? Actually cares about what I think, or do, or where I go—what I want to do with the rest of my life? Or is it just that you think Ted's trespassing on your personal private property?"

"That's redundant, and it sounds like a cop-out," he said, knowing the rebuke would anger her even more, but right now, it didn't seem to matter much. When she just glared at him, he stared back at her for a moment, regretting that he had been flippant. However, he knew the bitterness in her voice held something far more than the angry words she had just flung at him.

Guilty as charged came to mind.

"Sometimes I don't think I know you anymore, Bev. But I can't stop you from whatever you did, or you're doing, whatever. If you're sleeping with Ted, I guess there's nothing much I can do about it. But it's probably not a good idea to carry on in front of all our friends, the entire yacht club."

Beverly turned on him now, staring back defiantly. "So, is that it? It's okay to screw him, just don't embarrass you in front of our friends?"

He shrugged silently. He had not meant for it to come out like that. But there it was, how he really felt, so it was exactly what he meant.

"What is it you want from me, Jack? Because I don't think I know," she said, her mixed feelings of anger and despair obvious. Then Susan's warning went off in her addled brain again with her next thought, and it came spilling out on its own. "Ted says he's in love with me." Jack stared back, deadpan, unreadable. "And maybe I'm falling in love with him as well."

Jack swallowed hard and when he spoke his voice was as flat as his battered ego. "Have you been sleeping with him? You said you'd tell me if you'd had enough to drink, and that's pretty obvious tonight."

Beverly did her best to brush off his sarcasm and tried to decide how to answer. Lying was hardly a consideration, given her past track record with the ex-cop she was married to. She had tried little dumb things before because she'd been embarrassed by something. But it had never been anything serious, and he'd always read between the lines—just as he was now.

Tonight, however, she'd had far too much to drink to go there and was bound to say more than she should under the circumstances, and perhaps already had. The whole thing was making her sick and she needed to talk to someone before it all blew up in her face. Certainly not Susan. She was married to part of the problem. She did not recall ever feeling more alone or abandoned as she did at that moment.

Time seemed to hang in the balance until she found her voice again and said, "Jack, I really don't think whether or not I've slept with Ted is what's wrong with us. I know we need to talk about this, but right now, I'm tired, I've had far too much to drink, and I feel like the bottom of a birdcage. Could we please do this later, when we're *both* up for it?" Her stomach wrenched again. "And the smell of whatever it is you're drinking is making me sick as hell all over again."

He did not like her answer but noticed the frown lines in her face soften, the same face he had fallen hopelessly in love with so many years ago. If the determination in her voice wasn't enough, common sense told him that three o'clock in the morning was hardly the best time for either of them, especially in her condition.

"Sure," he said evenly. "Only fair. Later, when you're up to it." Then the makings of a crooked smile creased his drawn face. "In the meantime, do you want to fool around a little? It's been a while and you're way over your martini limit. Besides, you haven't told me to go fuck myself in a long time."

Just then, Maggie Mae stuck her head around the corner of the stairs. Jack patted the bed beside him, and she bounded up to lick his face before sprawling out full-length on her back between them wanting her belly scratched. With her legs in the air, Maggie Mae watched him, her floppy ears and sloppy chops billowing with the broad smile she was wearing.

Beverly recognized his stupid sense of humor coming out, even at a time like this. Maybe especially at a time like this. But she felt haggard, like she was being pushed into a corner. But there was no way she could have sex without confirming his suspicions and revealing her secret. Bev gave Maggie's rump a scratch and wished she could just take the "Fifth Amendment" and be done with it. But wasn't that what she'd been doing lately? She just didn't realizing it until now.

With a groan of resignation, she said, "Sex is something else we really need to talk about, Jack. But tonight I'd probably throw up all over you ... and the dog."

The
Morning After

Ten

t was past eleven thirty and the morning sun had just begun to warm the enclosed patio of the small boutique restaurant in the marina where the two women liked to go when they were not meeting for lunch and gossip with other members of what they loosely referred to as the Women's Social Club. There were only eight members in all. Membership was strictly by invitation to a privileged few, and only then when a rare vacancy came open.

Some of the influential women in town who had never been invited into the inner sanctum accused them of being haughty and condescending. However, truth be told, any of them would die for a place at the table where gossip flowed—about everything.

This morning, however, the two women sat alone at a secluded table. Beverly, who was suffering from the worst hangover she had ever had in her entire life, had managed to struggle into a tailored white blouse and black crepe slacks with a matching jacket, and had tried to do something with her hair. Her makeup had proven the most difficult, taking more time than usual, but she was forced to accept it as the best she could do under the circumstance. When she finally arrived twenty minutes late for her date with Susan, she was hiding behind a pair of large sunglasses that filtered out the painful late-morning glare of the sun, and helped to mask the colossal headache she was nursing. She had barely slept last night, was haggard, and racked with anxiety, all of which was mirrored in her personality that morning.

Susan had chosen a raw silk, beige jumpsuit with a contrasting floral design on a top that was purposely half a size too small for her enhanced bosom. She wore the zipper well down to reveal an ample amount of the cleavage provided by the substantial foundation garment it took to hold it all in place; a bra by any sense of the word, but not for the needy. She also wore an expensive wide-brimmed Panama hat of hand-woven palm fronds to top it all off. Her ruby lip-gloss matched her nails perfectly, and her long strawberry-blonde hair caught the shimmering sunlight and flowed over her shoulders like fire in a thorn bush. Susan was still the beauty she had been in her Hollywood days, just an older and wiser version.

Nonetheless, after last night Susan wondered if she wasn't beginning to lose it. She couldn't remember exactly how long it had been since Ted began showing the early signs of ED that had eventually rendered him impotent. At first, she suspected that his age was the culprit. It happened to everyone eventually, although she hadn't thought he was there yet. However, after his forced confession last night, it was apparent that *age* had absolutely nothing to do with it. Not only had he laid her good last night, but he was clearly doing just fine with her luncheon companion, who looked like death warmed over this morning. In the end, Susan was forced to accept the only possible explanation. It was she who was at the root of his temporary impotence, and his affair with Beverly had put an end to the problem.

Struggling with the troubling thoughts that she had been turning over and over in her mind most of the night, Susan said, "So tell me, darling, what is this all about?" Before Bev could answer, the waiter appeared to take their order—light salads, white wine for Susan, strong black coffee for Bev.

When they were alone again, Susan said, "I've been dying to find out what's going on. I was almost afraid you wouldn't show up today," She glanced ruefully at her diamond-encrusted Lady Rolex, a gift from one of the producers of her last film when it had won four Oscars and was nominated for Best Picture. It was just after twelve and the lunch crowd had already begun to pack the place.

For days, Beverly had been struggling with the idea of telling Susan about the affair she was having with her husband, but the awful scene with Jack last night had finally convinced her. She just wasn't sure how to go about it.

"I'm surprised Ted didn't say something," Beverly said, not having a clue where or how to start. "I can't believe you didn't pump him last night."

"I did scold him, of course, darling. You were both being very naughty. But he said you both had a little too much to drink and just got carried away is all. Of course, from where Jack and I were standing, that was putting it mildly," Susan hedged, sure that nothing was showing on her face. She was a pro at this sort of thing, and could cry on demand if the director was worth his salt and knew even half of what he was doing.

While Susan worked on her glass of white wine, Beverly nursed her black coffee, not sure if she believed her or not. The older woman noticed. "I really didn't press it," Susan said. "You know how men can get things all screwed up. Especially when it comes to something important like carrying on with your wife's best friend." With that bomb dropped, Susan stared at her intently for her reaction, but was unable to see beyond the dark glasses she was hiding behind this morning.

If Beverly had not been nearly brain dead, she might have reacted to the accusation and panicked. But she already suspected that Susan wouldn't be terribly upset when she told her, if her nerve held up that long. She may not like it, but she would have to accept it. After all, it wasn't anything she hadn't already done to Ted. She knew the hard part would be answering the all questions that were sure to follow and the intimate details she would demand.

"I hope you don't take this the wrong way, darling, but you look like shit this morning," Susan said almost sympathetically. She didn't like being vulgar, thought it was very unfeminine, but the comment was merely meant to emphasize her observation, not hurt Bev's feelings. "You must feel terrible."

"Thanks for the compliment, *darling*," Beverly croaked back, chin in hand, her elbow on the table.

"What's this all about? Is something going on with you and Jack that I don't know about?" Susan asked, careful to conceal what she already knew. She had Ted's version from last night and all she needed were the juicy parts from a woman's point of view, and she had vowed to get them out of her if it took all day.

"It's not about Jack," Beverly said, shaking her head. But it caused a stab of pain to go off behind her eyes, and she massaged her temples to ease it. She had been building up her courage for this all night but wasn't quite there yet, and the mother of all hangovers banging away in her head was making it almost impossible to concentrate.

When Bev hesitated again, Susan nudged her. "I know things haven't been the best between you two. And after last night, I'm beginning to think it might have something to do Ted."

Beverly's head was splitting, throbbing at the temples, but Susan's words jerked her back from the depths of the self-pity she was trying to hide behind. "I didn't think it showed that bad."

"Well, the two of you were a sight, darling. No question about it. And you got a very nice round of applause when you left." Susan eyed her, saw no change, and took the next step in the plan she had loosely come up with sometime during the sleepless night she had just spent. "I won't mention any names, of course, but some of the ladies from the yacht club already called this morning wanting to know what's going on. None of the Social Club regulars, of course."

Dark arrows of doubt shot through Beverly's clouded mind, not all of them caused by the gossip. She took a deeper breath than usual to mount a defense, but it was quelled when Susan held up a hand. "Personally, I wasn't sure what to make of it all. But I think Jack did. Of course, you know how he is, he didn't say much and I don't suppose he knows how Ted really feels about you either, unless you've said something."

Beverly nodded painfully. "Once, a while back, about the flirting business. We talked about it at lunch, remember?"

Susan nodded and smiled thinly at the euphemism. "Apparently there's been quite a bit of flirting *back* going on since we talked," she said dryly.

Their salads came and Susan sipped at her pinot grigio and looked around the small restaurant while she waited until they were alone again. "Are you sure you don't want a sip of wine, darling? A hair of the dog, as it were?"

Her hand went to the wide brim of her stylish hat as she smiled politely at someone they knew a few tables away. "It's Sally Keeler from the yacht club," she said under her breath, although the attractive athletic-looking woman was too far away to overhear them. "I understand she's in the market again since that artist fellow half her age she was shacked-up with ran off with one of the waitresses from Windows." Windows on the Bay was the upscale restaurant on the Embarcadero where the Women's Social Club met for lunch once a week.

Beverly made an ugly face, held her head with one hand, and then made a gagging sound. "I don't care if I ever have another drink for the rest of my life," she said with a grimace and took another sip of coffee that was now lukewarm. Her mind-numbing headache had not improved in spite of the Tylenol, and her stomach was still queasy. She could not remember ever feeling this awful.

"Oh, darling, what an awful thing to say." Susan paused, and then said, "So, tell me what this is all about." She began to pick at her food. When there was no reply, Susan put her fork down, stared at the hassled woman across from her and wondered if their friendship would survive the day. "Are you in trouble, dear? You know you can tell Susan."

Bev had been waiting for just such an opening—and here it was. She took in a deep breath to replenish her depleted oxygen supply brought on by her shallow breathing and silently exhaled, knowing it was now or never.

"Well, I'm not pregnant, if that's what you're worried about. Not yet, anyway," Beverly said, choosing her words, trying to make light of it. "This is really hard for me, Sue. But after I tell you what I have to say, maybe I *am* in trouble."

Susan tensed inwardly, the scratchy details of Ted's confession coming back vividly, ready for comparison. "Why don't you just take a deep breath, darling, and tell me all about it? You make it sound so ominous. You know you can talk to me. We've been best friends for ages. I've told you things I wouldn't tell my own sister."

"You were an only child, Sue, remember? You've never had a sister," Beverly said with a frown, recalling Susan telling her that she had been an accident. Her mother had also been in the movies, never wanted children, and blamed her ruined figure on Sue.

Susan didn't let the technicality discourage her and pressed on. "Is this about last night? You know, I'm really more upset with Ted than you, darling. I saw him feeding you all those terrible martinis. But I don't suppose Jack saw it that way." She wished the butterflies in her stomach would go away or at least settle down.

Beverly took another deep breath, trying to clear her head and keep her stomach from turning over at the same time. Then, bracing herself, she mustered all of her courage.

"What if I told you that Ted ... Ted and I were ... are ... having an affair?" The clumsy words came tumbling out of her almost on their own in clumps of doubt and wrapped in guilt. "And that I had too much to drink last night to hide it?"

Susan slowly put her salad fork down and allowed her chin to sag appropriately as if she were about to enter the first stages of clinical shock, her perfect stage face frozen in equal parts of curiosity and surprise. "So—oh dear. So, we're not just talking about the … the hugs and kisses now and then when he thought I wasn't looking?" She waited for the flustered nod she expected. When it came, she said, "But you said you could handle it—handle him, right?"

The frown on Beverly's face deepened as she continued with difficulty before she lost her nerve altogether. "Well, I—I guess I didn't do a very good job of that. In fact, not long after we talked about it the last time, things got a little out of hand. The way we behaved last night—*I behaved*—wasn't just because of the martinis." She hurried on, wanting to get this part over with before she could change her mind. But she knew it was already too late for that. There was no turning back now. "I've … we've been seeing each other at your place a few times when you've been gone."

"What do you mean you've been *seeing* him, darling? How long? What are we talking about?"

"A couple of times," she said looking down and shaking her head, trying to lessen the impact of what she was saying. "Three times, actually. And long enough to make a complete ass of myself last night. I've wanted to tell you for weeks. I've—it's been driving me crazy, between worrying about if you would really care and what Jack would say if he found out."

Susan's ears perked up even more. "What do you mean, *if* I would care? What's that supposed to mean?"

Beverly shrugged. "You said you and Ted have only been sleeping in the same bed lately, that you really weren't interested in … in sex, anymore."

Susan immediately regretted the subterfuge she had used several months ago to soothe her own ego, when all along it was actually

Ted who had not been able to rise to the occasion. However, since she suspected a more personal reason, she had been too embarrassed to admit it. In the back of her mind, she assumed that she might even be responsible for his wilted libido. It was something she had thought about most of the long night she had just spent but until now had simply refused to accept.

"Then you *are* talking about you and Ted—I mean *real sex*?" Susan said after a moment. "Who took the first step and when did it start? How long has it been going on?"

Beverly gave a guilty shrug this time. "When you were at the club a few weeks ago. I—I let him kiss me—then kissed him back, and well, it just got out of hand after that. I know I should have stopped him, but—"

"I have to say that I'm a little surprised you'd do something like that with my Ted or that you even *could*. He's so …" She did not finish. She didn't have to. They both knew exactly what she meant.

Beverly stiffened with embarrassment. "I really wasn't sure you would care from the way you talked. You said you and Ted were just going through the motions, that it didn't bother you that much." The next thought that flashed through her mind caused her to hesitate. "I even, ah, thought it might be … well, that your age might have something to do with it."

Susan visibly bristled at the rude inference. The tiny white lie she'd told about Ted had absolutely nothing to do with age, which was something they had never discussed before by mutual agreement. Ignoring the remark, Susan said coldly, "Actually, I'm more surprised you could manage."

Beverly did not answer, just nodded again, her breath catching involuntarily as she exhaled.

"In fact, it's a little hard to believe, unless …" Susan was baiting her, though she had confirmed Ted's story that they had been together on only a few occasions. "Most women couldn't just jump into bed with him. That's why I've never worried much about his straying." Susan gave her the twisted smile of a jilted housewife and tried not to seem too shrewish when she asked, "Exactly what did you do, darling? You and my Ted? That is, if you don't mind me asking."

"Susan—! Good Lord ..." But she expected nothing less and braced herself.

"Well, darling, since I'm the one married to the sonofabitch, I think I at least have a right to know what's going on."

"My God, I just told you!" Beverly said, totally embarrassed, not wanting to repeat her transgressions. "We're having an affair. I let him screw me, all right? And after I got over the shock, I went back and screwed him again." Her tone rose sharply with the anxiety and frustration that were choking her to death.

Her words hung naked in the ill-timed lull they caused. A few nearby heads turned, more at the timbre of her voice than the terse words she had spoken. The small café had filled by this time, and she glanced around, not sure how much of her outburst had been overheard, but found no one was glaring them.

Even with every detail of Ted's confession still vivid in her mind, Susan was still fighting off the shock of it all. "Had you and Ted been drinking when it happened?" she asked in a small voice, barely loud enough to be heard.

Beverly held her gaze. "Stone, cold, sober," she said more softly. "Not a drop. Now that I think of it, I could have used a stiff drink."

"And it was the first time that you ... tried, right?" It was actually something she had forgotten to ask Ted. She tried to see her eyes, but the outsized sunglasses made it impossible. They obscured half of her face, which had taken on a pallor that matched the white tablecloth.

Beverly shrugged this time, looking like she had just bitten into a ripe grape with a nesting hornet in it. Controlling her disappointment, Susan said, "At least it would have been an excuse. I didn't think it would be that easy for you, for anyone, actually."

"Oh, for God's sake, Susan! Please. You know as well as I do there is nothing *easy* about having contact sex with Ted," Beverly said quietly, careful not to raise her voice this time. "You better than anyone."

"Poor choice of words," Susan said with a sigh and a wave of her hand, and then stared down into her wineglass, gathering her thoughts. Then she looked up. "But that's why I've never worried about him getting even with me in spite of what I did. He's never done that before, not that I know of, anyway."

"He said that. He also says he's still in love with you—I guess with the two of us."

Susan made a feral sound at the back of her throat. "And what about you? Are you in love with him?"

Beverly nodded. "I guess … yes, think so. There's something about him, especially since we—since the first time. I can't seem to let go of it."

"You've tried—?" Her brow rose in silent doubt.

"Of course," she nodded, not wanting to meet her gaze, but needing to reassure her. "I didn't want to hurt you—or Jack."

"Then this really is beyond serious, darling."

Beverly took in another deep breath and looked at her now. "It's all so confusing. I don't know what to do anymore. But I don't think I can just stop seeing him."

"Now it sounds like you're asking for permission." She was glaring at Bev again. "My God, you've already slept with him. Is that what this is all about, this sudden confession?" Susan was no longer angry, just saddened and confused, and she felt a tightness in her chest as the reality of it began to overwhelm her.

"No," Beverly said. "I—I just needed someone to talk to. Actually, it was all beginning to drive me a little crazy. But I'm not sure what I want right now," she groaned, noting the open bitterness in Susan's voice.

"What about Jack?" Susan asked, her mind racing to keep pace with the aching feeling in her stomach. Her breathing had become noticeably shallow along with it.

Beverly waved off the question with a pained expression, not wanting to deal with that part of her life right now, not able to actually. *One problem at a time*, her rattled brain cautioned. And the problems between her and Susan were a long way from over.

There was a lull as both women struggled with their thoughts and feelings. "So ..." Susan broke the silence first, her brain playing catch-up as she took the initiative again, "... you were okay with Ted? Umm, I mean *all* of it?" Her look was as skeptical as the question was personal.

Beverly took a moment to consider how much Susan already knew, still unsure that she had not wrung the entire affair out of Ted last night. Deciding to stick with the truth, she nodded weakly, embarrassed by the new level of intimacy. "Not at first. Scared as hell, is more like it. I've never seen ... I mean, my God ... he's frightening." She hesitated before going on. "It may never have gone that far, but he doesn't take *no* for an answer very well either. And you certainly didn't do him justice, or you might have scared me off instead of arousing my curiosity."

"You tried to stop him?" Her brow knitted with equal parts suspicion and concern at the implication.

Beverly reconsidered what she had said and shook her head in retrospect. "No—not exactly I guess, not in those exact words. I suppose I thought it more than anything. I'm not sure. I just know I was scared to death. But just looking at him—at it—isn't something your mind easily accepts. I wasn't sure what he was going to do at first, even how far he would go."

"That's a bunch of horse feathers, darling." Susan almost sneered, but checked herself. "It's a woman thingy, something every girl learns by the time she's had her first serious date. Once they get your pants off, there's absolutely no doubt about what they want to do. The only question is deciding which of the three available places to put their thingies and how soon they can talk you into letting them put it there."

Susan could see that no further explanation was necessary and relaxed a bit. "So, I can see how it must have made you a little curious when I said he was like a mule," Susan said, recalling the boastful comments she had made in the past at several of their luncheons when the conversation had eventually turned to sex, as it sometimes did.

Beverly blushed and arched her brow with a grimace. It was answer enough. *Bitch!* Susan thought, knowing exactly what the look meant, having used it many times herself. "So, now it's my fault because I mentioned how well-endowed he is. Is that it?"

Beverly hunkered her shoulders, knowing she deserved her rancor. Susan saw the stab of pain in her face and decided if they were going to get through this, she would have to soften her approach. "Actually, I was just bragging a little when I said that, the mule thingy. I think mules are all female, actually—mollies or jennies, whatever they're called. Now that I think of it, it wasn't very romantic, either."

"Then how about a stallion?" Beverly mused, sensing a slight change in Susan's demeanor, the thought confirmed when she caught the whimsical smile on her face. Then, testing the waters to see if Susan's ego would allow her to be candid now that they were sharing her husband, Beverly said, "So, what about your first time with Ted? Where you able to just …?"

"God no, darling." Susan sighed, the mind-altering experience forever etched in her memory along with a sense of accomplishment when the long, painful struggle had finally ended successfully. "As a matter of fact, it took a while," she said with her usual open honesty. "I think it was about four months before he, you know, he was able to …" She didn't finish, her candor running out.

"My God, Sue. And you just kept trying—all that time?" Ted's memory was either starting to fade, or he felt the need to protect his wife's flamboyant image.

Letting go of the humiliating thought that her rival might be more capable, the strong sense of competition that she had been struggling with all night came flooding back over Susan. The expression that slowly glazed her face was that of a battle-scarred Hollywood starlet auditioning for her next movie, one that she would do anything to get.

The two women did a stare-down that Susan easily won, and she pressed on. "It must have been more than just curiosity for you to go that far once you found out how unusual he is," Susan said, stiffly. "We've talked about the boys before. I told you how handsome I thought Jack is, and you said you thought Ted was attractive. Why didn't you say something then if you were interested in him?"

"Because it wasn't like that. I wasn't curious before, not like that," Beverly snapped, not that she had the right, but Susan's self-pity was beginning to wear a little thin, adding to the throbbing pain that was still knocking around in her head. She took a breath and went on. "And there was nothing to tell, except for the flirting part, and we talked about that. I also said how lucky you were to have a man who loved you so much, and wondered why you didn't take better care of him. And I'm not talking about breakfast in bed here."

Susan tucked a wayward strand of reddish-blond hair behind her ear and doubled her efforts to preserve the modicum of rapport that still existed between them before it all came flying apart. "I'm not really blaming you, darling," she began slowly. "Believe me, I know how men are. A little squeeze here, a peck on the cheek there, and all the sudden they're madly in love with you," Susan said, sourly, as if she were talking about the enemy instead of one of her favorite subjects.

"He doesn't take no for an answer very well, either," Beverly added.

"Most of the time it's just flirting, having a little fun. God knows I've done my share. But I don't go around taking my pants off for just anyone." The moment she said it, she saw Beverly's brow arch. "Well, not anymore," she said, rolling her eyes in retrospect. "But I still don't understand why you were suddenly attracted to him? And, Bev, don't leave anything out. I really need to hear all of this if we're ever to get through this business without scratching each other's eyes out."

Eleven

everly knew that Ted was not the sudden attraction that Susan suggested. When she thought about it, her curiosity about him probably started about the same time as her troubles with Jack had begun. Which, she had now come to realize, was about the same time Susan and Ted's problems had also begun. Maybe she was sending out some kind of signal that she was not aware of. Perhaps Ted was too.

Nevertheless, she knew Susan's curiosity would demand all the lurid details once she had confessed to the affair with her husband. Beverly breathed out a long sigh of relief when she had recounted the first time they had been alone together. When she finished, Susan urged her on. "And you went back after the hanky-panky, the day he pounced?"

"Not right away. It took a while. God, I didn't know what to do, about him, about my own feelings, about Jack. The hanky-panky part was just the beginning, for me, anyway. I was thoroughly confused by it all, what we had done. Jack and I hadn't been getting along for months, maybe a year, and I didn't know what I wanted to do, except that I wasn't happy with the way things were," Beverly said, feeling a flood of renewed confidence now that it was all coming out in the open. All that was left was for her to satisfy Susan's feline inquisitiveness. Beverly was already breathing easier than a moment ago, aided by a strange calmness that had begun to settle over her.

"Didn't he call, trying to get you to come back?" Susan asked. "It's not like him just to give up like that. And, of course, with me in and out all the time, at the shop and working on the dance committee, you had plenty of opportunity. Actually, I thought you were upset over something when you hadn't been over for a while."

"The next day. And the day after, and the day after that. I don't remember how many times. Sometimes Jack would pick up and Ted would give some lame excuse for calling."

"Thank God the old fool had enough sense not to hang up when Jack answered," Susan mused. "That could have been a problem for you, darling."

Beverly shrugged in agreement, feeling comfortable with the male verses female attitude regarding such things. "Don't think I hadn't thought about that one. Jack even asked if I thought Ted was beginning to lose it a little."

"Then he was suspicious?"

"I don't think so. Other times when I did pick up, thinking it might be you wondering where I'd been and Jack was in the room, I pretended it was and gave some excuse just to get rid of him. It got to the point I didn't dare turn on my cell. Even when I was home alone I was afraid to answer the phone, not knowing what he might do." Her brow furrowed. "I was scared to death that Jack was going to find out, put two and two together somehow, or whatever it is cops do."

"And suspicious husbands, too, darling, don't forget," Susan added, possibly making more of it than Bev realized at the time. "But I think that was your guilty conscience talking to you, dear."

In the following weeks, Beverly recalled how she had struggled with equal parts of guilt and curiosity about Ted. Then, one day when Jack was out of town on a case, Ted had called again, pleading with her to come over just to talk. And she had gone back, knowing exactly what kind of signal it would send. One with *surrender* written all over it.

Susan had a sour look on her face as if she were having a gas pain. "You know we've never discussed age before, but he's so much older. God knows we hadn't done it in ages. I wasn't even sure he could anymore. I can only hope that he doesn't remind you of your father."

It was Beverly's turn to bristle, and she felt the hair at the back of her neck stiffen. "You're beginning to sound like Jack now. Why should Ted's age have a damned thing to do with it? And he doesn't look anything like my father, for your information." Then, deciding it was time to get it all out on the table, she said, "I think Ted's one of the sexiest men I've ever known. And, if you really want to know, he's doing just fine for his age—what the hell ever that happens to be."

Susan was surprised by the outburst and at her own composure, but the words tore at her just the same. She was more surprised that the two of them had not discussed the subject before, but decided to let the remark pass for the moment and tried another more subtle approach.

"You know you're gorgeous, darling. All you have to do is raise an eyebrow and you could practically have any man you wanted, married, unmarried, younger, older, whatever. If it's a fling you wanted, why didn't you pick someone closer to your own age? And, well, more average than Ted?" She hated sounding tacky, but could not think of any other way to say it. "What about the wine guy at the market? You said he flirts with you all the time." Susan paused a moment in thought. "Of course, there's a rumor that someone from the yacht club's been hitting on him lately."

Beverly felt the flush in her face and wanted to laugh at the same time. Susan still didn't get it. Ted was not a fling, a novelty to be tried out for a while and then cast aside when she got bored. "You make it sound like I was on the prowl, Sue." For a moment, she thought of sharing her innermost feelings with her, how intense their lovemaking was, the unbelievable orgasms he forced her to have, but she knew it would only serve to provoke her. "And I wasn't looking for an affair with the wine guy or anyone else," she added. "Besides, I'm old enough to be his mother—well, almost. Anyway, it's as if Ted ..." She did not finish and let the deeply personal thought drift away like a wisp of smoke.

"As if he what, darling?" Susan prompted, noting her emotion and was careful not to press too hard.

"It's difficult to explain," Beverly said, finally. "But I certainly don't want to come between the two of you. But you've never given me the impression that you'd really care."

Susan grimaced and wanted to choke on the irony. "Because I never thought I had to worry about him before, that's why," she croaked. "And sleeping with someone and seeing them are entirely two different things, in case you hadn't noticed."

Beverly shrugged off the angry-wife challenge and took another breath of the salty sea air that wafted onto the patio off the bay as she looked around at the other nearby tables. The place had begun to fill up at this hour, becoming as noisy as it was crowded, and no one was paying any attention to them except the busboy who had been eyeing Susan's cleavage every time he passed their table.

"Well, yes, but I couldn't exactly come right out and ask you if it was all right if I slept with your husband, could I. In a way, I actually thought I might even be doing you a favor, and Ted, since you'd given up sleeping with him for a while."

"Oh, how rational can we get, darling?" Sarcasm was dripping out of every pore in her body and was more than obvious in her voice. Clearly, Susan thought it was a cheap shot, an excuse to climb into bed Ted. But how many times had she done the same thing?

Damn all men, she thought bitterly. *All they want to do is screw you.* But, when she stopped to think about it, that probably wasn't such a bad thing.

Beverly did not try to defend herself; it was a battle she couldn't win, and wondered if things would be different between her and Ted now that Susan knew about them.

"And what about you, Bev? Weren't you doing yourself a favor too?" Susan let out a subdued neigh that sounded like a broodmare whistling after a passing bucket of oats. "Once you recovered, that is."

"Mmm …" Beverly moaned under her breath, admitting nothing, yet everything, her expression safely hidden behind her dark sunglasses.

After a moment, Susan reached over and grudgingly patted the top of her hand, noticing how smooth and tanned her skin was. Pushing her jealousy aside for the moment she said, "As a woman, darling, one who happens to have been around the block a few times, I understand how things can happen. But I'm sure you can imagine how I'm feeling just a little bit left out of all of this. Come to think of it, some of it is probably is my fault. You must have been curious after some of the silly things I said about Ted."

The slight change of attitude caught Beverly off guard. "Like what …?"

"You know, how unusual he is," she said rather unemotionally, for what they were talking about. "The mule thingy. I 'm actually surprised that you could manage."

"Frankly, so was I," Beverly said, recalling that Ted had said the same thing and concealing the feeling of accomplishment that was helping subdue her anxiety.

Susan wished she could see her eyes, but it was impossible, and then decided to ask a question she had thought about a number of times before Ted's confession last night. "Speaking of your, ah, success with Ted, Jack must have something to do with it, right?"

Beverly eyed her closely and decided that she was fishing again. "Not really. I guess you'd say he's average. Maybe more. God, Susan, I really don't know," she said at last, trying to imagine what *average* was. "I've never thought about it that much," she added, uncomfortable with the new level of intimacy between them and wondered why it was making her nervous, but she already knew the answer. She had never slept with another woman's husband before and then leisurely told her about it over a Cobb salad.

"Why is it you've never mentioned anything about Jack? We've certainly talked about the boys enough times."

"In the first place, *you* were always talking about Ted. And you never came right out and asked me about Jack," Beverly countered uneasily. "Or … I may have. And since you always seemed to be bragging about Ted, I didn't need to get into a pissing contest over something I couldn't win. Besides, I really didn't believe you. And comparing our husband's body parts actually makes me a little uncomfortable, if you want the truth."

"So, now it's my turn to be curious, darling, since I obviously don't know Jack nearly as well as you know my Ted. You definitely have the advantage," Susan said, the mixture of envy and sarcasm in her voice making it sound harsh.

"Would you like that? Sleeping with Jack?" Beverly asked, the thought of the two of them together had not occurred to her before. She had not had any seriously thoughts in that regard since the wild New Year's party a few years ago just before she and Jack had moved up from LA. In the past, however, she had noticed that Susan had made an occasional off-color remark to him, but she also noticed how Jack had ignored them and appeared not to notice.

"Don't be silly, darling, of course I would. I'd love it, adore it even. He's absolutely gorgeous. But the question is, would *you* mind if I did?" A vague idea had been flashing in and out of Susan's mind since last night, and she found herself laying the groundwork for something she could not quite put her finger on just yet, something she had not yet figured out. But the possibilities that were beginning to crystallize in her mind excited her.

"Right now—since it's you we're talking about, and with everything that's been going on—probably not, if that's what you mean," Beverly answered without hesitation and realized that it probably meant that she still had some serious feelings for Jack, perhaps more than she realized. She was beginning to see Susan in a new light.

Susan nodded thoughtfully, acknowledging the concession, but decided to pursue it. "You know I think Jack is dreamy. And I'd love to spend the night with him, several nights, in fact." Her eyes crinkled with the carnal smile that came over her, the possibility of revenge lurking at the corners of her glossed lips where the perfect amount of collagen added to her beauty. "And we already know how Ted feels about you, darling. At first I thought he might just be trying to make me jealous." Susan glanced away, suspecting that Beverly was watching her closely, but was able to see her eyes and did not want another one-sided stare-down with her. "I guess you could say I haven't been the best wife. But I do love Ted. Always have."

"I'm sure he knows that," Beverly said, unnecessarily coming to his rescue.

Susan sighed. "And now—? Well, now it appears that he's in love with a very attractive, younger woman who loves him back. That's never happened before."

Beverly considered the backhanded compliment for a moment and decided it was safer to let it pass. "This may sound a little crazy, and I don't want you to take it the wrong way, but ... well, you've had some experience. Have you ever been in love with two men at the same time? Do you think that's possible?"

The thought caused something to click suddenly in Susan's overworked imagination; it nudged at the same illusive thought that had been ghosting around in her addled brain since last night and abruptly popped into dim focus now with the question.

"Of course it is, darling. I could never sleep with a man I wasn't in love with, even if it was only for a few hours." Then the thin smile she donned said something else. "Or a few minutes even, depending on the circumstances. Some of them didn't even last that long." Parts of the nagging puzzle were definitely beginning to take shape now.

Beverly couldn't help but return the smile. "What are you trying to say, girl?"

"I have to admit this is a little embarrassing, but you already know that Ted and I haven't been very lovey-dovey, not like that anyway."

"For about a year," Beverly said, remembering her surprise at the confession she'd made some time ago. Why she remembered, she wasn't quite sure. Or was she?

"I don't remember exactly. But that's not really the point. The point is, darling, a while back I wasn't completely honest with you," Susan said with a pouty expression. "It wasn't because *I* didn't want to play house anymore. Apparently it was actually Ted who couldn't—with me, anyway. He just wasn't able to. And halfway measures aren't good enough for someone like him to ... well, you know, to get the job done."

"All or nothing at all, you mean? Like that—?"

"So to speak, because of his size," she said, and nodded, satisfied that Beverly had grasped the problem and was probably trying to picture it in her mind. "Now I find that he's doing just fine with someone else. The whole thing came as complete surprise."

So there it is, Beverly thought. And it confirmed Ted's story almost perfectly, but it did not make her feel any better. And the earlier "younger woman" crack had not been lost on her. "When Ted didn't have any difficulty like that, I sort of put two and two together and assumed it was the other way around. Not that it makes any difference," Beverly said honestly.

"You haven't been doing that well with Jack yourself, from what you've told me. How would it make you feel if he couldn't perform ... with you? Then you find out he's doing just fine with someone else? Like me, for instance."

Beverly knew her dark glasses were hiding what was showing in her face and nodded her understanding. "Not good," she admitted. "Crappy, in fact. But Jack's never had that problem."

"He's not Ted's age either," Susan reminded her. The hurt had begun to set in last night after Ted's confession had rolled out of him like a scene from a cheap romance novel. "I just thought there was something wrong with him. I even insisted he see a doctor, who did some tests and couldn't find anything wrong. So, since he seems to be doing just fine with you, it was obviously *me*. What else could it be?"

Susan tried to scrutinize Beverly, what she could see of her face not concealed behind her sunglasses. It was catty, but she was pleased to see the little telltale signs of maturity lurking around her mouth beneath the expensive makeup that wasn't all that perfect this morning. Neither of them looked their age. They were very much alike in that respect, except that Susan had undergone several cosmetic procedures in the past. However, it was somehow satisfying to know that Beverly's time to go under the knife was coming, just as hers had.

It was the price of beauty—at her age, anyway.

"I had no idea, of course. You said you just weren't interested anymore. I'm sorry," Beverly said apologetically. "I wish there was something we could do. I—I don't know what to say." The tension had been building between the two women like a bolt of unchained lightning, and Susan imagined that if she reached out to touch her, a great spark of static electricity would arc between them.

During the lull, Beverly sucked in her breath, knowing she had to finish with her story in order to put it all behind them, if that was even possible. Then, on a sudden impulse, she picked up Susan's half-full wineglass and drained it in a single gulp. With an equally huge effort she kept it all from coming back up, refilled the glass with a grimace, and held her breath a second time and gulped it down. After a moment, during which she was not sure if she would throw up, her stomach finally settled down and she began to pull her thoughts together.

She would see this through, somehow, someway.

"Oh, my goodness, darling, with the hangover you have? The rest of this must be really good," she said with a Machiavellian interest in the more intimate female version of the scenario she'd played over and over in her mind since hearing it from her husband the night before and already knew by heart. "But do me a favor and please take off those damned sunglasses you're wearing. I need to see your eyes for this, darling."

Beverly grimaced with the shudder that had begun churning in her stomach as the wine went to work on her.

Twelve

*W*hen she removed her sunglasses, Beverly was sure her eyes were as red-rimmed and puffy as they were earlier that morning before she left the house. It was late afternoon now as she looked around the restaurant at the thinning crowd and took another sip of wine. The first several swallows were already beginning to calm the fierce case of jangled nerves she was suffering from and had been steadily building in her throughout the nearly sleepless night she had just spent. She took a few minutes to order her thoughts, set her mind to the task, and then continued with her story.

"You already know about the first time," Beverly began slowly, "when he, we, got a little carried away after I let him kiss me."

"My God, from what you've said, you did a lot more than that. And once he unzipped your jeans it went way beyond flirting," Susan said, hoping she didn't sound bitter.

"Susan, I'm just trying to get through this with you! You wanted details, and I'm just trying to give them to you!" Beverly shot back. "And—"

Susan waved a hand in dismissal, cutting her off, pursing her perfect lips. "Never mind, darling. And no need to get huffy," she said, and poured another wine. "I didn't mean it like that, the way it sounded." She took sip to help quell the green-eyed monster again. "Well, you two had a pretty good time it sounds like. Knowing Ted, I'm surprised you were able to hold him off."

"Oh, he tried," Bev said, unable to hide the scowl and blushed with the thought, how he had tried to force her down onto the couch.

Susan caught the look and understood. "I can't imagine the nerve of the old bastard, pouncing like that."

Beverly exhaled audibly. "Then you can imagine how I felt. And I was scared to death you'd walk in the door any minute and say something to Jack."

"Darling, you know me better then that. And who knows, I might have joined in," she sniggered at the thought, but was hurt that Bev would dream that she would go to Jack. "But why didn't you just get up and leave if that's the way you felt?"

Beverly shrugged, still not sure herself, except by that time he already had her jeans half off. "I don't know what came over me. I thought about leaving when I first got there, when you weren't home. You know how he's been lately." The apology screwed up in her face could have easily been mistaken for the latent guilt she was feeling.

Susan chuckled in retrospect. "And how was Ted handling all of this? He had to be horny. It had been ages since he'd had a roll in the hay."

"There was some groping—on both sides, actually. That's when I found out that you had totally underestimated him."

"No one would believe the truth, darling. But you both … you know … like enjoyed?"

Beverly blushed again. "If you mean did we have an orgasm, yes—it, it was very exciting," Bev admitted after a moment, not knowing how else to explain it. "Once I got past the shock of what we were doing, it was pretty intense—for both of us."

Seeing her discomfort, Susan reached over and patted the top of her hand again, giving it a reassuring squeeze before picking up her wineglass. "Well, I'm not sure why you're so upset. It's only a love affair we're talking about. It just happens to be with someone else's husband, that's all. No one is going to die from it. It's probably even therapeutic in some ways, who knows. I didn't know why at the time, of course, but it's certainly been good for Ted. And now that you've told me, it's not even a secret anymore. Lord knows I've had my share of affairs—some of them more lovely than others. And if it had to happen, I guess I'd rather he did it with a friend rather than a stranger I don't even know. It's certainly not the end of the world."

Susan toyed with her salad. "Are you going to continue seeing him—carry this on? It's up to you, of course."

Bev was surprisingly relieved that Susan was not trying to dissuade her, to keep her from seeing Ted, and was just acting the way any wife would under similar circumstances. "That's the other reason I needed to talk to you. I don't know what to do, or what's going to happen with Jack and me. But I feel much better now that you know. But I can't keep it from him forever. He already suspects."

She chuckled. "After last night, darling, so does the entire yacht club." Susan sighed heavily and felt the bitterness begin to drain out of her like a tub of lukewarm bathwater. "So, what are we going to do about Jack? You haven't told him any of this, of course."

"Good God, Susan, no! But he's bound to find out later. Last night he practically accused me of sleeping with Ted."

"And—?" Susan gave a noticeable twitch at the thought.

"I was too sick from all the drinking, on top of the tension I've been under lately. And I remembered what you said just before we left the party. Anyway, by the time we got home I was a total wreck. I didn't know what to do or to say. I was throwing up all over the place and I think he felt sorry for me. I was able to put him off. But after last night he knows something's going on. It's the cop thing with him. He acted like I was a crime scene he was investigating once we got home. And he'd never believe me if I just denied everything. Not now, after last night. I was even afraid he might go to Ted or you if he couldn't get it out of me."

"But, darling, take it from someone who knows a lot more about men than you do, that's exactly what you have to do. Don't *ever* tell him that you've actually slept with someone else. They can't handle that sort of thing. Their egos get all inflamed and as big as their prostate glands and all they can see is another man in bed with their personal property." Her smile was weak yet knowing. "It's too bad, but that's how it is with men, the way they think. Once they put that ring on your finger they think they own you, especially what's in your panties." She cackled at the crass remark. "They're such little boys when it comes to sex, and so predictable."

"And when he brings it up again? What then?" she said, not sharing in the humor.

"Well, the first thing, darling, is to admit that you have feelings for Ted. And I *do* mean those kinds of feelings. That's important. He already suspects something, and it will help boost your credibility if you just admit it, tell him yourself." Susan brushed a strand of long hair off her face. "That will lay the foundation for everything else, whatever that happens to be. When he finally does find out—and if you carry this on long enough, he *will* find out, darling—it will make you look less slutty. That's just the way men think. And it has nothing to do with how long you've been together or how much they say they love you. That's just the way it is." Susan was feeling quite the sage and went on with a wry smile, "Nothing personal, but women can be a bit slutty at times. It can actually be fun, darling, if you don't over do it. Men are so juvenile when it comes to relationships. If they understood women half as well as well as we do them, there wouldn't be any more wars," she grinned.

Beverly was too frustrated to appreciate the humor. "Suppose he just comes right out and accuses me again? There's no way I can get away with lying to him. He was a detective for twenty years, and a

PI after that. Sometimes I think he can read my mind, that knows what I'm thinking before I do, sometimes."

"I don't know that much about cops, darling, but I do know men. And this is definitely a *man* thingy. When that happens, that's when you deny, deny, deny," Susan said emphatically. "It takes a while for it to sink into their thick skulls sometimes, but if you stick to your guns he'll have to accept it sooner or later. They can suspect all they want to, but it's the confession thingy they can't handle," she said, her tone motherly. "Just don't talk in your sleep, darling."

When Beverly did not reply, just stared at her through bloodshot eyes, Susan added, "Do you still love him, Bev, I mean *really?*"

Beverly blinked back her emotions; not trying to hide what she knew was in her face. "I used to adore him."

"Well, if you still have feelings for Jack, you should probably start taking your relationship a little more seriously before you lose him altogether."

Susan took some more wine. "So tell me, girl, what happened when you finally did go back?"

The Agony and The Ecstasy

Thirteen

The two women had only nibbled at their food by the time the table was cleared away and they sat alone again. The crowd had thinned; the strain they were under and had been weighing heavily on them was beginning to lift. Beverly's hangover had taken a turn for the better, now little more than a bad memory with the help of a second bottle of wine, and Susan had settled into a mood of curious acceptance.

"I didn't go back right away. I knew what would happen. And I was afraid of both Ted and Jack, obviously for different reasons," Beverly said, taking up where she had left off.

"So, when did you? I wondered why you hadn't been over," Susan nodded.

"He called again for the umpteenth time one day when Jack was gone, said you were off shopping for the day and that we needed to talk about us—about what happened."

"Yeah, right," Susan huffed. "The bastard. How long had it been since you'd seen him? Alone ..." She was trying to keep the chronology clear in her mind.

"Probably two weeks, maybe a little longer. I don't remember, exactly. I was worried sick about Jack finding out. And I thought Ted might break down and tell you what happened that day. You know how he can't keep a secret, especially about something like that. He called so many times, but I just kept making excuses."

"Well, he kept this one. He never said a word," Susan mused. "But he was a bit moody about then, now that I think of it."

"That's probably because you never asked him, or he would have told you. You know how he is. That's the difference between Ted and Jack—one of them, anyway."

Susan cracked a thin smile at the inference with an unfeminine grunt. "What did he finally say to convince you?"

"When he called that day, we talked for a while. With Jack gone, I couldn't use him as an excuse. And …"

"Don't tell me, and you wanted to see him again anyway, right?"

"The short answer is 'Yes,' I did. But it wasn't that easy. I knew what would happen if I went back after the last time, how far we went, and it frightened me to even think …"

"I don't have to guess why, darling," Susan said, and shrugged reflectively. "I had the same doubts myself at first. No woman in her right mind would ever believe that she could—well, umm, even possibly …"

Beverly took in a deep breath to help clear her head. "It must have been written all over me from the way he met me at the door. I felt a little—"

"Slutty is a good word for it," Susan finished for her. Only this time she wasn't doing her mind reading act very well.

Beverly ignored the sarcasm with some of her own. "I don't know, why don't you tell me? You've had a lot more experience at that sort of thing than I have."

Susan did not try to hide the scowl that curled up at the corners of her mouth and darkened her face. "Touché, darling. But that was a bit uncalled for. After all, this is about you screwing my Ted behind my back, not me and my past. Which, by the way, he has long since forgiven me for, however checkered it might have been."

Beverly stared at her. Her initial fear of the woman all but vanished. Susan stared back.

When the tension simmered down to a slow boil, Beverly said, "Actually, I was thinking of something more along the lines of overwhelmed, if you really want to know."

Susan shrugged, accepting the stalemate for what it was worth. Beverly had nowhere near the experience she did, but she had to give her credit, the woman was a lot stronger than she realized, possibly even dangerous. Susan was beginning to wonder if she was past her prime, or if she was just getting soft.

"So, what happened then?" she asked dryly, already knowing the answer, but needing to hear her say it, the sting of punishment in her words.

"So—" Beverly continued with a difficult sigh that had embarrassment written all over it, "you were gone for the day, Jack was out of town, and we ended up on the couch—naked."

Bev's words were candid, but without rancor, and the honesty of them took Susan by surprise, causing her brow to kick up curiously and her pulse to jump at the same time. "Oh my," she puffed, as if she had just heard a juicy piece of gossip. "Well, I ... I really need to hear this part, dear. Could you go back ... and start with the getting naked part?"

There were no formalities this time when she entered the kitchen that day. Ted closed the door behind her, swooped her up into his arms, her own curling around his neck. He clutched at the sides of her breasts before moving down to her waist, then over the wide saddle of her hips, pulling her body firmly into his. They kissed hungrily, eagerly clinging to each other until Beverly felt her knees begin to weaken and she pushed back, struggling free of him.

"My God, Teddy," she said, breathlessly, "let me in the door first."

"God, I've missed you, kitten," he rasped and tried to kiss her again, but she pushed him back. His strained expression was hidden behind a sheepish grin, that wasn't working. He was in his usual Berkeley sweatshirt and pants, his hair still damp from the pool, where he had just completed his daily workout.

"It's good to see you, too." Bev broke free and brushed past him into the living room. She was casually dressed in a soft cotton-cashmere sweatshirt and jeans, her dark honey-blonde hair flipped, and wafting Chanel all over the place.

Ted followed, taking her in his arms again. She pushed at his shoulders and tried to step away, but he pulled her down onto the couch. "I'm sorry, I don't know what's come over me. I've been going crazy thinking about you. I guess I can't believe you're really here." He worked to control his stressed and shallow breathing, his tone growing more intense by the minute as he tried to quell his excitement, but that wasn't working either.

"Well, I know what's come over you," she said more seriously than she felt, looking down at the evidence that was impossible to conceal.

Fourteen

As Beverly held his gaze, her mind was abuzz trying to decide exactly why she had come back. There were so many reasons, none of them justified, yet all valid. She finally pushed away all of the guilt-ridden feelings she had been struggling with since the last time she had been alone with him, along with any thought of leaving.

Since the first time they were together, she had struggled with the thought that she would eventually come back. Now that she had, she was fighting back the nagging guilt that had kept her away. Beverly softly touched Ted's face and then gently kissed him. Her lips parted, inviting him, wanting him. Still, she tensed when his hands slipped under her cashmere sweatshirt and began to fondle her, instantly causing her nipples to harden. After a moment, he unfastened the clasp on her bra, releasing her breast from their bondage of silk and lace. He explored each one tenderly at first, and then cupped them firmly with more intensity, kneading the soft flesh in his large hands, feeling her heat, her heartbeat, as he rolled the firm nipples between his fingers. Then he pulled her top over her head, unfastened her jeans and slid them down over her long legs. Consumed with passion, she unconsciously raised her hips and her panties followed.

Completely naked, her silky hair cascaded over her bare shoulders as Ted pressed her back onto the cushions. "My God, Teddy …" she panted when she was splayed out before him, looking up at the looming hulk towering over her. He kissed her again, and she did her best to fight off the fog that was smothering her thoughts.

Ted pulled back, his gaze riveted on her naked body, and quickly began to strip out of his warm-up suit. When he finished, her eyes went wide in disbelief, fascinated and frightened at the same time at what she saw. Her heart was pounding wildly and she broke out in a light sweat as Ted positioned himself, daring her, pressing her there, hard, promising everything, demanding the impossible.

In a sudden burst of panic, Beverly roughly pushed him away. "Wait, Teddy! Stop!" Then, just as suddenly, clutched him to her. "I—I'm going to … Oh, Jesus!" Bev moaned throatily, quivering in her panic, her nails digging into his upper arms. "Oh, God, Ted—yes!" She gulped the air she needed to help clear the heavy veil of fog that was engulfing her and grasped him to her breast, her eyes rolled back in her head, her back aching, her hips thrusting upward into him.

Fifteen

She did not know how long she had been trapped beneath him panting like a caged animal, waiting for her orgasm to subside, finally returning her to reality. She had never experienced anything like it before, and was relieved when there was nothing left except a series of tiny electric shocks that left her covered in sweat, limp and drained, her skin burning and sensitive to the slightest touch.

When she could finally breathe halfway normally again, she gave Ted the half-lidded, crooked smile of a drowsing cat.

He had been watching her intently, waiting for her to come back to him. "Looks like you just had a very good time," he said with a satisfied grin.

With her passion ebbed and temporarily satisfied, she was suddenly aware of the bulky fullness in her. She thrust her hips into him to be sure and was instantly stunned by the sharp stab of pain. "My God, Teddy, did you—? Are you—? Oh, my God!"

"Can't you tell, baby girl?" he said, proudly. "I knew you could," he purred at her, nearly half buried, his smile huge. "My turn now, baby," he said and slowly began where he had left off when she had unexpectedly checked out on him.

Ted knew he was going to hurt her this time; there was no way around it. But he didn't invent this game, he just knew how to play it. As he began, Beverly's hips rose naturally, melding into the contour of his body. But when Ted dug his knees into the cushions and pressed firmly against her, she grunted loudly when he reached the depth she was accustomed to and there was no further progress. Ted shifted his bulk and pushed harder, causing her to recoil.

"Ahh—Jesus, Teddy!" Beverly moaned, her head arching back. He hunched his shoulders and pushed again, harder this time.

"Oh, Christ!" she gasped, sucking in more air against the pain that was radiating all the way up into her chest. She had already broken out in a light sweat that plastered her hair to her forehead. Trembling, she squinted up at him, her eyes slitted open as his hips moved painfully into her again. Beverly was beginning to understand why Susan had always come back to him. He was electrifying, a fantasy she'd never dreamed possible. She just wasn't sure if she would faint before he finished with her and ruin everything.

Ted looked down at the sizable gap between them as he pulled back to gauge his progress. "Sl-ow-er …" she groaned, her breast bucking in unison with the motion of his hips.

He glared at her, panting, unable to speak for a moment. Beverly was fighting to control the scream lurking at the back of her throat and threatening to gag her just as he lunged again.

"Aaaughh—!"

The scream leapt from her uncontrollably.

"Jesus Christ, Ted! Stop! You're hurting me!" The tears began to stream down her mottled face.

Startled at the sudden outcry, Ted hesitated, saw the anguish in her face, but began again almost immediately. She tried to protest again but could barely manage a curdled growl that served to heighten his passion, making him even more determined. Beverly grimaced as another wave of magnificent agony swept through her entire body, hating it, yet loving it at the same time. She pushed at his upper body in a futile effort to dislodge him. But her strength ebbed as a wave of nausea suddenly gripped her. She groaned and clawed at his back until he snapped out of his stupor.

Ted raised his damp body to look down. He had seen the same look on other women—face flushed, a dull, blotchy mottling under a sweaty sheen—but none more beautiful then hers. Beverly shut her eyes again. Her lips curled back in a grimace, a tiny trickle of blood showing where she had bitten her lower lip.

"You okay, baby girl?" He breathed heavily. A drop of perspiration dripped from his nose onto her cheek. He mindlessly bent to lick it off, savoring the salty bittersweet mixture of sweat and makeup, her warm heavy musk wafting, making him dizzy.

Unable to speak, Beverly grunted at him, her eyes open now but dull and flat, her face a mask as she tried to suck more air into her starving lungs.

"You want to stop for a minute, kitten?" he panted. He could tell he was over halfway.

His voice seemed far away, yet his breath was close and heavy on her face, that of a spent athlete. She shook her head with an effort, knowing what that meant, afraid to close her eyes now, afraid of passing out.

"*Oh God, not now. Please don't let me faint!*" she begged her subconscious, but the words came whispering out of her loud enough for him to hear. She was at the end of her tolerance, needed for it to be over, yet knowing that he would not stop until he had finished with her.

Bev lost track of time as they lay motionless, his hot, sweaty bulk pressing her deep into the cushions, her raised knees agape and stretch to the limit, the corded tendons of her inner thighs as tight as steel cables, distorting the little tattoo she had beyond its design. She cradled his muscled torso, her eyes mere slits as she glared up at him, afraid to move until her labored breathing began to wane along with the burning inside of her.

Ted shifted his weight slightly to ease the strain on her heaving chest. He waited for her to say something. When she did not speak, he slowly began to press himself into her again, straining to hold back the flood that was building in him, holding back until he totally engulfed her.

Beverly clenched her teeth tightly, the muscles in her jaw rippling, as her head bucked rhythmically to his motion. She cried out again, the bite of her nails meaningless as they cut into the soft flesh under his arms. He saw her grimace. The tears had stopped, but he knew the pain she was feeling. Determined to put an end to it, Ted arched his back and drove his hips into her with a final powerful thrust.

"Aaaughhhh—!"

Beverly's scream was loud enough to arouse the neighbors as the lightning bolt of white-hot pain struck deep inside of her. She bolted, clawing at him, trying desperately to dislodge him, to retreat, but it was useless. She was pinned helplessly beneath his bulk and groaned loudly as another sharp stab of pain overtook the first, then teetered on the edge of consciousness but hung on. They remained motionless for a moment, her chest heaving as she gulped in the air she needed to survive.

"You okay, baby girl?" He watched her for a long moment; his groin now pressed hard against hers.

Beverly felt the gorging fullness of him. She tried to suck in more air, but his dead weight was pressing her heavily into the cushions nearly collapsing her lungs. She forced her eyes open and glared at him, her face beet red now, her hair plastered over her sweat-soaked face. His broad chest heaved with his own labored breathing, allowing her to take only small breaths. Bev's mind swirled between the encroaching darkness she felt closing in and the intense pain where she judged her uterus used to be.

Beverly saw his strained expression through the fog that had come over her. She did not know how much time had passed, but the panic that gripped her moments before was no longer sending off a Klaxon of alarm bells in her head. Her fear of him had gone from fantasy to reality—and she had survived.

Ted noticed the change in her expression. "Better, baby? Want to stop for a minute?" She had screamed so loudly that his ears were still ringing.

"Did you—? Have you … finished yet?" she croaked weakly.

He shook his head. "Close. The worst is over."

She shuddered. "Then you have to set up—let me catch my breath," she panted, her breathing less labored now but still difficult. The pain had subsided considerably, and she guessed that something resembling the fat end of a baseball bat had deadened every nerve inside of her, making her numb. She could only hope that she was bleeding all over his fucking couch! Let him explain that one to Susan!

"How's that?" Ted sat up a little and pressed his hips tightly into her, but he could go no further. "How're we doing?"

She winced, but managed a nod, feeling the pulsating end pressing hard against her sternum, sending a quiver up her spine and fueling the small fire that was lurking somewhere in the shadows. She curled her legs over him, locking her ankles, making it impossible for him to maneuver, allowing the good feeling in her to take hold. There was another jab of pain and she took another deep breath to quell it.

"Aside from feeling like I've just given birth to a fifty-pound kid, Teddy, I think I'm fine," she rasped, using the back of her hand to mop the stinging sweat out of her eyes, hoping he was right and the worst was over. She could feel him about to explode.

Sixteen

Ted managed a twisted grin, the respite helping to pull him back from the edge. Then Beverly finally relaxed the grip she was holding on him and lowered her legs, the signal for him to begin again. Ted snuggled his face back down into the hot, Chanel-reeking curve of her neck and slowly began to work on her, taking the long deep strides that he had not been able to before.

Beverly lost track of time, and after several long minutes said, "Can't you—why haven't you finished yet?" She felt as though she might fade again, wincing with the burning inside, but grateful that it had lessened considerably, replaced by the enormous fullness of him. She could feel the prickly sex flesh that covered her from head to toe now and usually preceded an orgasm and wondered if that was possible after the way he had been mauling her.

Ted shrugged like a naughty boy. "I guess I don't want it to be over, kitten," he said, maintaining the slow rhythmic motion of his hips, but the strain was obvious in his perspiring face.

"Well, for God's sake, Teddy, just stop that! Either come or get off me," she huffed at him, blowing a damp strand of hair out of her eyes. But it was an empty threat, meant only to hurry him. Then Bev let a thought slip out that she had been mulling over in her mind while trying to dodge the pain he was causing her. "Is it ... I mean, am I ..." She suddenly winced and sucked in her breath when he went deeper. She waited until he resumed his natural rhythm. "Am I ... like Susan?" she finally managed, but it did not come out as seductively as she had intended.

Ted knew it was a trap, a trick question, and looked down into her blotchy face with a half grin. "I guess so. Sort of, maybe," he admitted, "but different. You're a much bigger girl than Sue."

It wasn't the answer she expected. "Whatever that's supposed to mean," she scowled at him, and tried to concentrate on the little inner spark that was definitely building in her and promising something more.

He grinned at the sour look on her face and the way she had said the words. "I didn't mean *there*." He gave his pelvis an extra nudge to emphasize where *there* was. "I just meant that Susan's pretty small, and you're a much bigger girl—all over."

She knew the *all over* part wasn't exactly true. Susan was at least a "triple-D" cup, while she was several sizes smaller. "Well, at least there're two of us big enough to handle you now," she said, alluding to the alterations he had just made in her, and then gasped as he plunged even deeper. "My God, Teddy!" Her voice sounded like a feral cat as the air went out of her and she struggled to catch her breath.

Ted was watching as her chest rose and fell with the rapid motion of her breathing when a sudden wave of nausea threatened her again, every nerve in her body jagged and raw. When it passed, Beverly said, "So, what about Sue ... the first time?" She tightened her arms around his neck and gazed into his blue eyes, her hips slowly moving with his now as he worked on her; surprised that she had asked such a question.

Without interrupting his slow, steady pace, Ted tenderly licked a dollop of sweat off her chin then kissed her puffy red lips. "She couldn't do it the first time we tried. It took her a while."

Beverly managed a tight smile that helped mask her pain. "Dare I tell her that I won first prize—when I can walk again, that is?"

She was already near exhaustion when he kissed her again, his hips rhythmically drawing back nearly a foot before gliding all the way into her again, his tongue reaching the place where her tonsils used to be when she was a kid, helping to rekindle the tiny flame that was still smoldering in her. She did not gag this time and wondered if she would get used to the rest of him as well.

After a moment, she broke away and said, "Why don't we stop talking so much and—"

As quickly as the words came out of her mouth, she immediately regretted them.

"Aahhh—!"

Her eyes closed tightly against the pain, saliva flicking of from her swollen lips. Then her nails clawed at him, the ache heightening her desire. There was no way to fake what had suddenly exploded throughout her entire body like a river of molten lava.

Weak from exhaustion and numb from her waist to her knees, Beverly knew he had bruised her thighs and her breasts and everywhere else on her body he had mauled her to prevent her escaping, and had made other permanent alterations in her.

As she waited for him to recover from the gushing, convulsive spasms that were still causing him to twitch, she thought of Jack. She wondered how long she could keep her new secret from him and about their future together. More than that, she wondered if he would even care once he found out. The thought saddened her as much as Ted thrilled her.

The Third Visit

Seventeen

A brooding afternoon haze had drifted over the water filtering the soft rays of the fading sun that streamed in through the large glass portals from which Windows on the Bay took it name, casting long shadows across the dining room. In the distance, several great blue herons raced to beat the fading light that was fast turning into the gray shades of dusk, back to their nests high in the distant trees at the water's edge.

The day had grown late by the time the two women had moved from the small café in the marina that served only breakfast and lunch to their favorite restaurant on the Embarcadero to complete the unfinished business that still lay festering between them, threatening both their marriages and their friendship.

Beverly was edgy. Her nerves were still jangled, only partially calmed by the wine they'd had at lunch. She was near exhaustion, while Susan was sure if her stomach knotted up just one more time she would probably throw up. But the short time it had taken them to change venues had proven a welcome respite from the tension that had been steadily building between them all day.

It was too early for dinner and the place was nearly empty. The two women had taken their favorite table in the far corner near the windows that looked out over the harbor with a view of the returning fishing boats. Seagulls were cawing and darting overhead as bait tanks were cleaned and flushed overboard while other crewmembers on deck were busily filleting the catch of the day that would soon be for sale at dockside.

Beverly and Susan settled down in the soft afterglow of late afternoon to finish their business in relative privacy, which was just the way they wanted it. The only distraction was a young couple at the bar who had been having a not-so-private discussion since they had arrived and the young woman's distraught voice easily carried across the large dining room.

"But you said you loved me!" the girl cried, her tears flowing into the half-empty margarita on the bar in front of her.

"I know, honey, but—" The young man grimaced, the pilsner of draft beer in front of him untouched.

"We're supposed to get married!" she protested, nervously twisting the small solitaire engagement ring on her left hand.

"But that was before, honey," he groaned defensively.

"Before what—?" her haggard voice rising to just below a screech.

"Before … um … Darlene," he gulped helplessly.

The girl went rigid and then livid with rage, making it obvious that she knew exactly who *Darlene* was, and sprang from her seat, nearly falling off the barstool in the process. She tossed what was left of her drink full in his face, twisted off the tiny ring and threw it at him as well, sending it skittering down the bar.

"You—bastard! You—you're nothing but a big, red, hairless asshole!" she belted at him and trotted unsteadily out of the restaurant before he realized what had happened.

Wendy, the bartender who had been at Windows forever, casually shook her head as if she had heard it all a hundred times before. She dutifully retrieved the ring, placed it and a fresh bar towel in front of the young man before she began to wipe down the bar while the rest of the kitchen staff went back to work after the outburst as if nothing had happened.

Paul, the maître d', who could easily pass for the club's bouncer and always had a ready smile, looked around and caught the two familiar faces eyeing him from across the room and helplessly raised his hands. "What can I say?" he mouthed in their direction, shrugging his broad shoulders.

Beverly and Susan smiled and waved back, knowing he would send over a round of whatever they were drinking with his compliments to compensate for the disturbance. Windows was not only one of the finest restaurants on the California coast between Los Angeles and San Francisco; it was among the classiest.

Susan twiddled her fingers at him. She liked Paul, but her brow was still arched at the creative curse the girl had just hurled at her ex-fiancé.

"Kids," she said aloud, and watched to see what the young man would do next. But he just sat there, wiping himself down. "I'll bet even a Shanghai sailor's never heard that one before," Susan ventured.

"She was cute, poor thing," Beverly mused. "I wonder what Darlene looks like?"

"I don't know, darling, but he's a cutie-pie," Susan said with an appraising eye focused on the young man.

"Lecher," Beverly said. "Or is it lecheress?" The accusation was prompted by the look on Susan's face. She knew it was a masculine insult, but at the moment could not think of the female equivalent. *Bitch* would have been appropriate, but the way things were between them, an innocent insult could easily be misunderstood.

An awkward silence fell between the two women as things settled down to normal in the bar. Paul had gone back to taking reservations over the phone and greeting early diners, while Wendy was busily making curlicues out of lemon rinds that would grace various cocktails she would serve throughout the evening. The sounds of pots and pans clanging in the kitchen, mixed with the jabber of the cooks and waiters and the rest of the serving staff picked up again and wafted out into the dining room like a well-oiled machine as they all went back to work.

Both women were frazzled by the ordeal that had taken up most of the day, and had switched to black coffee that was strong and steaming hot, the caffeine helping to sooth their jangled nerves. Susan finally broke the truce they had silently lapsed into by mutual agreement.

"So, tell me, darling, how do you really feel about my Ted? Are you serious about him?" Beverly looked surprised at the open-ended statement and the possessive tone that went with it. "I know this is hard for you, but we've been gone most of the day, and we need to finish this before the boys turn in a missing persons report on us." Her cell had chimed a dozen times or more over the course of the afternoon, while Beverly had turned hers off hours ago.

Susan cleared her throat when she did not answer. "Do you plan on seeing him again?" But she knew it was a silly question the instant it popped out of her mouth.

Bev glanced at her to make sure she was serious. She was. Yet, in spite of the confession that had caused a wide range of emotions between them all afternoon, they were still more or less on friendly terms despite the fact that she was sleeping with her husband. Bev studied the older woman more closely now. She could not be sure, but there was probably at least ten years difference in their ages, yet it hardly showed—unless she wanted to get picky, and she did not have the energy for it right now.

"I felt like a teenager again," Bev mused awkwardly in retrospect, breaking her silence. "It was like the first time … all over again."

"You mean like losing your virginity?" Susan chuckled lightly, caught a bit off guard. She was still trying to organize a plan that had been trampling all over her imagination since last night and was finally starting to take shape. But too many parts were still missing for her to bring it up just yet.

"In a way," Beverly said. "I've never known anyone— anything, really—like him before. I could barely get out of bed for three days," she added in a smaller voice.

"Welcome to the club, darling," Susan said, her own first time with Ted never to be forgotten. She took another sip of coffee that had begun to cool. "After the first time, I think it was a week before I'd let him even come near me again. But it was all fun and games after that."

Beverly nodded. "I'm sure he dislocated my uterus and maybe a few other things in there. But I still can't imagine you ever leaving him and running off to Hollywood."

"That's because you've never been in the movie business, darling. It's a dog-eat-dog business, I know. But I suppose I inherited from my mother. It's also quite addictive seeing yourself up there on the big silver screen, and people making gaga eyes at you in the supermarket." She sipped her coffee with a far away look in her eye. "I was young the first time," Susan said, recalling her own deflowering. "Sixteen or seventeen. I'm not sure, exactly."

"Who was the lucky boy?"

"Actually, it was a man, darling. Well, almost, anyway. He was my cousin, for goodness' sake. Four or five years older than me, and so handsome. I let him chase me all over the bed until I caught him." She chuckled with the memory of her initiation into the magical state of womanhood.

"Ted said his first time was with his auntie." He had told Bev about his father's youngest sister when he was a teenager, and she wondered if it was just a coincidence or if incest ran in their respective families.

Susan nodded, a bit surprised, and wondered what other family skeletons he may have revealed. "I'm surprised he told you about her."

"I asked him about the other women in his life," Beverly offered.

"Then you know she walked in on him. Caught him, you know ... like playing with himself in the john." Susan made a suggestive movement with her hand and wrist as if she were holding a garden hose and milking a cow at the same time. "He was young, just a teenager, not much older than I was the first time. She was in her twenties, I think. I guess Teddy was pretty well developed even then. She'd probably never seen anything like that before and did a real number on him."

"How long did it last?"

"The number? About an hour or so, to hear him tell it. You know how girls are. The poor thing must have been in a complete frenzy."

"I meant the relationship—"

"Oh, that. Only a few months, I think." Susan grinned mischievously. "He says she got pregnant and moved out."

"His—?" Beverly frowned noticeably at a part of the story Ted had failed to mention.

"Her boyfriend's, he says. But who knows."

"So, there may be a little Teddy running around out there somewhere," Beverly said reflectively.

Susan smiled at the thought. "Hardly little anymore. That was a long time ago." Then she glanced up at Bev curiously. "Did he mention anything else—about me, for instance."

Beverly came instantly alert, but kept it from showing. "Some ..." she said, but her smile said it might be more.

"About Hong Kong? What happened with my leading man?"

"He's the one you went off to Kenya with." She recalled that part of the story. "That was your last movie, when you won all the awards?"

"Well," Susan frowned, "it was the reason I went with him that I'm talking about," she said, a bit sullen with the thought. "That's when I thought I was going to lose Ted for sure," she said, warming to the story. "We were doing some post production work, retakes and background stuff, things like that after the main shoot had rapped. Something wasn't right with the music; I don't remember what that was all about exactly. But we all knew we had a good picture in the can with a better-than-even chance of winning some awards. But there was some damned *windy hill* they couldn't decide on that was important to the plot. The hill thingy seemed a little silly to me, but they agreed that everything had to be just so. They couldn't seem to find the perfect location they were looking for in Hong Kong and were about to wrap it up and go looking elsewhere. There was talk of going to Bali or some other tropical island over there, which would put them way over budget.

"Anyway, we were all sitting around Gaddis one night over dinner—that's the famous French restaurant at the Pen ... the Peninsula Hotel, Kowloon side, where we were all staying—trying to figure it out when he asked me if I wanted to go on hiatus with him to Africa when the filming was done. Well, the man was so charismatic and charming and so good-looking, it was hard to say no. But I told him I was a married woman and couldn't be gone that long. Well, darling, he just wouldn't take no for an answer. We had all been drinking pretty heavily with no early call to worry about the next day. And by the time dinner was over, the dear man actually crawled under the table and started ... you know, started doing all those yummy thingies right there. Do you believe it? And he refused to come out until I either said yes or had a climax."

Beverly nearly choked with laughter. "Had you been sleeping with the guy?"

"My God, of course, darling. Every chance I got. But so were some of other girls in the cast. Anyway, there were eight or ten of us around the table, cast members, writers, producers, a few technical people, like that. And everyone was laughing so hard at all the noises he was making down there, it was mortifying, completely embarrassing."

"Oh, my God ... what happened? What did you do?"

"Well, I had to do something, for goodness' sake. I couldn't just sit there while he … and I couldn't fake something like that in front of everybody. My God, if I tried, they would have sent out for a camera crew and insisted on two or three retakes. So, as you well know, darling, Susan went to Africa right after they found their damned high and windy hill."

They laughed together this time, so hard their sides began to hurt. When they had settled down, Susan said, "It's funny, but you never forget your first time. No matter how many come along afterward. Don't you agree, darling?" She was feeling a bit chattier now. The wine at lunch was doing its job.

"I couldn't do it the first time."

"Oh, you poor darling, how awful for you. Who was the boy? He wasn't like our Teddy, was he?" Susan's grin was genuine and motherly, that of a senior wife in a harem.

Bev immediately caught the inference that she had apparently attained *family* status, and they were no longer merely adopted sisters now that they were sharing Ted. "Hardly," Bev said, raising a brow. "He was actually the proverbial *boy next door*. I was nineteen. We'd dated during my senior year in high school. Then he went off to the navy. When he came back and it got really serious, we tried every chance we got until one night in the backseat of his car it just happened—unexpectedly. All of the sudden, there we were, acting like grown-ups and doing it like crazy."

Susan laughed. "I used to love doing it in the car. Still would, I think," she said with a grin. "It was so intimate, being all closed in like that. Made me feel like I was doing something very naughty. Which I was, of course." She laughed again. "Especially at the drive-in movies where other people could peek in. I just love being naughty sometimes. Don't you, darling?"

Beverly smiled demurely. "So, how many men have you been naughty with, girl?" Susan had told her some of the stories, but she had never asked for numbers before in spite of her curiosity.

"Too many to remember, that's for sure, darling." Susan smiled shamelessly. "And what about you? There must have been lots of men in your life."

Beverly groaned, but not because she could not remember. "Not that many," she admitted, as if it might be a character flaw. And compared to Susan, perhaps it was.

"Well, you poor thing," Susan said, pursing her lips but smiling inwardly. Sex was something she never tired of. "Thank goodness you kept trying, dear. Men can get so creative once a girl lets them get past second base—you know, the boobies thingy, feeling you up. Lucky for us that men like boobies," she said, as if she needed to explain.

Beverly had not heard the cliché about the "bases" since high school, but didn't go there. "Why do you suppose that is? Why are they so infatuated with a woman's breast?" she asked curiously.

"I'm not sure," Susan said thoughtfully. "But after spending two or three years with a nipple in their mouth, it's bound to be habit forming later on in life. And it always leads to something else," she said with a mischievous grin. "Maybe that's part of the grand scheme of things."

Bev saw the humor, but said more seriously, "That's probably part of it. But I think once they discover the difference between a boys and a girls, it probably has something to do with the male dominance thing, too. And once you let them ... you know, do it, feel you up, they think it's okay to do everything else."

Susan chortled in agreement. "That's exactly what I meant, darling. By the time they get to third base, playing with your titties, they simply won't take 'No!' for an answer because they think you've already said 'Yes!' to everything else and all they want to do is get your panties off after that." She eyed her closely now. "But every girl learns sooner or later that there are other places ..." Her voice trailed off, not needing to finish.

Realizing that Susan was on another fishing expedition, Bev

said, "I finally figured that one out—what goes where—if that's what you mean." Bev finished her coffee and tried to decide if she should have another drink and wondered why Susan was getting a little pushy again. She'd hoped they were past that.

"I'm sure you did, dear. I just meant there are other interesting ways of doing things that men like to try when they get like that, which is most of the time." Susan noticed Beverly's brow twitch as they stared at each other across the table.

"I think I've figured that one out too," Beverly said with a slight edge in her voice now. "I guess it's just human nature, the way we affect them."

"And what about Jack, darling? Is he adventurous as Ted at times?"

"Not really," she said, knowing full well now what she was fishing for. "He's pretty much the missionary type." Beverly was purposely vague and fought off a wave of embarrassment at what Ted must have already told her.

"Have you noticed that about Ted, how he likes to explore different, shall we say, alternatives?"

"We've hardly been together enough to get bored with plain old-fashioned sex, Sue," Beverly answered defensively and saw the flash of resentment lurking behind the forced smile Susan was wearing.

"Yes, well, I suppose that's true." Susan paused, knowing that Bev was holding back and wondered why. Ted's account of their last rendezvous had been much more detailed and graphic. She glanced away with a scowl and then looked back at the younger, very attractive woman who overnight had gone from being her best friend to her arch competitor.

Then Susan's expression noticeably hardened. "That brings us to my next question, darling ..."

Eighteen

"*E*xactly what else do you intend to do with my Ted, darling ... besides *fuck* him again?"

Beverly's temper flared with the bluntness of the attack. "Damn it, Susan, the last thing I intend to do is take Ted away from you ... even if I could." Then her instant rancor faded as quickly as it had come on. "You never use that word."

"I've just never liked the sound it," Susan said, her mood patronizing. "I've always loved doing it, though."

Beverly tried again. "It's just something that happened. I don't know why, but it did. I guess he needed something. I needed somethig. Christ, we both needed something. You haven't made love with him in practically a year, and I don't know how many months it been since Jack and I have slept together. But I don't plan on running off with your husband. I already have one of those. And right now, damn it, that's one too many."

Inwardly, Susan relaxed slightly in spite of Beverly's flare of temper, letting her defenses down a notch, but nothing showing in her face as she switched tactics. "Men—! They should come with instructions."

When Beverly did not reply, she heaved a sigh. "I think I might have made a serious mistake a while back. In the first place, I never thought you were attracted to Ted when I mentioned how gifted he is, not like that anyway," Susan said, as if the whole thing was suddenly her fault. "In the first place, he's quite a bit older than you. And you and I were such good friends. We felt so comfortable with you and Jack that I guess I just rambled on a bit from time to time. And I suppose I was bragging a little, too. It's just that he's so amazing. But it's frustrating to be with someone like that all these years and not being able talk to someone about it."

Beverly caught the *past tense* reference to their friendship, but also noticed that her mood had mellowed slightly since she had practically bitten Susan's head off just now. "You mean your remark that he's hung like a mule?"

Susan shrugged with a thin smile. "Even then, I never dreamed you would ... the two of you, that is ..."

Beverly shrugged her shoulders, understanding. "I really didn't believe you, anyway. Even after I found out, I think I was more frightened than anything else. But I have to admit, I think I've fallen in love with him. Maybe even before we started seeing each other and I just didn't realize it. But I never wanted to hurt you, Sue. We've been friends too long. I hope you believe that."

"I love you too, darling." Susan could not help the condescending look she gave her, and wondered how she could possibly think that sleeping with her husband wouldn't hurt her. But, to be honest, she knew there was another side to it, and said, "I have to admit I haven't seen him this happy in a long time, maybe in years, since the two of you ..." She didn't finish as another thought smothered that one.

Susan already knew the rest of the story, including something that had surprised Ted as much as it had her. She had not always been able to avoid *that* kind of sex, even with Ted on occasion, although he was certainly a challenge. It was definitely not her favorite. And since the regular way was so much fun, she had only tried it a few times to see what all the fuss was about. However, she knew that most men liked variety in their sex life and thought differently about it. And apparently so did Bev.

"I know you might feel I'm being too personal, darling," Susan said, changing the subject, "and maybe I am, but if you and Ted went beyond what the, ah, the missionaries allow—you know the man on top, woman on the bottom thingy—it wouldn't surprise me. In fact, it would be just like him. I just never saw the point in it myself when the regular way is so lovely. I've always found that there's something incredibly sexy about having a man on top of you instead of behind."

Beverly had been expecting this moment since she decided that Ted had caved in last night and told her everything. "It was me— something I asked him," she said, feeling her embarrassment flush into her face again, and decided it was time to put this entire business behind them and get it over with. "I suppose all of this is about the hot tub?"

Susan stopped breathing for a moment.

Nineteen

The restaurant had started to fill by the time darkness settled over the bay and Beverly had finally finished with her full confession, complete with all the lurid details. The best part, she judged, was that they were still on speaking terms.

"I know you're upset, but I'm glad you're not angry," Beverly said, breathing a sigh of relief now that the ordeal was behind them. Somehow, she had even managed the last part, a tale that would have left the missionaries breathless. Her headache was completely gone now, and she felt as though a huge weight had been lifted from her shoulders. She had not felt this good in a long time. Her appetite had even returned; of all things, she was hungry.

"Goodness' sake, darling, I wish I had been there," Susan said, still panting from the tale. More bizarre, and greatly adding to her excitement, was the uncanny idea she had come up with, and all the erotic images that went with it, while listening to Beverly's story. But her scheme involved Jack and she knew that would be the hard part, making her wondered if it was even possible. However, the erotic thought of the four of them together greatly titillated her. All she had to do now was to think of a way of explaining it to Bev without sounding like a complete lunatic.

"You mean like a '*mouse in the corner?*'" Beverly asked.

"My goodness no, darling, not at all," she said a bit overexcited, her head was spinning with possibilities. The pitch of her voice surprised even her and she glanced around, and then dropped her tone a notch before continuing. "I mean being right there—with you. That's the sexiest story I've ever heard."

Beverly was surprised by her enthusiasm and tried unsuccessfully to suppress the part-frown part-smile she was wearing. "You can't be serious? You mean like the three of us—as in ménage à trois?"

"Well, darling, it seems the least you could do after screwing my Ted when I wasn't looking. Call it a favor if you want to, or even payback." She was not glaring, her look friendly, yet serious. "The thought occurred to me that it could certainly be more exciting if Jack were interested. How do you think he would feel about something like that, dear? But that would make four of us. You speak a little French, darling, went to that snooty cooking school in Paris. How do you say the foursome thingy?"

"Good Lord, Sue, I have no idea." Beverly noticeably gasped, reflecting back on her two years of high school French and the week she had spent at Cordon Bleu, neither of which included such things. She was on the verge of shock and trying to hide it, her brain racing, struggling to keep up, trying to comprehend. "I don't think there is such a thing. I guess you would just call it an orgy."

"Oh no, darling, that's much too vulgar for what I have in mind. Have you two ever tried that sort of thing, by the way? You know, with another couple. With Jack—or before?"

Beverly's color deepened enough to be noticeable and she hesitated, but not because she had to think about it. It was partially the reason she and Jack had decided to move up to the Central Coast. They had come close one night with two other couples and decided it was time to move on, to leave LA behind and all the temptations that went with it.

Susan caught the change in her expression, her left eyebrow kicking up with interest. "Mostly talk," Bev said in response to the look she was getting. "Joked about it some, but nothing serious."

"Well, darling," Susan said, staring at her with the tiniest smile, "I think I see something a little more interesting than *just talk* on that pretty face of yours." She nudged Bev gently. "Certainly more serious." Apparently, there was a side to Beverly that she wasn't aware of. And possibly Jack, also.

"There was one time before we moved up," Bev began slowly, feeling more comfortable talking about it now that things had settled down between them, most of the ordeal behind them. "It was at a New Year's Eve party and we'd had way too much to drink. We took our motor home to the Rose Parade in Pasadena every year and invited my brother and his wife and another couple to come along. Jack had rented our regular parking spot on Colorado Blvd. We got there around two in the afternoon and started drinking margaritas. By time midnight rolled around we were all pretty much in the bag."

"Sounds like fun, darling," Susan smiled. "My kind of party. So it was the six of you?"

Bev nodded. "We had rented space in this used car lot facing the parade rout, practically on the sidewalk. The streets were all blocked off for the parade the next morning. The place was jammed with people coming and going, milling around all over the place. It was New Year's Eve and most everyone had been drinking all day. Everybody was partying, happy, and having a good time. There was a big street party going on practically in front of us. They could see us inside the motor home with our drinks watching them. Somebody in the crowd would do something silly and we'd wave and laugh, they'd laugh and make faces at us, and we'd toast them and cheer. They'd do the same to us. Then one of the girls in the crowd decided to flash us, pulled her sweater up right there on the sidewalk and danced around with everything hanging out. The crowd cheered and hooted. Then another girl did the same. Then some guy with them mooned us. Everyone was having a good time and laughing; people were toasting each other and urging us to join in."

"My goodness, darling, and did you?" Susan asked.

"Well, as I said, we'd all had a lot to drink by that time, and my brother's wife, Lucy, did better than that. She said something about the girl's boobs weren't as big as hers and got right up in the windshield and took her top off. Stood there wiggling her shoulders like a belly dancer. People outside started banging on the hood, hooting and hollering, and cheering her on."

"Oh, good Lord," Susan giggled, "was brother upset?"

"Hardly. He turned on the overhead lights for her. Lit her up like a Christmas tree. Well, that did it. The crowd went berserk. Everyone outside roared and cheered and were clapping until Kathy, our other friend's wife, stripped to the waist and did the same thing."

"You've got to be kidding, darling," Susan laughed. "She bared it all, too? You *were* having a good time. So, it sounds like you were the only one with all your clothes on?"

"It gets better," Bev said with a guilty sigh. "I couldn't be left out of all the fun, so I stripped down to my jeans. There we were, three pretty-well-put-together broads standing in front of this huge windshield with all the lights on, our boobs hanging out all over the place, and drawing a huge crowd. Some of the guys were even cramming dollar bills under the windshield wipers."

They laughed together until Susan finally said, "And what were the boys doing while all of this was going on?"

"Well, Brother Billy said the last time he'd seen me without a bra I only had starter titties and that he was impressed how well they turned out. Then, as we began to get dressed again, Bill started teasing Lucy, took her sweater and bra away from her, trying to kiss her, playing with her boobs. She was pretty drunk and finally got tired of chasing him around trying to get her things back, and took the rest of her clothes off and dared him to do something about it. They ended up on the dashboard in front of the windshield—screwing."

"Oh, Jesus, no!" Susan croaked in disbelief, holding a hand to her mouth. "You can't be serious. What happened—I mean with the people outside …?"

"Well," Bev continued, "it got so bad Jack finally got up and drew the curtains when people began jumping up on the bumper for a better look. It got a little strange after that. Kathy was way over her limit, all but falling down by this time, and Paxton, her husband, scooted Bill and Lucy over, stripped her down the rest of the way, got naked himself and started with her right there beside them."

Susan's eyes were huge orbs. "And you and Jack just watched all of this?"

"Not exactly. But at least Jack was a little more discreet. We stripped down and used the couch."

"Oh—my—God, darling, what a story," Susan said, nearly breathless. "How marvelous. Too bad everybody was too busy to take pictures. You didn't … I mean, the six of you … did you like— itchy-switchy at all?"

"Good Lord, Susan, no. But I think the others wanted to. But something like that could only go so far. Billy's my brother, for God's sake. Not that we didn't play doctor and show-and-tell when we were kids. And Paxton's a nice guy, but he's a client of Jack's. Besides, after all the fun and games, we weren't that drunk anymore, everyone had pretty much sobered up."

"Did you get together after that, darling? All of you?"

"Well, that's the thing. I think we were probably both tempted. Kathy called about a week later. Said they were having dinner with Bill and Lucy and wanted us to join them. I didn't have to ask what was for dessert. She made it pretty clear without saying so. Then Bill called a day or so after their dinner party, and Paxton mentioned to Jack what a good time they'd had together. Invited us again the following weekend—of course. Jack and I had already talked about moving out of the big city, out of the rat race, and that was about the time we figured a change of scenery might be a good idea. We both love LA, the theaters, shopping, all the restaurants, sailing to Catalina on weekends, the beach and mountains both close. We were born and raised there, but it was just getting too big and crowded."

"Well, darling, we still have to figure out a way of getting Jack interested in our little arrangement. Of course, you'd have to tell him about you and Ted first."

Beverly blanched. "Yeah, right, Sue! I can just hear myself now: 'Oh, by the way, Jack, did I mention that I'm thinking of screwing Ted? Susan wants in on it too. Would you care to join us?'"

Susan's smirk turned into a wanton grin to which she added a chuckle. When she settled down, Beverly said, "But it wouldn't surprise me if most married couples haven't at least thought about that sort of thing at one time or another."

Susan nodded. "I'm sure, but I've never encouraged Ted along those lines, if we could even find someone for him. And you can't exactly hold auditions for that sort of thing. He's not exactly easy to sleep with, as you well know," Susan said. After a moment, she asked, "Has Jack ever said anything about me like that, darling? Sexually, I mean?" She pushed back a reddish blonde curl from her forehead that was crowding her vision and tried to look poised, but was having trouble. "Maybe something you haven't mentioned before?"

"Ah, well, not exactly. Only that he thinks you're attractive, of course." She purposely left out, "For an older woman," that had accompanied his remark. She knew Susan hated the "old" word and never used it. "Oh, and that he thinks you have great boobies, of course." She glanced at the woman's large breasts that were doing their best to peek out of her top. "Wondered if they were real."

"And ..." She squinted at her suspiciously.

Beverly shrugged. "I told him the truth. That you'd had a boob job."

Susan shrugged; there was no need to suffer over it, the damage already done. Apparently, nothing was sacred. "Nothing about what a great little butt I've got? Nothing—?"

Bev tried to be diplomatically now. "Actually, he sort of prefers something a little north of a size four." She almost added, "Like mine," but didn't go there, since it would sound as if she were bragging.

The comment garnered one of those looks from Susan that had been flying back and forth between the two women all day. She judged Beverly was probably a perfect size nine and would die for just a peek at the bare facts. "Well, maybe that's because he's never seen me naked, dear. Of course, you know I think Jack is gorgeous. And I'm not so sure he wouldn't be the tiniest bit interested, even if the size of my butt's not exactly what he's used to."

At that moment, Lex, one of the waiters, appeared from around the corner with carafe of hot coffee and headed their way. When he heard Susan's remark, his thick brow kicked up as he spun on his heel and headed back for the bar. Susan looked after him. "He's so cute, don't you think, darling? Like a big, cuddly teddy bear," her gaze lingered on his retreating buns.

"Jack would never agree to something like that," Bev said, ignoring her lechery. "And where would it lead?" She was still trying to sort through some of the crazy thoughts that were spinning around in her head. She found it hard to believe they were having such a conversation.

"Wherever we want it to, darling. Now that we know Ted's thingy isn't broken, it could definitely help us with our problem." Susan did not bother to mention that the problem in question was well on the mend since he had awakened her out of a dead sleep sometime before dawn to prove it. He had begged her forgiveness, and when she had sleepily accepted, more out of exhaustion than pity, spent the next hour making up for lost time. In fact, she was surprised at how soar it had left her.

"And it certainly wouldn't hurt you and Jack either," Susan

added. "Especially when he finds out how naughty you've already been." Chris, the sommelier, recognized the two women and waived from the bar. Both smiled back, Susan more brightly, and waived. "Isn't he the one with the nurse?"

"Na-uh. The nurse belongs to Lex, the 'teddy bear.' Chris belongs to Vikki, the cute girl from the wine shop downstairs."

"He's as cute as Lex. Maybe even younger," Susan said with an appraising eye.

Bev sipped her coffee, but it was cold and didn't taste good. "I haven't a clue how to even bring up such a thing with Jack. I can't just ask him to jump in bed with the three of us. I'm not even sure if I could do that."

"Do what, darling? The jumping in bed part or the screwing after you got there?"

"Screwing your freaking husband in front of my freaking husband, that's which part," Beverly huffed, her voice up, not sure if she was serious. Lex had started their way with another pot of fresh coffee, and again spun on his heel and darted away, eyes to the ceiling at what he'd just overheard.

"But suppose he went along with the idea. I admit it sounds a little kinky, but you have to agree that it has a certain charm. It certainly does for me." Susan giggled after a moment. "What do you think, dear?"

Beverly frowned. "I don't know what to think. My brain's fried. I can't imagine—"

"Oh, for goodness' sake, it should be a no-brainer for someone as bright as you. You're already sleeping with both men. And in love with both of them to one degree or another. I don't see what the problem is." From the look on her face, it appeared that Beverly was at least considering the possibilities, and Susan quickly went on. "And while you're at it, don't forget to include us in the bargain, darling—you and me. Men like seeing two ladies together like that. It could be exciting when you think about it."

"Susan? For Pete's sake—!" Beverly looked at her strangely now. "Sleeping with Ted, even with Jack and Ted, is one thing. But another woman …?"

"Oh please, Bev, give me a break. And I never said a thing about sleeping. It goes on all the time. We've known each other forever, for goodness' sake, and we're already sharing one of our husbands. How much more friendly can you get?" She blinked back the slight disappointment she felt. "Besides, if it's one thing I'm not, it's a lesbian, darling. Although, I have no problem with two ladies like that. I just meant the two of us could put on a little show for the boys. It would be good fun, and men love it. They like to watch two girls together, naked. They think it's naughty. But most of all, they don't feel threatened by it. Especially if they get to—you know, do you afterward, or during, or whenever." She grinned again. "Besides, darling, you never can tell. It might be interesting." The look on Susan's face changed slightly; her full lips held a sultry pout, leaving little doubt that perhaps she had actually thought of the idea before.

"Hello, Bev! Susan!" The two women looked up to see both Lex and Chris cautiously advancing on them from a few steps away, each holding a carafe of coffee and reasonably sure that they had once again overheard at least part of their conversation.

"Oh, you naughty boys, there you are again," Susan said and grinned coyly at them. "Sneaking up on us like that. Shame on both of you."

"I brought reinforcements this time," Lex said as he poured for Susan at the same time Chris refilled Bev's cup. "Out alone tonight are we? Where're Jack and the coach?"

"Lady's night out," Bev smiled.

"From what I've heard, dinner with you two tonight sounds interesting," Chris said to Beverly in his usual low, easy voice, but loud enough for Susan to hear, his dry sense of humor coming through as always.

"Don't you dare repeat a thing we've said," Susan said in mock distress. "You know how this town likes to gossip."

They had already turned to leave when Chris looked back over his shoulder, holding a finger to his mouth. "Our lips are sealed," he said and disappeared around the corner.

They sipped their fresh coffee, and after a moment Bev said, "I still have no idea how to bring up such a thing to Jack." She sighed, picking up their conversation where they had left off and using the argument as a hedge to buy time to think about what Susan had said before they were interrupted. "He'd never agree to it. I know him." Beverly looked at Susan in a slightly different light now, a myriad of thoughts spinning through her mind.

"Then we'll just have to get a little creative," Susan said, refusing to accept defeat without even trying. Then another idea occurred to her. "You know, there's a good chance Jack might agree if he already knew about you and Ted when you ask him, that he had nothing to lose and everything to gain, since you're already seeing him."

The doubt on Beverly's face was obvious, showing up first in her eyes. "What ever happened to, 'Deny, deny, deny?'" she said incongruously, her mind in a spin.

"Well, this definitely changes things a bit, darling, don't you think? And Ted certainly isn't the problem here," Susan offered.

"There's no way. I don't think I could ... could ask him something like that. Even bring it up."

"But you're okay with the idea, darling, willing to give it a try? The four of us—or any combination that makes everyone happy?"

Beverly hesitated and then managed a nod, more to put the troubling thought aside, knowing she could always change her mind. Then she saw the sly, mischievous grin that did a slow crawl across Susan's attractive face. "What are you thinking, you bitch?" she said, her eyes crinkling with a half smile.

"Just how exciting it would be," Susan said. "The four of us. Together. Like that ... naked ... screwing. It's supposed to be every man's fantasy."

"Then you'd like to sleep with Jack?" Her voice became serious again as she tried to picture them together, naked—Susan on her back, but Jack nothing like Ted.

"Of course I would, darling. Don't be silly. I've told you before, I think he's divine. And I'm talking hot, wet, sex, here."

"He's not like Ted … not that way."

"Half—?"

"God no! Not even," she said, and shook her head. "Well, maybe lengthwise."

"Well, I'm sure he makes up for it in other ways." Susan paused, then said, "By the way, I have a small confession to make, darling."

Beverly twitched, watching her closely; unsure of what she was about to hear. "I thought this was my turn in the barrel."

"It's not as serious as all that. But last night I had a good talk with Ted when we got home and we made love for the first time in nearly a year. He told me all about the two of you. I didn't say anything right away because I needed to hear your side of it. I … I'm sorry. I hope you'll forgive the subterfuge. But now that I've told you, I think we understand each other much better and we can start over again. No more secrets. What do you say, girl? Susan still loves you."

Beverly had always suspected the ex-movie star had the survival skills of a saber-toothed tiger in her Hollywood days—and apparently, she still did. She had an Oscar to prove it.

"Sure, don't mention it," Bev said. "Thanks for fessing up. No more secrets."

The Interrogation

Twenty

$\mathcal{A}$t seven-thirty, Jack was already at his desk in the offices of Investigative Services, Inc., with a cup of strong black coffee in one hand and a handful of phone messages in the other. He had already walked Maggie Mae, his pushy St. Bernard, shaved and showered and tried to make dinner plans with his wife—who had been beyond bitchy lately and ready to fight at the drop of a hat—before leaving for the office.

Just because he had been around women his entire life, did not mean that he understood them.

One of the messages caught his eye. It was from Andy Anderson. They had been partners out of Hollywood Division and had remained friends after Andy was hired away by a popular rock star at ten-times his cop's pay to head up his personal security detail in Las Vegas. By the time the King of Rock and Roll had died unexpectedly a few years later, Andy had already made some good contacts in the casino business and opened his own PI business. Andy was doing well in Vegas and they often exchanged pro bono work. Jack figured he needed a favor and would definitely get back to him.

He hurriedly flipped through the rest of the phone messages, mostly from Hollywood entertainment types he had known for years who needed to talk to him ASAP. In the twenty years he had been a detective in the country's third largest city, Jack had met most of the A- and B-listers in Hollywood and their attorneys. When they needed help—and it seemed that most celebrities always needed help—they seldom looked beyond someone who had been around for a while and they already knew.

In fact, Jack came from long line police officers. His grandfather had walked a beat in LA's seamy Skid Row district, and had risen to the rank of Deputy Chief in the raw days of the late 1920s when the City of Angels was still in its relative infancy. Like father like son, Jack's father had also retired from the Department some thirty years later as Deputy Chief of Detectives.

However, the real hero in the family was his Uncle Stoney, Sgt. James Addison Stonebreaker, the big six-foot-six, three-hundred-forty pound giant of a man, who had met his untimely death in the line of duty in the late 1930s. While on foot patrol in one of Chinatown's tong-ridden neighborhoods, Stoney had been in the process of breaking up a street fight singlehanded. Standard operating procedure for the time was to stand back and wait for the paddy wagon to arrive, then pinch the winners and call the ambulance for those who were left littering the streets. However, according to the official police report, a crowd had gathered and become unruly, and Stoney decided to break up the melee without waiting for his backup to arrive. He grabbed the first two punks he could get his big hands on by the scruff of the neck, shook the first like a rag doll, and threw him nearly halfway across Sunset Blvd.

However, before he could do the same to the second young man, he had sunk his teeth into the big cop's forearm in his attempt to escape the same fate as his partner-in-crime, who was by that time lying unconscious in the middle of the intersection of Sunset and Grand.

But the cannibalistic attack had only served to piss the big man off and when he drew back his ham of a fist to prove it, the dirt bag had pulled out a knife and stabbed him. By the time Stoney had shaken him off and pulled the knife out of his shoulder, the guy was already hightailing it up Sunset Blvd. Rather than shoot a fleeing suspect in the back, Stoney had pulled out his old .38 caliber Smith & Wesson with a six-inch barrel and threw it at him, hitting him square in the back of the head, knocking him out cold.

The gun that had belonged to his father and had not been fired in twenty years, suffered only a few scratches. But a week later, Stoney died at the age of forty-nine of sepsis—acute blood poisoning—from the bite he had received. Over three hundred people attended the funeral and a short time later the case was closed when the suspect was convicted of murder one in the death of a police officer.

Business at ISI had been good from the day they opened the doors. The new PI business employed six ex-police officers, a former attorney, who hated going to court and needed more excitement in his life, and a retired judge who handled all their trial preparations.

However, not everyone who worked for ISI came with a sterling reputation. A good example was one of their best investigators, an ex-cop who had lost his pension for sleeping with another man's wife and then lying about it at the divorce trial to save the lady's reputation. Jack had met the woman, found it hard to blame the guy, and offered him a job.

Judge Birch Donovan, however, was one of Jack's favorites and had known his father before him. Jack had appeared before the judge many times, and they had shared many a drink over the years after a long day in court. He had not won every case he took before him, but they liked the same Irish whiskey and each other's company, and had always been honest about their differences. It was over a glass of

Jameson one night that Birch had confessed to thoughts of suicide after his wife of fifty-three years died unexpectedly and he needed a reason just to get up in the morning. Jack offered him a job and promised to piss on his grave if he did anything stupid.

The "Judge," as everyone called him, had started his law career as a deputy sheriff in Orange County just south of LA, passed the bar and went into criminal defense work before his appointment to the Bench by a close friend, then California Governor Goody Knight.

However, it was hard to think of the Judge without recalling the first time he had appeared before him. He had called him into his chambers before trial and admonished him that just because he had known his father for twenty-some years didn't mean that he had a free ride. He needed to do his homework just like every other cop who brought a case before him.

Jack assured the Judge that he expected no favors, just a fair trial. With that said, they had discussed guns, whiskey and women in that order, and if Jack thought he should use a powerful Plus-P ammunition in the snub-nose .38 Colt Detective Special he carried in open court in the ankle holster under his robe. Sighting its tremendous stopping power at short range, he did, and hoped that no one who came into the Judge's courtroom was foolish enough to prove him right.

The case at hand, however, involved a minor traffic accident in front of Barney's Beanery in West Hollywood and a good-looking hooker Jack had arrested for DUI and possession of a controlled substance for sale. The working girl had been stoned out of her mind and packing nearly a pound of cannabis in her car.

The assistant DA assigned to prosecute the case—a short, older guy in a rumpled suit on loan from Santa Monica who Jack knew by reputation for winning drug cases—had asked him if he recognized the hooker's defense attorney when he walked in wearing a pinstriped navy blue suit and a flamboyant necktie.

Surprised, when he sat down at the opposing counsel's table next to them, Jack surmised he was the real reason the little guy from Santa Monica with the reputation for putting drug dealers away had been assigned to the case in the first place. He wondered at what price a high-powered San Francisco lawyer like Melvin Belli was paid to represent a not-so-famous small-time prostitute who was suspected of being a mule for some drug cartel in the off hours when she wasn't hooking.

After jury selection and several hours into the trial, Jack also wondered why the visiting DA was needling the notorious attorney throughout the morning session by referring to him as "Mr. Belly." The guy had tried many high-profile cases, been on TV and in the news so often over the years, that everyone knew him and how to pronounce his name. And it certainly wasn't "Belly." He was so well-known in fact, that many of the state's law schools now taught a class in "trial tactics" using his techniques.

After the noon break, the DA was at him again. By this time, however, and apparently concerned that the prosecution's continued veiled impertinence may influence the jury that appeared to leaning in his direction during the morning session, Mr. Belli roared at Judge Donovan, "Your Honor, I must protest! My learned colleague on the other side of the aisle knows perfectly well how to pronounce my most illustrious family name, which is well recorded in the law libraries of this great state."

Well aware of the famous lawyer's exaggerated ego, and somewhat amused all morning by the prosecutor's antics, the judge had been expecting the outburst long before this and asked attorney Belli exactly how he wished to be referred to and he would be happy to so instruct opposing counsel. "The name, your Honor, as everyone in this courtroom well knows, is pronounced B-e-l-l-i, with a long 'I' at the end." He drew out the ninth letter in the alphabet in low baritone usually reserved for juries.

To his credit, the judge did a good job of containing

himself—something he'd probably learned as a cop years ago, since he was like God Himself in his own courtroom and had no need to be diplomatic—and asked the little guy from Santa Monica what he had to say for himself.

Jack had never heard such an uproar of laughter in a courtroom when the assistant DA stood respectfully and replied with a satisfied look on his face: "Well, your Honor, I really must apologize to the court for mispronouncing my learned colleague's illustrious name. But, if that's how he pronounces it, then I must have had 'spaghett-eye' for lunch."

During the trial it was shown that the car was a rental and the defendant claimed never to have looked in the trunk where the drugs were found. Further, on advice of learned counsel, she had also refused a blood test on religious grounds.

"Not guilty," the judge had decreed, throwing the case out after closing arguments with a nod toward the prosecutor's table—and Jack, reminding the investigating officer that in the future to dot his "i"s and cross his "t"s.

Surprisingly, one of the highlights of jack's career in law enforcement involved a good deed he had done for one infamous Meyer Harris Cohen, aka: Mickey Cohen, one of LA's most notorious gangsters.

Jack had been transferred to the patrol division to pull his annual month of graveyard in a patrol car on the Sunset Strip that the brass figured gave old timers, plainclothes detectives and uniformed officers alike, a better grounding in a new law enforcement concept known as community policing.

Jack and his partner, an overweight uniform who had been behind a desk far too many years, had been cruising by the Gayety on Sunset Blvd, an all-night joint that stopped serving booze at 2:00 a.m. and turned into an informal gathering place for much of LA's underworld. This also attracted some of the city's rich and famous who came to ogle and hobnob on the edge with the likes of Benjamin Siegelbaum, better known as Bugsy Siegel, and the even more infamous Alphonse Capone.

The end of that era was followed by the appearance of Mickey Cohen, a pudgy little gangster out of New York who moved west to further his career in crime and to avoid becoming beholden to the five mafia families who ran most of the organized crime in the country at the time. After years of failed attempts to put him behind bars, the only charge the feds could nail Cohen with was income tax evasion, in spite of the half-dozen murder charges that had been brought against him.

Among other lesser-known transplanted East Coast thugs who migrated to Las Vegas and then to LA, was a slippery character known as *Louie the Ice Pick*, the underworld's go-to thug for collecting past-due gambling debts in the late sixties. They found Louie one night in an alley in a dumpy Hollywood neighborhood south of Sunset Blvd. where he had gone to collect a gambling debt from one of Cohen's mobsters—his own ice pick sticking out of his ear.

But it had been the notorious Mickey Cohen himself who had run out into the middle of a deserted Sunset Blvd. around 3:00 a.m. one morning and flagged down Jack's patrol car. Cohen held court at the Gayety almost nightly, usually between 2:00 and 6:00 in the morning, and parked his big, bulletproof, Cadillac at the curb in front of the club in the care of a like-sized thug in a black suit with a bulge under his left arm. In a panic, Cohen reported that his little white Lhasa Apso pup had gotten out the window of his car and gone missing. The dog's name was Missy and a generous reward— the thug in the suite had gladly offered to pay—was offered if they happened to see the mutt while on patrol.

Less than an hour later they saw Missy, who turned out to be a boy dog, since they found him with his leg raised on the bushes at Ciro's, the famous night club farther east on Sunset. Ten minutes later, and in full uniform, Jack waltzed into the late-night den of inequity with a fluffy white snowball under his arm and asked for Mr. Cohen's table. The reunion was jubilant, the reward proffered again, and again declined.

Being a cop in a big city was a tough business, but they did not always do bad things to bad people. The proof of that was the reunion at the Gayety, which had not been nearly as tasking as Jack's explanation in the captain's office a week later. A heavy package in brown-paper wrapping arrived at the Hollywood station addressed to "Detective Sergeant Edwards" with a return address of: M. Cohen, 546 Beverly Glenn Blvd., Hollywood. It was, however, a known fact that every cop in LA who'd been on the job more than six months knew where the pudgy little gangster lived in the Hollywood Hills area above the city. The creep was even listed in the phonebook. When the suspect package was opened by the bomb squad an hour later after the total evacuation of an entire building, they found the most beautiful matched pair of nickel-plated, model 1911 Remington Colt .45 semi-automatic pistols with carved ivory grips that Jack had ever seen, and would have killed to have in his collection. Accompanying the gift was a personal "Thank You" note from the grateful gangster that briefly corroborated Jack's story about finding his pooch. The confiscated pistols turned up on a wall at police headquarters—in the chief's office no less. Jack wound up with the "Thank You" note signed by M. Cohen that he still had in an old scrapbook somewhere.

In Uncle Stoney's day, the pistols would have found their rightful home among the rest of the family's heirlooms, the old badges and service revolvers every uniformed member of the family had worn for over five generations.

Jack often wondered what Stoney would have said about the way things turned out. The only thing he was sure of is that it would not have been printable.

As Jack shuffled through the rest of the messages, there was a tap on the door. Lindsy, who ran the office and held the place together, stuck her head in. "I just checked the e-mails, boss. Something you better look at." Her voice was a tip-off that something was up.

Lindsy Evans was smart, had a good grasp of the law, and fiercely loyal. She was a tall, attractive divorcée in her forties with a great figure, who helped run the often-hectic business as if it was her own, and made the best coffee in three counties. She was also engaged to his partner, Ransome Wahlrode III, a six-foot-six ex-federal DEA agent with whom he had become close when they worked together on several inter-agency drug cases before going into business for themselves and opened Investigative Services, Inc.

Jack swiveled around to the credenza behind him and toyed with the mouse on his computer for a second until the office e-mails popped up. "What's going on, Linds?" he said without looking at her. "What am I looking for?" He suspected from the tone of her voice that some Hollywood big shot had his butt in a wringer and needed help before his current mistress could blackmail him for more money than he was willing to part with. In the early days in Hollywood, they would be out in the waiting room ringing their hands waiting to see him, sometimes three and four deep. But since their move to the Central Coast to escape LA's jammed freeways, the half-hour waiting lines at Starbucks, and a social life that had become somewhat awkward and had begun to go south, the only walk-ins they had were a few local attorneys and an occasional distraught housewife who thought her husband was cheating on her. Most of the time, neither could afford their services.

"Jack," Lindsy said softly and waited for him to turn around.

She almost never called him by name during business hours, and when he finally turned toward her, it was clear from the look on her face that something was definitely wrong. "What is it, Linds? What's up?"

"I had to open it. It came in with the regular office e-mail. I wish I hadn't. But the minute I saw what it was, I shut it down right away." She told him what to click on and watched while his fingers flicked over his keyboard. After a few seconds, he paled as the blood drained from his handsome face, matching the gray at his temples.

"You put a trace on it yet, kid?" he said in a dead monotone, not taking his eyes off the big-screen.

"Already on it, boss. Shouldn't take long," she said. "It was local. You—"

"Give me a minute, Linds," he said, cutting her off, staring at the large thirty-two–inch monitor that was big enough to pull up half a dozen e-mails at a time, but after a few keystrokes, it was crammed full with just one. "And let's keep this between us for now. No need to bring Randy in just yet, okay?"

"Roger that. But if it's blackmail or some kind of extortion, he'll scream his head of at both of us for keeping him out of the loop. He'll want to nail this while it's hot," she warned. "It has to be some sort of trick photography. I mean Bev wouldn't ..." Her uncertain voice faded in wonder.

"It could be anything," Jack said, his eyes still glued to the screen.

"Whatever you say," Lindsy said. She looked like someone had just kicked her in the guts when she closed the door behind her. She wanted to cry, but she would settle for just finding the low-grade SOB who had sent the cell phone pics. From the little she had seen, it looked like the photos could have been doctored. But what if they weren't? What in the world was Bev thinking of? In that case, someone was possibly laying the groundwork for a case of blackmail, and she wondered how long she could keep it from Randy. She knew he would want blood when he saw them.

She just had to find out whose blood it would be.

Twenty One

Jack needed to get out of the office. He had been trying to concentrate on work, but his mind kept going back to the anonymous photos they had received earlier that morning; his years of training as a detective ubiquitous as he juggled all the possibilities. And as he methodically analyzed what little evidence he had and began to formulate a plan, it became obvious exactly where he should start.

By late morning, the trace Lindsy was running still had not turned up anything, and it had become increasingly difficult for him to concentrate on anything else. He had poured over each of the electronic images, using an app called HPMI, an acronym for High-power Magnification Imagery. It eliminated all of the guesswork.

He first determined that they were untouched and undoctored originals. The close-up details generated were nothing less than remarkable, making the enlarged digital images even sharper than the originals, instead of being blurred and grainy as most enlargements turned out. After adding the highly magnified versions to the originals already transferred to his cell phone, he finished his sixth cup of coffee, which tended to jangle his nerves more than settled them. Then, putting the next part of the plan he had come up with into action, Jack jumped into the Jag and headed into town on a mission, leaving instructions for Lindsy to call him the minute anything came back on the trace.

Twenty minutes later, he parked in front of a row of trendy shops just off Highway 101 that ran through the center of town, and entered one of the fashionable storefronts with gold leaf on one of the large bay windows that said it was the home of Central Coast Antiques. Inside, he caught a glimpse of the attractive owner and headed in her direction.

She was a petite woman, somewhere near middle age, with a shapely figure and long, strawberry-blond hair that fell down her back in soft wavy curls. She had a narrow waist, slender hips, and a look about her that made you wonder if she was shopping in spite of the chunky diamond she wore on her left hand.

Susan Davenport glanced up from what she was doing and brightened when she saw Jack headed her way. "Well, hello there, handsome," she purred at him. "What brings you into town this time of day?"

"Hey, Susan." Jack greeted his wife's best friend with a thin smile. "Glad I caught you."

"So am I, darling." She smiled sweetly at the not-so-subtle double entendre she tossed out and leaned over the glass countertop to give him a peck on the cheek. This morning she was not surprised he was in a dark mood. "At least I think I am," she added. "You look like something's going on that might be interesting." Susan folded her hands over the stack of invoices she had been poring over, giving him her full attention with a rather seductive smile as a bonus. She loved intrigue and felt her heartbeat quicken slightly. "So, what's up, big guy? Do you want to tell Susan all about it?"

"I think we need to talk, Sue. It's about the other night," he said, noticing how she often referred to herself in the third person.

"Bev, right? Your wife, my best friend. And the party—with Ted."

"What makes you say that?" If he had been suspicious before, she just dumped a gallon of high-test fuel on the smoldering fire he was harboring.

"What else would bring you all the way into town at this time of day, darling? Bev's told me what a workaholic you are, the long hours you spend investigating all kinds of naughty things people do. By the way, how is the PI business these days? You're not here checking up on *me*, are you?" She grinned invitingly.

"Busy," he said with a slight frown, sidestepping the humor. "What makes you think I'm here about Bev?"

"Well, darling, you're certainly not after me—although it's a delightful idea." She batted her long lashes at him, insinuating more. "And she was being very naughty the other night. I had a long talk with Ted about that when we got home. I'm surprised it took you this long to come around." Her smile was all honey now. "Are you sure Ted didn't hire you to spy on me? Because I was thinking of doing the same thing to him after the party." She smiled sweetly at her own humor, but at once saw that he wasn't in the mood.

Jack said, "I know you and Bev talk, tell each other things." His brow knitted, his tone way offbeat from his usual ubiquitous self-assured personality.

Susan's antennae shot up as she tried to assess how much he knew, or thought he knew, or if he had talked with Bev before showing up unannounced. Playing it safe, she said, "Well, go ahead and talk, darling. I'm all ears. What is it you want to know?"

"It's kind of personal," he said, glancing at the clerk who was the only salesperson on duty and the few customers who were milling around the shop at that hour of the day. "Can we go somewhere?"

"Of course we can," she said, with a glance at the Lady Rolex she was wearing. "But it will cost you lunch, darling. I just love that little Italian place over by the train station."

When Susan reached under the counter for her handbag, she noticed that her heart was beating double time.

Twenty Two

Ten minutes later, they were sitting in the staid clubby bar at Café Roma, a popular Italian bistro at the Union Pacific station a few blocks away. Five minutes after that, with only small talk between them, they were sipping a pricey sauvignon blanc when Jack retrieved his cell from his jacket pocket, flicked a button, and handed it to Susan.

"These came into the office anonymously this morning. Apparently from someone at the party the other night."

Susan took the phone, steeled herself against a shiver that started up her spine, knowing what she was about to see, and studied the small screen. It was Beverly and Ted, just as she suspected, sucking face in living color on the dance floor at the yacht club party. She did not particularly like the euphemism, but it was what kids called French kissing these days. The photos automatically began to blink from one to another.

"Oh, my," she lamented after a moment with the sincerity of a well-trained actress.

"It gets better," he groused. "Push the red button at the bottom."

She found the button and pressed it, and the screen came to life, smoothly scrolling through the remaining photos she was already familiar with. Then it transitioned into a live-action movie mode that was even more shocking. This was followed by a series of graphic close-ups of the first photos that she had not seen before, and left little to the imagination.

The tight shots showed the deep flush in Beverly's face not visible in the others. As they swayed to unheard music, Bev's eyes were closed, her arms tight around Ted's neck, his hands groping her below the waist, pulling her into him as they kissed. Suddenly, the screen zoomed into a tight head shot. The picture was so clear and sharp you could see the tiny nearly invisible lines under Bev's makeup, their tongues hungrily crammed into the other's mouth. The view slowly panned down to capture the erotic motion of their grinding hips that caused Susan's breath to catch in her throat—and a twitch somewhere else.

After a few moments, the screen froze on one of Ted's hands as he clutched Beverly's breast. Susan handed the cell phone back to him and noticed that her hand was twitching slightly. "Well, my goodness, it certainly didn't look nearly that interesting from where we were standing the other night. You're the private detective here. Who do you suppose sent these? There wasn't a ransom note or something with them was there?" she said, showing what she carefully judged to be the proper amount of curiosity for what she had supposedly just seen for the first time.

"We're still checking, but I'm not sure I even want to know. It really doesn't matter who it was." Susan breathed a little easier with an unnoticed sigh. "What I want to know is how long this has been going on, Sue. And if you knew about it." He paused for a moment, fixing her with an icy stare, giving her a chance to defend herself. But he saw the denial in her face and went on before she could get the words out. "You don't seem all that upset," he added, studying her as if she were the suspect in a crime scene investigation.

She knew she was dealing with a professional and caught the look, disappointed that she had underplayed the part enough that he had noticed. "I know this looks bad, but aren't you taking it a bit too seriously, darling?" she said. "After all, Ted is probably twenty years older than her. And they'd both been drinking quite a bit— especially Bev."

"I'm not sure that's the point at all, Susan," Jack said plainly. "A blind man could see there's something going on, has been going on for a while, and it has nothing to do with Ted's age or how much they had to drink. Not to mention doing it in front of the entire yacht club, or that you didn't know about it. She said you two talk about everything. She even said she might be doing you a favor, since you weren't particularly interested in that sort of thing anymore."

"Sex—?" Susan gulped, surprised at the remark, but did her best to keep it from showing. "Did she really say that I wasn't interested … in sex?"

Jack nodded. "And then some," he said, the muscles in his jaw rippled with his growing frustration. Under normal circumstances, he would not be so forthcoming with their bedroom conversations, but Bev had already crossed the line and he was just doing what any suspicious husband would do, especially one who happened to be an ex-cop. He was investigating.

Susan started to speak just as the waiter brought their food and waited until he had refilled their wineglasses and departed before she said, "Have you asked Bev if she's been seeing Ted? I mean that way … like that?"

"Yes, as a matter of fact. Oddly enough, the same question had occurred to me, too," he said, the irony in his voice obvious. "One night she brought up how Ted's flirting was getting a little too friendly lately. Apparently, he told her he was in love with her and she said that she'd discussed it with you."

"Well, the love thingy is nothing new. But why in the world would she bring that up if she were trying to hide something?

Unless …? Did you ever think she might be trying to make you jealous?"

"Actually, I think I pissed her off at dinner the night she mentioned it. One of the girls at Windows was showing off her goodies and I guess she thought I was paying too much attention."

"Ah, the new girl—young, dark hair, with great boobies, right?" The girl had also caught Ted's interest recently, but she was so young, Susan had only scolded him for over-tipping her, not for his gawking. "We—women, that is—can be like that sometimes," she said. "In her case, it's probably good for business."

Jack nodded and made a face, remembering that he had also padded his bill that night. "I asked Bev if she'd tell me if she had sex with Ted."

Both of Susan's brows rose in unison at the comment. "And—?" This was an interesting detail Bev had failed to mention before. She nibbled at the vegetarian salad she liked so much with the special Italian dressing, waiting for his to answer. However, any appetite she had arrived with nearly an hour ago was history after viewing the graphic photos she was familiar with and the close-ups she had never seen before, and wondered how he had managed to do that.

"And, she quibbled about what I considered having sex was." Jack took a sip of wine. He had ordered the calamari, but had not touched it. "We finally narrowed it down to the usual things, and she said it depended on which one of them she did with him and how many martinis she'd had when I asked her."

"Oh, dear." Susan stifled a giggle. "But that sounds like Bev, all right. And how did that work for you, darling?" she said, neatly putting the ball back in his court.

"My God, Susan, you're beginning to sound like Dr. Phil on TV now. I tried to talk to her about it again the night of the party when we got home, but she was sick as a dog in the car and a couple more times after we got back. I agreed to put it off until she felt better. I've just been waiting for the right time to bring it up again."

Susan fixed him with an accusatory stare. "You mean you're

waiting until she's had one-too-many martinis again. You know how they affect her. That's taking unfair advantage, darling."

He nodded awkwardly this time. "We haven't exactly been on the best of terms since the party. And I don't suppose she's in any hurry to bring it up again. But now, with the photos …"

"And how long has all this been going on between you two?"

"For a while, before the dance the other night." He caught the glint of skepticism in her eye. "Maybe longer, six months or so," he corrected himself, but her suspicion only deepened. "All right, maybe it's been a year. Christ, I don't know. Long enough for her to make an ass of herself at the party," he said, his frustration obvious now. "You probably know better than I do."

"Maybe, darling, but you sleep with her, not me." Nevertheless, Susan did know how long it had been, and it was a lot closer to a year than last week. Knowing he would be uncomfortable discussing their sex life, she still needed to see how candid he intended to be. "If it's been that long, I'm a little surprised it took all this time for you to realize how unhappy our girl is in her marriage."

"I thought the husband was supposed to be the last one to know," he countered, his irritation mounting steadily. "That doesn't mean *you* didn't know about it."

"And if I did, that doesn't mean I'd tell anyone. Especially her husband, for goodness' sake," Susan said, the words coming out as smoothly as if she'd rehearsed them from one of her movies.

He fully expected she would try to stonewall him. "I don't even know why I'm here. I know you two are tight, and you'd probably consider yourself a traitor or something if you said anything. But Ted's your husband, for God's sake. And we're not exactly strangers."

"Then you really don't think it was just the martinis? She had a pretty good hangover the next day at lunch as I remember." She almost blushed at the understatement. In reality, she had never seen anyone that hung over, not even after one of the wild studio parties she'd attended.

"Even if it was, what about Ted? He can handle his liquor pretty well, and he was just as bad; all over her out there in front of God and everyone." As an incentive, he added, "If you can help me out here, I don't need to say anything to Bev about it. It'll just be between the two of us." He held up his right hand in the form of a Boy Scout pledge. "Word of honor." He thought about many of his clients over the years who had struggled to find the truth while trying to decide if they should go through the emotional and financial rigors of divorce. They just needed to know for sure before making up their mind. Now, it seemed it was his turn.

Susan drained her glass and waited while he refilled it at the same time he waved off the waiter who had been standing idly by and started their way when he picked up the bottle. It was getting late and the lunch staff was waiting for them to finish.

"Well, darling, I guess there's no harm in telling you something you apparently already know—or at least suspect," she began slowly, and saw the anxiety leap into his face as soon as the words came out. She did not want to appear too cooperative, or that it was exactly where she had been leading the conversation since they arrived at the restaurant. "Of course, I wouldn't want to get Bev into trouble, darling. She's my very best friend. I've never had a sister, but it's like family with us."

He waited, anticipating the worst, needing to know the truth, but dreading it all the same. "Then it's true? Bev *has* been doing you a favor?"

"It's more like what it's done for Ted than for me, darling. Although, I'm not complaining, mind you. I don't remember the last time I've seen him this happy. He even cuddled with me after I scolded him the night of the party. I almost forgot how good it felt to, you know …" She trailed off, not needing to be that personal to get her point across and possibly raise any further suspicion.

They had never had a reason to speak this frankly before, and when he raised a brow, she didn't try to hide her true feelings. "At the risk of sounding crass, darling, I think a good schtupping would pretty well describe it," she said and shrugged her narrow shoulders, her cleavage moving seductively with the effort. "But it was better than that, really. Anyway, it was like old times."

"You want to tell me about it?" He wasn't interested in her private sex life; it was his wife's extramarital sex life he wanted to know about.

"About them? Or Ted and me, darling?"

He gave her an unmistakable look that she read perfectly. But she did not want to appear too eager and knew that once she started there would be no turning back. She would have to tell him everything—which was exactly the way she had planned it.

"Bev said it began one day when she came over with a basket of goodies. You know how she loves to cook and how good she is at it, always bringing over something new to try on us."

Jack knew. He had walked the streets of Paris alone for an entire week that winter she had attended Cordon Bleu and had been battling his waistline ever since.

"As it happened, I was out that day and Ted was home alone. She came over and I guess one thing led to another. He told her he was in love with her, and they got into a little heavy petting, and he just pounced, right there on the library sofa, to quote a line from an old movie I was actually an understudy for. But it was actually the living room sofa, since we don't have a library."

"Heavy petting?" He coughed up the words, ignoring the nostalgia. "That's something kids do, for God's sake. And why all the sudden? We've been friends, known you and Ted, for years. If she's so hot for him, why now? Why not before? Jesus, for that matter, why at all?" He seemed to cringe inwardly with his next thought. "No offense, but he's old enough to be her father."

Susan gave a silent shrug, her mouth down-turned. "I'm not offended, darling, but you have to remember it wasn't exactly my idea either. But I guess she felt safe with him. Neither of them have been all that happy in their marriages lately. And maybe she thought she could be naughty with Ted, without getting into too much trouble since he is older. She could play around the edges of sex with him, all the excitement, even the fear of being caught that goes with it, and not have to go all the way; could stop any time she wanted to."

"And did she tell you how far that was?" he asked, hating that he needed to know.

She pursed her lips. "It's not my place to get into the nitty-gritty part, darling. Bev will have to supply you with the juicy details if you really want to know. Personally, I don't think that's as important as what prompted her to do it in the first place. Maybe she just wanted to see what it would be like to have sex with an older man, to experiment. She might even have been comparing the two of you."

Her words sent a chill through him. "Do you know whose idea it was to start playing grab-ass?"

"Ted's, I'm sure, as I understand it. But he says he's been in love with her. I spoke to him about it, and they both gave pretty much the same story. That's really what lunch was all about with Bev the day after the yacht club thingy. She said she needed to talk, to get something off her chest, which turned out to be the affair. And, as I said, he's been in love with her for years. I guess the opportunity presented itself that day. He knew things between the two of you weren't going that well, and he just decided to go for it. You know how you men can be sometimes."

"She said he was in love with her. I just didn't think it had gone that far." He sighed. "Do you know how long it's been going on?"

"The huggy-kissy stuff—? Probably way before the library sofa thingy, darling. About a year or so, maybe. Ted would give her a peck on the cheek, sometimes on the lips when he thought I wasn't looking. Bev said she could handle him, that it didn't bother her. He even gave her a pat on the fanny from time to time, I guess. He pinched her once, though. Did you know she how she hates that, darling? Thinks it's terribly chauvinistic."

Actually, he had no idea, since he could not recall ever pinching her there—somewhere else, maybe. But when he thought about it, he may have bitten her there once. He shrugged and waited for her to go on.

"Funny, because she said she'd always taken care of it without involving me. We even laughed about it over lunch. Neither of us could believe the gall of the old bastard—pardon my French. I mean, she's really too young for him. Of course, since his shenanigans didn't seem to bother her, I wasn't worried about it. I wasn't really worried about either of them because of the age difference.

"And, no need to repeat this part to anyone, darling, but confidentially, he hasn't been able to perform—you know, like that—for sometime now. But I guess she was probably flattered by all the attention he's been giving her lately and begun to flirt back a little. Even asked me not to be angry with him. And, as I said, as long as it wasn't bothering her I didn't see any real harm in it."

"Do you know when it got serious?" If he was right, it was about the same time she became almost impossible to live with, started undressing in the closet, and sometimes even went to bed without saying "Good night."

"You mean the full-body contact part? I don't think it's been going on that long," she said, answering her own question. "Not like that, anyway. A few weeks, maybe a month or so. I knew, of course, what's been going on between the two of you and thought at first that she was just having a little fun with Ted, being naughty like girls do sometimes; a little flirting, nothing serious. I even thought she might just be trying to make you jealous. And he's a big boy and knows better than to play with fire, especially with someone like Bev."

"What's that supposed to mean? What's so different about Bev?"

"Come on, Jack, you know very well what a hottie she is— with a dynamite figure. She could probably have any man she wanted, just for the asking. That's why I think she was playing it safe with

Ted. He was older, and married, of course. And not likely to get her pregnant—unless she's on the pill, which I doubt."

"And knowing all this, you trusted her—with Ted?"

"Of course I did, darling, but it was more like I trusted Ted. He's not exactly what you'd call average, if you get my meaning. Then there's the ED thingy lately. But that's really another story and not what we're talking about right now."

But he knew exactly what she was talking about after Bev had made it crystal clear the night she had told him about Ted. It was the same night he had first suspected that something serious might be going on between them. Jack paused for a moment and then went back to what he really wanted to know. "So, the day she came over and you were gone is when it actually got serious?"

"That's what she said. Ted too."

"Did she say where I was?"

"Out of town on business." She thought of adding "again," but did not, and instead said, "She's complained before about you being gone so much."

Jack was smart enough to stick to the subject and did not take the bait. "And you believed her—them?"

"What's not to believe, darling? There was no reason not to. Bev and I have always been honest to a fault with each other. Especially about something as serious as this. And, of course, Ted confirmed her story—from a male point of view, anyway. I realize that's like comparing apples and oranges sometimes, I suppose."

"When did she tell you all of this?" He knew he was sounding like a cop again. But that's what he was, and he didn't know how else to handle it.

"At lunch that day, the day after the yacht club dinner, when the pictures were taken." She indicated his cell phone that was still open on the table, beckoning to her. She wanted to see the close-ups of Ted and Bev again, but did not ask for fear of betraying her true motive for them being there.

"Did she say why the confession all the sudden? Apparently, it's been going on for a while."

"Not really that long, darling. She said they'd only been together a couple of times after the patty-fingers thingy that day. The confession was a total surprise to me too. She must have realized, even through her alcoholic haze, that what they were doing out there on the dance floor was a dead giveaway. I guess you even said as much when you two got home that night, because she asked my advice about what to do, how to handle what was going on with her and Ted—and you. And she couldn't really do that unless she told me about the affair, could she."

Jack grunted, his mind in a jumble as he tried to put it all together. But her logic was reasonable. He was a sucker for logic. You couldn't argue with it. It was the reason people acted the way they do.

"And now we have the pictures. As you said, there's no denying them," Susan said, focusing on the one thing that had helped her decide how to tell him about the affair. What she was not sure of was how much he needed to know if she were to convince him. Susan studied the deep hurt in his face before she continued.

"I have to confess I advised her to deny everything. Women have a way of working these things out between them, but I know men look at it very differently."

Jack slowly shook his head. "Bev's always been her own person. It was part of what we had between us." He looked up from his plate where he had been playing in his food. "So, sometime after that is when they saw each other again?"

"At my place." She nodded and continued. "At least they didn't go off to some sleazy motel, somewhere people might see them. They hadn't seen each other for weeks after the first time, and apparently Ted kept calling her every chance he got trying to get her to come back to the house."

"Thank God for little favors," he said sarcastically. "But I thought that was a little strange, too—all the phone calls, I mean."

She nodded again, understanding his cynicism, even agreeing with it. "Must have started you thinking …" She eyed him before continuing. "Then one day when you were gone he called again and she decided to go back. Just showed up at the door. I haven't really gone into that part of it with Ted, except that they took off all their clothes this time. I guess it doesn't really matter." Susan took a deeper breath than usual before going on this time. "The fact is, she did go back, and it was only for one reason this time. That was when they—well, you know what I mean, the first time. I guess she had a pretty difficult time with him."

He blanched. "She actually told you that? How … how hard it was for her?" Jack was incredulous at the thought.

Susan smiled anyway, in spite of the look on his face. "Girls talk, darling—it's you boys who don't. We always want the details, to compare. But it was my fault this time. I insisted, actually. We can be like that sometimes." Susan stared at him over the rim of her wineglass, a bit defensively now. She noticed that he had not touched his food. She had done little more herself. "Looking back, I suppose I helped it along a bit without realizing it. Bev admitted the other day that some of the things I said about Ted made her curious."

Jack glared back at her, his unspoken question obvious. She went on. "I guess she excited him quite a bit. What can I say? But, no, we weren't comparing *size*, if that's what you're thinking, even though Ted is quite unusual in that department, out of the ordinary, you might say. That's what I meant a few minutes ago, about him being rather exceptional. He's just not that easy to be with. In fact, it had something to do with why I married him. He was at Berkeley when we met in my senior year and he asked me to marry him. I wasn't exactly looking forward to the boring life as the wife of a college swimming coach. But then one day I saw him in his Speedos and it helped to change my mind."

Jack was at a loss for words now and knew it showed. Apparently, it all boiled down to an older guy with a big schlong was banging his wife. And once she got over the shock, she decided she liked it and had gone back for more.

When he said as much, Susan said, "From a woman's point of view, darling, it really isn't that simple—liking sex or not, I mean. When it comes to Ted, it's also a matter of being able to." Her expression took on a more serious cast now, and she lightly cleared her throat. "This is kind of personal and may hurt a little, but we might as well get it all out as long as we're talking about it. And, in a way, I suppose you actually have a right to know. Bev would probably be too embarrassed to say anything, but I can back her up from personal experience."

She saw his eyes narrow and went on. "Bev said that Ted causes her to have the most intense multiple orgasms she's ever experienced in her entire life." She paused long enough for that to sink in, before adding, "And, I know our girl well enough that she wouldn't say something like that, especially to me, unless it was real, darling."

So, Jack thought, not only did she like it, but she liked it a lot. The visions running through his mind were not only maddening but strangely erotic. "Is she in love with him? Or is it just that he's … big."

Susan chose her words carefully now, fully aware that his ego was on the line. "Of course, darling, that's what I wanted to know, too. But, yes, she did say that she's fallen in love with him. But now I guess it's both of those things; being in love with him making the other possible."

She saw the hurt darken his face even more, but went on. "And for the record, darling, Ted's way beyond *big*. He's the next thing to impossible for almost any women. Take my word for it. The good part is, I also asked Bev if she was still in love with you, and she didn't say no. Just that she used to adore you, was confused by it all, and wanted to know if it was possible to be in love with two people at the same time."

"And …?" Her description of Ted took a couple of twirls around in his imagination.

"Well, I not only told her I thought it was possible, but that it happens all the time," Susan said with some authority. "Apparently, Ted's been seriously attracted to her for some time now. But he told her he's still in love with me too. So I guess he feels the same way." She let the last part hang between them for a few seconds while she sipped her wine. "When I asked Bev if she intended to continue seeing him, she said she was worried about you finding out. I don't think she wants to hurt you, Jack. And that's a good sign."

"... Of a guilty conscience, maybe," Jack said, his ire showing through. "You mentioned they were only alone a couple of times?"

Susan smiled weakly now, betrayal written all over her at what she was about to say, but knowing it was necessary if he was to believe her. "The last time was the day she told you we were going shopping in Santa Barbara. She told me she couldn't get away and actually spent the day with Ted at our place again." Susan shot him a mischievous grin. "... In the hot tub no less. Ted tells me our girl likes to be a little adventurous at times, in a different way. Did you know about that, darling?"

Jack's cell phone buzzed just then. He saw it was Lindsy and held up a hand. "It's the office. Give me a sec." He partially turned away from her, pressed the send/receive button, and held the phone to his ear.

"Yeah."

Susan picked up her wineglass, looked around the empty bar, and surveyed the darkened dining room beyond. Jack listened briefly before clicking off, and turned back to Susan. "Sorry about that. Business." He took a sip of wine before picking up where they left off. "I'm almost afraid to ask what you're talking about," Jack said, looking at her curiously now. "It has to be something I've been neglecting, no doubt?"

Susan's grin was puckish. "I'm going to let you figure that one out on your own, darling. It doesn't happen to be one of my favorite thingies. You know her better than I do when it comes to that sort of thing. But from what I'm told, it has nothing to do with the missionary position that, uh, I understand you're so fond of."

"Good God, Susan! Is nothing sacred?" He gasped. "She talked about that? How we make love, for chrissake?"

Susan's smile went from impish devilment to prudently sagacious in a heartbeat, in spite of the fetid look that had come over him, and she raised her glass in a toast, which was answer enough. From his expression, she could tell there was going to be a scene when he got home. It would take him about twenty minutes to get there, giving her more than enough time to call Bev with a heads-up—unless, she thought, unless she could strike a deal for the plan she had been working on since she'd opened her e-mail this morning and saw the candid photos the commodore's wife had sent to her.

"It doesn't seem fair for you to just barge in on Bev and confront her with all of this," Susan said to him in preparation for what she was about to suggest.

"Who the hell's being fair around here? Looks to me like everyone's in on this conspiracy except me," he said bitterly. He knew it wasn't Susan's fault, though he was finding it hard not to take it out on her.

"Still, darling, it doesn't seem right." She was skillfully pleading her case without seeming to take sides. She knew exactly what he was feeling. It was the same way she had felt at lunch the afternoon Beverly had confirmed every word of Ted's confession to her the night before—and more.

After the long moment it took for Jack to bring his temper under control, he said in a less sarcastic tone, "What did you have in mind, Marquis of Queensbury Rules?"

"Better than that, dear." Her smile had victory written all over it this time. She knew at that moment that she had won the battle she had been waging against almost impossible odds. "How about I call her when I get back to the shop. In return, you can tell her all about our luncheon date and what we've been talking about."

"All of it—?" He was taken aback by the offer.

"As I said, darling, it seems only fair." Susan's grin turned cheeky as she studied him with her slate-gray eyes, a steely glint flashing from them. Susan was a beautiful woman, but her expression could take on a blunt edge when necessary. And right now, that was exactly what she needed. But he could not begin to guess why.

It took only a few seconds for Jack to decide. He was already in a lose-lose situation, and being fair didn't have a thing to do with it. But he suspected there was something else lurking behind the beautiful, yet stern, facade staring back at him; exactly what, he wasn't sure, but he had the sinking feeling he was about to find out. Lindsy had just confirmed the results of the trace she had put on the e-mailed photos they received that morning. They were sent from a cell phone listed to one *Theodore Travis Davenport*. And he'd bet his last dollar that *Theodore* didn't know a damned thing about it.

"Yeah, sure," he said finally, "why not? Only fair, right?"

With that battle over and won, Susan was anxious to get on with the next one and the rest of her plan. She could only hope that Beverly picked up when she called with the news—and that she was sitting down—because she was probably going to pass out when she heard what she had to say.

Susan steeled herself for the bombshell she was about to drop in Jack's lap. "There's something else we should chat about while we're on the subject, darling."

"There's more?" Jack said from behind the blank look he put on that was doing its best to mask his suspicions. "What more could there possibly be?"

Susan's expression turned playful, lighting up what had once been a million-dollar smile that had lately settled for being just plain sexy at this stage of her life. "Oh, but this is the best part, darling. I always like to save the best for last. Don't you agree?" She literally cooed at him, batted her long lashes, and pursed her full, glossy lips that perfectly matched the color of her beautifully manicured nails.

His gut churned at the tone of her voice, his gaze steady but benign, giving nothing up. "So, chat away, darling," he said, not mocking her, never suspecting what she was about to tell him.

Twenty Three

Susan idly swirled what was left of the wine in her glass and noticed how nicely the leg clung to the faux crystal the little bistro used for stemware. They were still at their table in the bar, and Susan used the few moments of silence that had fallen over them to collect the same thoughts she had been formulating and rehearsing since sending him the revealing photos earlier that morning. She'd failed to consider the possible consequences of using Ted's cell phone until it was too late, and hoped when she was finished with what she was about to say that it would no longer matter.

She still wondered how he had managed the extreme close-ups and the graphic movie sequence on his cell phone, but guessed it had something to do with the fact that he was a private eye who probably knew how to do all of those complicated thingies. At the risk of sounding rehearsed, she resisted the urge to clear her throat before looking up to make eye contact with the handsome man sitting across from her. When she did, she found him staring back at her with a strained look on his face.

"This may sound a little personal at first, darling, but I want you to hear me out before jumping to conclusions." She paused for effect, taking his silence as tacit acceptance. "Ted and I have been sleeping together, but that's about all. Things haven't been very lovey-dovey at my house for a while, and—"

"I thought you just said the two of you were 'cuddling,' I believe was the term you used," Jack interrupted, his attention to detail kicking in.

Her hand went up to stop him before he could go on. "I know, darling. And we are cuddling—now. What I was about to say is, until Bev came into the picture. If you recall, I also mentioned that the cuddling part came *after* she and Ted began seeing each other. Actually, Ted and I hadn't done anything like that for quite some time. The times we tried he just wasn't able to, you know, to perform, rise to the occasion, as it were." She noted the stoic look he was giving her and hurriedly went on.

"Being a woman, of course, all I have to do is show up. We can even fake the rest of it if we need to. And I don't know of a single woman who hasn't at one time or another. It's not that it isn't lovely, mind you, it just goes with the territory sometimes. But men, of course, are different. You not only have to show up, but you have to, um … perform, so to speak. Naturally, the poor darling blamed himself. He's such a sweetheart that way. As you might expect, we've been together so long that I suspected I might actually have something to do with it, that it was me all along, and not him. He works out all the time, swims his laps every day, rain or shine. He doesn't use any sort of medication that might affect him like that."

Jack resisted the urge to ask Ted's age, eyed her curiously, and instead let his skill as a professional interrogator form his next question. "Assuming that's true, you think his ability to perform has something to do with Bev?"

"It makes perfect sense to me, darling. He seems to be doing just fine with her according to both of them. The only answer left is that it has to be me, that for some reason I just wasn't able to arouse him any more. God knows I haven't always been the perfect wife. But if there's one thing I've learned over the years, it's how to persuade a horny producer or director to give me a part in their next movie." Her gaze grew hooded as she watched for his reaction. Her last remark was intended as a bit of advertising just in case he was interested in the rest of what she had to say, and she noticed his brow tweak slightly.

Jack said, "You must have a good reason to think that." He still did not know where she was going with all of this or if it had anything to do with the anonymous photos she had sent him. But he sensed a connection and hoped it wasn't revenge; a way for her to get even with Ted.

"Well, it seems pretty obvious to me. Our girl is not only younger but terribly sexy, if I do say so myself." She looked away, her smile twisted slightly, leaving him to wonder how much older she was than Bev. He looked as if he was about to ask when she seemed to read his mind and said, "How much younger is none of your business. Anyway, it seems like Ted and I have been together forever, and I guess it just goes to prove the old adage that familiarity really does breed contempt." She looked up now. "And from what Bev tells me, he has apparently been able to fill some sort of a void in her life as well, certainly in her sex life."

Jack felt her twist the knife she had already stuck in him with her comment about Bev's intense, multiple orgasms. "Why are you telling me all of this, Susan? What's going on? What's this all about?"

"What I'm trying to say, darling, is apparently more than you realize," Susan said, but still purposely vague. What she was about to say wasn't something she could just spring on him from out of the blue without laying some groundwork first, some sort of preparation, not if she hoped to convince him that she had not completely lost her mind.

"Bev tells me she's been unhappy for some time before becoming involved with Ted. I originally thought it might just be a father figure thingy with her. But that doesn't seem to be the case at all. She thinks he's sexy, and he makes her feel needed, not to mention, umm—very satisfied—if you get my meaning."

Susan cocked her head with a bright little smile at the obvious implication. It was one of those feminine gestures she had that was very attractive. She went on. "And now that she's recovered from the initial shock, I think sex has a lot to do with it too, darling. I know it does for Ted. I won't tell you exactly how he described it because it was a bit too graphic for my taste, but very masculine," she added, her expression turning a little sour at the thought. "And he definitely doesn't have the same problem with Bev that he did with me."

"So, what's the point? I still don't know why you're telling me all of this?"

"Only because it takes two to tango, darling, to borrow a phrase. And I never would have stopped dancing if it weren't for Ted's problem—with me." She flicked her brow at him several times in quick succession in a sexy "come-hither" fashion, her knee lightly touching his under the table. "You wouldn't care to give a girl a few dancing lessons, would you?"

Jack shifted slightly in his chair, disappointed that she was trying to use him as her revenge, the reason behind the photos obvious now. She was getting back at Ted. "No offense, Sue, but thanks anyway," he said ruefully. "Some other time, maybe. Right now, why don't you just tell me what all of this is leading up to. What's on your mind? I was a cop too long not to know when someone's holding out on me."

Susan was almost afraid to continue. She turned her head now so he wouldn't see the deep breath she needed to help calm the case of nerves that had come over her, caused by a sudden panic with "Moment of truth!" written all over it. From the beginning, she knew Beverly could not handle this part, and she had racked her brain for days for a way of telling Jack about their plans for the four of them. Then, just as she was about to give up, the photos had shown up in her e-mail folder that morning like a gift from heaven. Or was it hell? In reality, it was a gift from commodore's gossipy wife, and she wondered if the shrew would ever know how much she appreciated it, or the flash of genius her poisonous e-mail had inspired her to. Heaven or hell, she thought, she was about to find out.

Susan lightly cleared her throat and prepared to come straight out with it. "I have a proposition for you, Jack." She waited for her words to settle over him, knowing that countless possibilities were probably clicking through his mind at the speed of light.

Jack cracked a weak smile, as if he did not know that getting even with Ted had everything to do with it. "And what might that be?"

She managed another strained breath, then said, "Well, darling, the way I see it, for some time now you and Bev have not been getting along. There's been little or no sex at your house and all the other wonderful, cuddly thingies that go with a loving relationship. Am I right?"

He stared at her, unblinking, no answer was necessary or expected. Susan hurried on; thankful her voice had not cracked so far. "Bev says she used to adore you, and the sex was always very romantic and satisfying—for both of you. What if you could go back to those good times the two of you had together? And all it took to get there was a little *understanding*, some *tolerance* and getting a grip on that super ego you men seem to carry around with you all the time?" She smiled sweetly, already feeling better. "Not to mention expanding your horizons and having a little fun while you're at it. Does that sound like something you might be interested in, darling?"

Definitely, this was not what he expected. "Maybe you better define understanding, tolerance, and what you mean by getting a grip."

She smiled inwardly with more confidence now, liking the way he got straight to the point. But that was Jack, and exactly what she expected. "Well, as it stands right now, out of the four of us only Ted and Bev—and now me, thank God—are getting along and enjoying each other's company so to speak. And not nearly often enough for any of us. As for you, lovies, it's been the big ziparino! Now that I think of it, darling, you don't have something going on the side do you? Bev says you're out of town a lot."

He stared back at her malevolently; his unspoken answer loud and clear. She was pleasantly reassured when there were no sign of guilt showing in his face. She knew he was waiting for her to continue, for something more, but nothing in the world could not prepare him for what she was about to say next.

"Beverly and I have thought of a way to change everything. It's a simple solution, and lots of couples do it all the time. It's even accepted in certain therapeutic circles as being quite healthy and very effective when it comes to mending troubled relationships."

"Why don't you stop beating around the bush, Susan," he cut in, tired of her talking in circles. "What the hell is it you're trying to say?"

Susan openly gulped in a breath this time, not caring if he noticed. "Simply put, darling, Beverly, Ted and I think we should all get together in a kind of ménage à trois, I guess you could call it, except with the four of us. I don't know how to say the 'four' thingy in French, darling." She tried a light smile on him this time but saw it wasn't working for him, and could tell that he had just entered a state of shock. "Bev doesn't either, by the way. Isn't that silly?" She hurried on. "I guess you could just call it a ménage à trois, plus one. Bev called it an orgy, but that isn't what I have in mind at all. I looked it up on the Internet. It's actually called 'polyamory'—that's Latin for being in love with more than one person at the same time."

Susan breathed a huge sigh of relief now that it was finally out in the open, the idea now squarely confronting him, forcing him to deal with it. All she could hope was that his wounded ego wouldn't screw things up. Since coming up with the idea, it had so captivated her—filling her imagination with all manner of delicious thoughts and possibilities—that she'd hardly been able to sleep. Susan tried to breathe more normally, but that wasn't working either. She felt as though she had just confessed to robbing Fort Knox—to an ex-cop, no less.

Jack tried to keep his jaw from dropping, which sagged noticeably just the same. His brain began to click off a whole series of questions, some of which he had not thought about since the New Years Eve party a few years ago. "You're saying that you want the four of us, you and Ted, Bev and me together for group sex?"

Susan glanced around, but the restaurant was quiet, almost empty by this hour. The bartender was washing glassware at the far end of the bar, and no one was close enough to overhear them except one of the busboys who was busily cleaning tables across the room and paying no attention to them.

"Well, yes, darling, something like that, but it's not that simple, really," she said quietly and kept any doubt from showing in her face, confirming that he was on the right track. "But I think it would be just fine once we get past the shocking part, you know, the awkwardness, like taking off all our clothes for the first time. After that, darling, we should just be like one big happy family." She watched him, but nothing changed. The shock that had all but paralyzed him was still in evidence.

"Anyway, does that interest you even the tiniest little bit? Something you might consider—circumstances being what they are?" Her voice almost cracked under the strain this time, but her stage presence held and she was able to maintain the sweet look she was wearing as if she had just invited him to high tea at a nudist colony. "And don't forget the important part is it could help get you and Bev back together," she reminded him as a further enticement.

He stared at her for what seemed like an eternity before it all began to sink in. But his biggest doubt, the serious thought that flashed into his mind, led the way. "And Bev's okay with all this? You've discussed it with her?"

"After she got over the shock of the idea. And Ted, too, of course," Susan said, instantly relived that he had not rejected the idea out of hand. "Or I wouldn't be here, right now." Her grin broadened. "Which is something you're in right now, am I right, darling? The shock thingy?"

He watched for something else to show up in her face. After a moment when there was no change, he said, "So, you're actually talking about the four of us?" He did not know if he was stalling to give his addled brain a chance to catch up, or if he could not believe what he had just heard.

"Together," she confirmed with a perky smile.

"At the same time." His mind demanding confirmation.

"In the same bed." Her smirk turned seductive, an eye twitched in anticipation.

"Naked!" he said, sure now that he was stalling.

A grin exploded across her pretty face. She was pleased at his quick grasp of the delicate situation they were discussing. Actually, she was surprised that he was able to think at all.

"Doing the big nasty, darling," she offered with finality, dispelling any possible doubt, but could see that there was no need for that now. "That's what the polyamorous thingy is all about; couples falling in love with each other. And don't forget the fun-fun-fun part," she said, beaming at him and at all the delicious possibilities the idea conjured up in her twirling imagination.

Jack was obviously having a little trouble breathing himself now. "I can sort of see Ted and Bev—sort of. But you and me? That part's all right with you?"

"Oh come on, Jack, please. Didn't Bev tell you I think you're gorgeous?" Susan grinned openly now and batted her long lashes at him. "She told me you think I have great boobies, but my butt is too small."

In fact, she had told him that. He got a stupid look on his face, checked out her cleavage, and knew she was right again. "What about Ted? How would he feel about you and me …?"

Susan held her napkin to her mouth and cleared her throat again, feeling the tension flow out of her. She and Ted had, of course, discussed that very thing. And in view of the affair he was already having with Bev, had readily agreed. Susan said, "First of all, since Ted and I made love the other night, I feel like he's actually come back to me from some strange place he's been. I can't be sure, of course, but I think it's because of Bev." She took a sip of wine and went on. "All I know is that it's real. He says he still loves me, and I believe him. Now, it seems he's also in love with Bev, and they can't just let go of that, not now anyway, maybe ever. I don't know where all of this is leading, but I'm certainly willing to go along with it for now. And, from what I understand, you were on the road to divorce long before Ted came into the picture. I'm not sure if this is going to work, or even exactly how it works, but considering what's at stake, I'm more than willing to give it a try, and I think you should too, darling. The four of us all have a great deal invested in our relationships. And, my goodness', we've already been friends for years. I think we owe it to each other to try to work this out. I know you're taking all this very personally, darling, but you have to realize that it's not just your problem. What we decide will affect all of us."

She paused, trying to evaluate what was showing in his face, to decide if it was rejection, acceptance, or something in between. Right now, she would settle for simple recognition. However, no matter how hard she tried, it wasn't working. What she saw was not good or bad, a yes or a no. For her own peace of mind, she also needed to make sure that if he turned them down, that it was not because of her.

She tried to think of something else that would help to convince him, and after a moment said, "You and I haven't fallen in love yet, darling, but I'm certainly looking forward to it." She seductively raised one perfectly pencil-enhanced brow to him.

A sudden thought flashed through his mind. "You said you and Bev talk. Do you know if Ted ... if he's the first time? Or has she ... have there been others?"

"Now, darling, I don't want you to take this the wrong way. But all I can say is there has never been the slightest hint that Bev's ever done something like this before, been unfaithful to you. But I have to admit that I've never come right out and asked her about it, either. There was never any need to. And we've certainly talked about my trips to the casting-couch enough. You know how curious women can be. If there had been the slightest hint of an affair, I would have pounced on it, gone after her for the juicy details. But, to be perfectly honest with you, I'm really not sure."

He analyzed what she said, the way she had said it, and weighed it against what he already knew. "So, as her best friend—the sister you never had—tell me what you really think."

It was not the actress, but the woman who answered. "I really don't think so, darling. She said she adored you until the last year or so. And I honestly think Ted just happened to be in the right place at the right time. She needed that male intimacy all women crave, and apparently has gone missing in your relationship. She felt safe with him. He was convenient, and was the lucky guy she just happened to turn to. I think our girl has far too much class to be just sleeping around, that sort of thing." Her gaze was steady. She could see the turmoil he was going through.

Jack listened in silence, waiting for her to finish. Susan read the look on his face. "Well, darling, that's it in a nutshell." She sighed with relief. "It could work, you know. It could be good for all of us. And everybody's already doing it, except you and me. And I'm looking forward to that part." She grinned at him good-naturedly, but unable to completely hide the lust that was lurking just below the surface.

It was Jack's nature to challenge the obvious, to look for alternative solutions, a possible hidden motive. "And if I don't go along?" The question hung between them in the still, aromatic air in the bar that smelled of aged wood and spirits.

"We talked about that possibility, darling," Susan said evenly. "The three of us have agreed to give this a try. And I suppose that's the way it would end up if you're not interested or can't handle it for reasons of your own. But it would be so much better for all of us if you would at least try. We could all help each other over the rough spots that way. I really have a good feeling about this, Jack. I could work for you and Bev, for Ted and me, for all of us."

"For Ted, anyway," he said sarcastically.

That did it, by God! Susan thought. She had done her level best to approach this in an entirely adult, intelligent and logical manner, giving due consideration to what she knew to be the typical male point of view, one that she personally considered a bit stupid a good deal of the time, but at the same time understanding that they just couldn't help it. That was the way men were wired, the nature of the beast. That was not to say that she couldn't be quite taken with their controlling and dominant personalities at times, especially when it came to sex. And it always did. It was one of the things that made life interesting.

But she had just spent most of the afternoon trying to reason with Jack and was rapidly growing tired of his self-serving, chauvinistic, male attitude. He was not the first one to have his wife jump in the sack with another man, and he certainly wouldn't be the last. And the world was still spinning around, just not the way he wanted it to.

Deciding now that it was all or nothing and going in for the kill, Susan said, "You better snap out of it, big guy. Get a grip on that bruised ego of yours and wake up to the fact that your competition has the best of both worlds here. Ted's already sleeping with your wife, for goodness' sake. What's more, it appears that once she got over the shock, she not only loves it, but him as well. Now, I don't like it any more than you do. In fact, if you want the truth, darling, I'm jealous as hell over the whole damned thing. But if you really want to do something about losing your wife, you had better consider what I've just said very carefully. Bev and I both think it could be good for the two of you. It's certainly already helped Ted and me. In that sense, it's actually proof that this polyamory thingy works."

She waited for him to react to the logic of her outburst, but no such luck. He just numbly stared at her and she went on. "With that being said, darling, unless there's something about *me* you don't like, I suggest you think about this very carefully before you say no to a perfectly marvelous idea and turn down a wonderful opportunity for all of us."

His expression changed instantly at the suggestion that it might be personal, that his reluctance might have something to do with her. "Susan, that's not it at all. This has nothing to do with you, believe me."

"Well, darling…" she said rather haughtily, "I'm glad to hear that." With an effort, her face softened slightly, the dark frown she had taken on disappeared and the makings of a tiny smile worked its way into her pouty lips. "So, how about it, handsome, what do you say? Do you want to dance, or are you going to sit this one out?"

The Phone Call

Twenty Four

"Bev, darling, it's me! Thank God, you're home! I've got the most marvelous news!"

"Oh, hi, Sue. I've been trying to call you."

"And I've been trying to reach you for over twenty minutes, darling. The line's been busy the whole time. Is Jack home yet?"

"No. I haven't seen him since he left for the office this morning. We had a spat over dinner plans tonight and he left in a huff."

"Oh dear, he's had more than enough time to get there."

"Ted said you were at work. We talked for a while. I was about to try the shop again. You sound excited about something. What good news? What's going on, girl?"

"Sorry, but there's no time for all the details right now, darling. Jack should be home any second. I need to tell you something. He showed up here at the shop a little before lunch today, and—"

"—Why in the world would he do that?" Beverly cut her off, a suspicious edge in her voice.

Susan sounded out of breath. "I'm about to tell you, darling, as soon as my heart stops beating so fast. I had this marvelous idea. You know how we've been racking our brains for a way to tell him about you and Ted and the little talk we had about the four of us getting together the other day, and it just came to me out of the blue. That ninny from the yacht club sent me some terrible photos—and I'm talking real close-ups of you and Ted at the party the other night and—"

"What ninny? What pictures? Who sent them …?"

"That busybody, of course, the commodore's wife. Who else would bother? But listen, darling, Jack should be home any minute. The photos are on his cell phone."

Bev felt suddenly panicked and slightly nauseous. "My God, Susan, how do you know that? How could that happen? Why …"

"Because *I* sent them to his office this morning on the chance that he'd call me before talking to you or Ted," Susan said, abruptly. "And it worked perfectly. Everyone was watching you two the other night. The old witch must have taken some pictures and e-mailed them to me this morning thinking I'd be all honked about the way you two were carrying on. That's when it dawned on me that it was the perfect way to break it to Jack, to put him in the loop for our little, ah, the arrangement we talked about. I told him all about you and Ted, everything you told me, the whole works."

"Susan! For God's sake!" Beverly yelled at her. She could feel the panic beginning to crawl over her like a heavy shroud, as if she had just been bitten by a pit viper; betrayal lying leaden in her stomach. "What am I supposed to do now? Why in the world didn't you talk to me first? How could you possibly do something like that?"

With the questions popped at her in rapid fire, Susan said, "I was going to, darling. But I was sure he'd call me first, and then I was going to call you. But instead of calling, he just showed up here at the shop. So we went to lunch and talked for three hours. This is the first chance I've had to tell you."

"My God, I can't believe this. And why did he come to you?"

"He obviously wanted to know about you and Ted, to see what was going on before confronting you with it. And I just planned on him acting like a cop. Which is exactly what he did. Men are such little boys when it comes to sex. As I said before, darling, they don't handle this sort of thing very well. Especially if they think you're trying to hide something from them. They always suspect there's more to it than there really is, except in this case, there really is," she said, nearly out of breath. "I was sure he'd want to find out all he could before confronting you; it's the cop thingy again. And I knew that Ted would be the last person he'd go to. I was the only one left. And it worked perfectly. Aren't you excited, darling?"

"Excited …? I—I think 'scared to death' is more like it. And right now—I—I—I think I'm going to throw up," Beverly stuttered, her voice quivering now. Yet Susan's bubbling enthusiasm bolstered her the tiniest bit. At first, her initial panic had threatened to smother her. But she knew this was bound to happen sooner or later.

So here it was—sooner.

He was not going to commit murder over it, she reasoned. Mayhem, maybe. "I—I don't know what to say," Beverly managed in a state of near shock, most of the emotion already drained out of her. She was now trying to ward off the severe case of rigor mortis she felt headed her way. She had been worried sick about Jack finding out. Now, some mysterious photos had apparently changed it all from a possibility to harsh reality. She racked her brain trying to remember exactly how she had behaved that night and then realized that the four 007 martinis she'd had made that all but impossible. What she did remember was dancing with Ted as if they were in their own little world, all of the worries and complications her life suddenly nonexistent, and not caring about anything else. Even with her foggy memory, she knew the photos had to be undeniable. Maybe Susan had not betrayed her after all.

"You didn't go into all of the details, I hope," Beverly said, recalling the thoroughly detailed and revealing conversation she'd had with Susan the day after the Commodore's Ball, the thought causing her panic to well up all over again. It had taken nearly all day, but she had told Susan everything, her confession graphic and embarrassingly candid.

"I made it very clear about the four of us, and he didn't ask for any of the juicy details about you and Ted. Men don't seem to do that sort of thingy, darling, just us girls. But I had to tell him everything, be quite frank with him, if I was going to pull this off," Susan replied quickly. "I had to make him understand that it was our way or the highway, or he might have just walked out on me and the whole idea right there. But I was counting on the fact that he's still very much in love with you and didn't have much choice if he was going to avoid losing you altogether. Something he did ask, though. He wanted to know if you were okay with the idea. Of course, I told him that you were, that I'd talked to Ted, and that we'd all agreed to it. I even told him how much better Ted and I are getting along now since the two of you … since you've been seeing him. And it worked, darling. It worked perfectly."

"You told him everything? My God, Susan!"

"No-no, of course not everything, just times and places mostly. But you know me, dear. I would have, but the poor darling didn't even ask about the juicy parts, certainly not the ones you and I would have. I think the shock might have been a little too much for him, sort of bowled him over. But I did mention the hot tub thingy you told me about. Personally, I thought that part was yummy, but I didn't tell him that or what it was, only that it had nothing to do with the missionaries."

Susan paused breathlessly when she sensed Beverly's panic in the huge gulp of air she took in. When there was nothing on the other end of the line except heavy breathing, she added, excitedly, "And he knows I'm calling you, darling. In fact, it was his idea. But here's the best part. When it was all over, I came right out and asked him about the four of us getting together for you-know-what."

"*You did what?*" Beverly's voice rose sharply out of control, another wave of panic overtaking her. "Oh my God, Susan!"

"That was the whole idea, darling. And he agreed! He said 'Yes!' He's willing to at least give it a try, for goodness' sake! Isn't that marvelous?"

Beverly gasped now, not believing her ears. She could not breathe for a minute. It was so unlike him, the man she thought she knew so well all of these years.

"I couldn't just blurt it all out right away, mind you. It took some finesse, some explaining at first," she said proudly. "But in the end, I guess he figured he had nothing to lose and everything to gain if he at least gave our idea—the foursome thingy—a try." She was breathing heavily now herself with the excitement of it all. "Anyway, we're in. All we have to do now is get the four of us together to discuss the details—a few ground rules are in order I suppose—and let the games begin."

Before Beverly could collect her wits and get a word in edgewise, Susan rushed on. "And I say the sooner the better, darling, before he has a chance to think about it and change his mind. So, I suggested that we start off with dinner tonight, the four of us, and he agreed! Did you hear me, darling? He actually agreed! Tonight!"

Beverly grunted numbly with a pain that resembled something similar to childbirth.

"After dinner we can all go back to my place. I'll take care of everything. Don't you worry about a thing."

He actually agreed! The thought of what that implied raced through Beverly's mind like Halley's Comet, flashing impossible images at her in rapid succession, all of them embarrassing.

Just then, she heard the familiar chirp the Jaguar made when the alarm was set. Maggie Mae got up and went to the kitchen door that led into the garage, tail held high, twitching with anticipation, her head cocked as she waited. "He just drove in," Bev said breathlessly. "I'll talk to you later, I guess. Oh God, tonight, I guess," she said with a quiver in her voice that was half panic and half determination and clicked off.

Beverly had been preparing a triple dark-chocolate cake recipe she had clipped from one of her gourmet cooking magazines when Susan called. She covered the mixing bowl with plastic wrap that contained the egg yolks she'd saved and placed it in the frig and then turned to wash her hands just as Jack came in and Maggs began to whimper and wag like she had not seen him for a year instead of just a few hours.

Beverly did not turn around but could feel his eyes boring into her back, and it seemed like forever before he spoke. "I just saw Susan in town," he said, patting Maggie affectionately, ruffling her floppy ears. There was a heaviness in his voice.

"I know. Almost an hour ago … she just called." Beverly still did not turn around and was surprised at how even and steady her voice was. She did not want him to see the guilt she knew was written all over her, or traces of the inner fire that threatened to consume her. Her head was still spinning from the telephone conversation with Susan, the reality of it all beginning to settle over her through the murk that was fogging her mind.

"I stopped by the office on the way." He waited for her to turn around, but she did not move. "I guess we need to talk … about this."

"Susan said that's what dinner was about tonight," she said stiffly over her shoulder. She finished washing her hands and began to dry them on the dishtowel.

"I meant us, you and me—before dinner," he answered and gave the big St. Bernard another scratch behind the ear. She looked up at him adoringly. Someone still loved him, he thought.

"Sure, where?"

"Down here's okay. Let me run upstairs for a minute and change."

She waited until she heard his heels click across the Italian marble floor as he exited the kitchen, Maggie Mae's nails making a *tickita-tickita* sound hot on his heels, before she went to the bar and poured two glasses of wine.

Beverly settled herself on the large, curved sofa in the living room to wait for him. Her heart was beating like a jungle drum as she placed the glasses on the coffee table in front of the black granite fireplace that was framed in polished brass and set to automatically come on when the temperature got down to sixty-eight. But the day had been much too nice for that.

Until now.

The Confrontation

Twenty Five

Beverly had never known such an all-consuming passion was possible before Jack. The second they met the chemistry between them was instantaneous. She had been married in her twenties, which had lasted just two years, and Jack was recovering from a bitter divorce after a long-term relationship with his high school sweetheart. They were both at a turning point in their lives, and they came together as if it had been preordained.

Now, Beverly was at a loss to explain how it had all come down to this, waiting to discuss how they were to move on with the rest of their lives—with Susan and Ted. She wondered what had changed. How had they grown so far apart over the last few years? And why had she come to resent him in the first place? But she knew the answer. It had been slowly creeping between them since they moved from LA. And why was he always right—about everything? *Damn him*, she thought, for always being right. But she knew that was only part of it, and wondered if Ted was actually the face of her revenge?

Bev heard his footsteps on the circular staircase that came led from the library. She brushed a strand of hair back from her face where she knew the tension and anxiety she'd been trying to ignore since talking with Susan had taken up residence and must be showing. She tried to concentrate on the wine she had brought from the bar instead of her unsteady hands.

"I know it's a little early, but I thought we could probably use a drink," she said when he came to sit beside her, but not too close, and managed not to glare at him. She hated that her hands were trembling, that this was so hard for her, not sure if it was guilt, resentment, or just plain anger that was causing it.

Maggie Mae flopped down between them, her big head propped on one of Jack's feet. He scratched behind her ear before reaching for his glass. He had changed into a pale-yellow Ralph Lauren polo, cotton chinos, and a pair of Top-Siders with air socks. "Maybe we should go a little easy on the sauce," he said stiffly. He sensed that her tension matched his own.

There he goes again, Beverly thought, *giving orders.* The maddening part was that he was right—again. Subduing her frustration she said, "I was surprised when Susan said you agreed to … to tonight." She did not look at him, not wanting to see what was sure to be in his face. But it wasn't him she was afraid of; it was what they were talking about that scared her.

"I'm really not sure what I agreed to," he said and wanted to get straight on to the part about her sleeping with Ted, but he knew that wouldn't work. Lately, any direct confrontation between them would completely shut her down. She might even tear up on him, provided she still cared enough to do that. The thought was probably unfair, but he thought it anyway.

"What *are* you sure of?" Beverly glanced up with a puzzled look, her right brow arching suspiciously.

The raised brow was one of her *tells*. It usually meant that she didn't agree with him, but was listening. It was a look he had come to know well lately. "Only that we're supposed to get together with Ted and Susan tonight. Then after dinner …" Her other brow joined the first when he hesitated. "... and the four of us go back to their place. I went along, but it wasn't because of any particular desire to see Susan naked, or watching you and Long John Silver get it on. It was because I didn't have too much choice in the matter since you seem to have a pretty good head start on me."

"Much choice—?" Beverly said, her leaping sarcasm masking the tinge of guilt she felt. "As far as I know, nobody's forcing you to do anything, Jack." She ignored the 'head start' crack, recognizing it for what it was—the casting of bait upon the waters—and refused to take it. Nevertheless, since Susan had told him about her affair, it felt like a giant weight had been lifted from her shoulders.

Jack took a sip of wine and made eye contact, something she had not been doing lately. "The way I hear it, the three of you were going ahead with or without me, one way or the other. You don't have to be a psych major to see where that would lead."

"You mean us? Divorce ...?"

"That's pretty much it, I guess."

"And you don't want that, even now that you know about Ted? Is that what you're saying?" This was only one of the many questions that had began roaring through her mind since talking with Susan a few minutes ago.

He was instantly encouraged, but only slightly optimistic. "If you want to know the truth, Bev, I'm shocked as hell about Ted. I mean ..."

"If you dare say he's old enough to be my father, I'm out of here," she said, ready to take flight.

He stared at her for a moment, taking note of what must be a raw nerve with her. "Look, Bev, in spite of what's going on with us, I still love you. I don't like what you've done, but it's that simple," he said heavily. "I can't just chuck away half our lives, all the time we've been together. I even accept half the blame for the way things have turned out. And I think down deep—I hope, at least—that you still have some feeling for me, for us. I know this may sound a little crazy, but I thought about this whole thing on the way back from town. Since it's already happened, maybe it actually is a chance to put things back together like Susan said. It sounds weird, but I guess she could be right about it being therapeutic in a way, or whatever it was she called it. 'Recommended in some circles,' I think she said. And since you've already … umm … been with him, well, it's not like I'm going to prevent some big catastrophe."

He still didn't get it, she thought furiously. He just didn't understanding! It wasn't just about sleeping with Ted; it was the fact that she *wanted* to. And that infuriated her more than anything else. She knew she was glaring, skepticism written all over her, when she said, "Exactly what did Susan tell you about Ted and me?" She felt awkward asking the question, as if it was too personal, even between husband and wife.

He saw her smoldering mood staring back at him. "Pretty much the whole thing, I guess. According to her, anyway." The resignation he felt showed up in his voice. "There's more …?"

"Everything—?" she demanded, ignoring his question.

"How would I know? Not a blow-by-blow, if that's what you're worried about," he said, the double entendre not funny or meant to be. Then he added, "Do you women really talk about things like that? I mean … your sex life—all the details? Who did what to whom and how?"

Beverly gave him a *"What if we do?"* face. "Venus and Mars," she said with a shrug. "I'm just trying to figure out what got you to agree to tonight. I told her you'd never do it … ever. In fact, I was sure of it."

"Are you sorry I did?" He searched her face for something else now, but all he saw was defiance that accompanied the icy silence that had suddenly fallen between them. After a moment when it was obvious she did not intend to answer, he tried again. "Are you in love with him? Susan says you are."

Beverly felt the heavy weight of the guilt that had taken up permanent residence in her conscience since she started seeing Ted; it was nestled right next to the ton of relief she felt now that it was no longer a secret. She still could not believe they were having such conversation. "Did she say how she felt about that—Ted and me?"

"Said she didn't like it either, but was dealing with it. Are you—?"

"I'm … I'm not sure, but yes, I suppose I am," she said and shrugged without realizing it. "Otherwise I wouldn't have …" She purposely did not finish the thought. "That's how we came up with the idea about the four of us. I'm just not sure how to handle it, all of us together … like that. But it's the only way we could think of to make it work. Susan said she explained all that to you. Didn't she?"

Jack nodded. "I guess I'm just not clear about how to go about it." He paused and then said, "What about Susan and me? That part's okay with you? Or maybe from what the two of you have said about Ted, you'd be too busy to notice."

Beverly's eyes flashed at the provocation, and then narrowed. Maybe Susan had revealed more than she thought. "She told you about that? About him, how he is?" When he nodded, her curiosity switched to Susan. "I know you think Sue's attractive, her big boobs and all. Would you like to sleep with her?" She'd asked him before and wondered if the answer was still the same.

"I haven't thought about it that much," he said, which meant that he probably had. But the truth was that he had considered it in some detail during the drive back from town. He guessed there was really no way to know how any of them would react until tonight, when it actually happened. "You're okay with the idea—Susan and me, and you and Ted, of course?"

"I've already said I'm not sure what's okay anymore. All I know is, the way things are between us is not the way I want to spend the rest of my life."

"As long as we're on the subject, mind if I ask if this has happened before? Or is Ted the first?" He already had Susan's take, but he needed to ask her face-to-face. This time it was the husband in him needing an answer, not the cop demanding it.

Beverly glared at him, fire in her eyes, resentment plastered everywhere else. But when she thought about it, she would have asked the same question, and calmly said, "No, it hasn't." Then added, "Do you believe me, Jack?"

His smile was sad, but a smile nonetheless. "Yes, of course I do. Since everything seems to be out in the open now, it doesn't make much sense not to be honest with each other."

Her mouth twitched with the unjustified resentment that was tugging at her. She took a deep breath and tried not to glare at him. "What about you—?"

He shook his head with a tight grin, expecting the question. "Susan asked me the same thing. Said I was gone a lot and wanted to know if I was seeing someone on the side."

"Are you—?"

"No, of course not. I told you, Bev, I love you. But since you seem to have fallen in love with Ted, it makes me wonder … about us."

She had not told him that in a long time, that she loved him, and said, "I'm sorry, I … I just don't know. I'm not sure how I feel anymore, about you or us." But she resented the inference that she was no longer in love with him because of Ted. They both knew better. The trouble between them had started long before he came into her life. "Was that all Susan said about us, Ted and me?"

He refused to let go of it. "I'd like to know if you're still in love with me, Bev."

"And I just told you, *I don't know.*" She refused to be bullied any longer and glared at him, but for the first time tonight she felt like crying.

A shadow darkened Jack's already troubled face, but he forced himself to let it pass. "Susan says Ted told her there's something I don't know about you that has nothing to do with the, ah, the missionary position."

Her stomach wrenched to think that he and Susan were already that intimate, to have discussed such a delicate matter, but the sigh it caused was barely audible. "This is probably not a good time for that," she said evenly. "But I hope you understand that Ted isn't just a whim. I'm not just sleeping around, Jack. I—I like being with him, the way he treats me when we're together—and all the rest."

The words were like a stiletto in his guts. "Susan says you mentioned that he's been doing a pretty good job ... with the rest of it ... whatever that is. Apparently you've discussed having sex with him." Her glare caused him to pause for a moment before he added, "How many times have you been together?" He knew she consider it too personal for the way things were between them, and the scowl on her face proved it.

Her eyes darted up from the sanctuary of her wineglass where she had been avoiding his gaze. "You mean how many times Ted and I have ...?" She couldn't finish. No matter what she said, she knew it would sound like what she and Ted had together was something dirty. Her expression hardened even more when she said, "What difference does it make? He screwed me, okay. And I screwed him back. More than once."

Beverly bit the inside of her lip, hating that she felt obliged to answer him, while his own dull mask was doing its best to hide his pain. What did he expect her to say? That after she recovered from the first time, she had gone back for more? That he caused her—No, damn it! he *forced*—her to have such incredibly long, intense orgasms that they rattled the very core of her being and left her drained and satisfied? That any normal man would never be able to satisfy her again, at least not in the same way? Or that when she begged for more, he had hungrily obliged and it started all over again until she wanted to scream? No, she thought, not if she cared about tonight, if she expected him to show up and not march straight upstairs and start packing.

Despite the confusion that had been running roughshod over her and clouding her mind since receiving Susan's call, Bev was actually looking forward to the evening, to seeing Ted again without the nagging guilt that went with it and was still hanging on. She knew that Susan would not have a problem being with her and Ted. And the way she had manipulated Jack into agreeing with their scheme was nothing short of amazing. But both Ted and Jack were still problematic with respect to seeing their wives with another man. That was yet to be seen, and she wondered how the coming evening would affect all of them.

Bev noticed Jack staring at her blankly, waiting for her to continue. "Jack, this isn't getting us anywhere," she said finally, her flash of anger dissipated. "I'm not trying to be coy. But I just don't see the point. Not right now, anyway."

He shrugged, doing his best to let go of it. "Then you *are* in love with him?"

"A few days ago I would have said I'm not sure," she said with a sigh, her voice heavy, tired from the emotional strain she'd been under the past several weeks. "Maybe not like it was between us in the beginning, before. But we both need to know the answer to that one."

Jack could not remember the last time he felt this crappy, and then realized that was an understatement. Shitty was more like it. He was losing the woman he loved—if he had not already lost her—and was not sure he could live without, not to mention that he had just signed up to watch Ted screw her silly. Then, changing the subject back to the reason they were having this discussion in the first place, he said, "What about tonight? What are we supposed to do?"

An even stranger look came over Beverly. She'd had little time to think things through, and what they were talking about doing tonight was just beginning to catch up with her. However, that he would even ask such a dim-witted question made her wonder which of them was the more confused. How many answers were there for what you could do during group sex? As if she even knew!

When he saw her reaction, Jack held up his hands. "Sorry, I didn't mean that the way it came out. I just wondered if you knew where we were going, dinner, afterward, what the program was."

Beverly stared at him for a moment to make sure he was serious. When she decided the question was so dumb that he had to be, she said, "I'm not sure. Susan said she'd take care of the details. Dinner somewhere in town—Windows, I suppose—and then back to their place for ..." She didn't finish because she had no intention of trying to explain what was supposed to happen after that—even if she could.

Jack nodded, not knowing what else to say.

Beverly saw something else in his face, a sadness, maybe pain, she thought, perhaps even pity. "Jack, are you sure you're okay with this?"

He managed a tired smile, gently stroked Maggie's broad head, and let her lick his hand. "I don't know, kid. We've never done anything like this," he said, shaking his head, "only kidded around some that New Years Eve." Still, he remembered how intense it had been with two other couples in the same room. "I know I don't want to lose you. Not sure I could handle that. And if this is what it's going to take to make you happy—us happy, I mean—maybe even keep us under the same roof for a while longer, I guess it's worth a try."

Then, his ubiquitous sense of humor surfaced through the mire he had sunken into. "I've learned one thing, though. Men can be such jerks sometimes, husbands, and should ask a lot more questions about things ... what their wives like—and need. Besides, I haven't seen that gorgeous butt of yours in a while, even if I do have to wait in line."

The
Arrangement

Twenty Six

"So, my darlings, where were we …?"

A very radiant Susan Davenport asked of no one in particular. They all knew she was referring to the subject of their unfinished dinner conversation that had dominated the entire evening. A curious pall had come over them since returning to the house, each knowing the other's thoughts. No one had been able to think of anything else all day and their mood remained thick with anxiety.

They were at the Davenports, in the cozy family room surrounded by expensive antiques, sipping coffee. Dinner had been at Windows on the Bay, their favorite restaurant, and it was after eleven by the time they had returned. Over the course of several hours, they had shared two bottles of white wine to celebrate the occasion and to help quell their apprehension. However, the tension in the room was still crackling like a downed power line on wet pavement.

As usual, the dining room at Windows was crowded. Tuesday evening was oyster night in the bar, and with the tasty mollusks at half price, the place had been jam-packed. The crowd had made it difficult to discuss their reason for being there without being overhead, forcing them to be discreet, carefully choosing their words when the discussion turned delicate or to a subject not normally included in the average dinner conversation.

As a result, the mood at the table had been rather stilted and businesslike most of the evening. Jack had suspiciously eyed Ted for the first time since learning that he was having an affair with his wife. Ted had eyed him back with his usual affable grin. The two couples had agreed that there needed be rules if they were to avoid the inevitable pitfalls associated with such a delicate relationship. They also understood that as their familiarity grew and the honeymoon was finally over—which they judged would take at least several of their special evenings together—things would be much more relaxed. "It will like being married all over again," Susan had said, "but without all the inconvenience of a divorce."

"You mentioned we should come up with a name, something to call it," Ted said from the couch across the room. "I'm just not sure why. Who else are we going to talk to about this, anyway, that it has to have a name?"

Susan had served fresh coffee and little sweet cakes she had stopped for on her way home from work, since Bev had been too frazzled to prepare anything that required more than opening a packaged mix. Beverly sat next to Ted, with Jack across from them by the fireplace in a not-so-comfortable eighteenth-century Louis XV wingback covered in plush burgundy velvet.

With the evening's frustration beginning to show, Susan made an unladylike noise in the back of her throat. "Ted, we need to call it something," she reminded him in a wifely tone of voice. "We can't just call up with, 'Oh, by the by, darling, how about our place for a little group sex tonight,'" she lectured with a slight lilt in her voice, since it did sound rather sexy to her. "Suppose we had to leave a message and Rhonda happened to be there and heard it, for goodness' sake?" Rhonda was the housekeeper Susan and Beverly had shared for years. She was a pretty girl and they both loved to death. Just not that much.

"She'll probably find out anyway," Ted countered, dryly. "She was doing the wash the other day, and when she saw that I hadn't been wearing pajamas lately wanted to know if I'd been sleeping well."

Susan scowled, hoping that one didn't get back to the commodore's wife. Actually, she was too keyed up right now to worry about it. She was bubbling over inside and much more excited than she was letting on. Notwithstanding the initial shock of learning that her husband was having an affair with her best friend, she was very pleased that she had only experienced the slightest hint of jealousy all evening—so far, anyway. Once she recovered from the episode, she had to admit that it was probably more envy over her younger rival than anything else.

She had also considered the possibility that it may be her past catching up with her. Strangely enough, in spite of her live-and-let-live attitude, Susan really did not believe in feeling sorry for herself. She was more of a realist than that and had always been of the mind that everyone controlled his or her own destiny. You needed to take advantage of the opportunities that life presented, *carpe diem,* seize the day, go with what felt good, and try not to hurt anyone in the process. If you could do that, everything else would turn out for the best—most of the time.

"And what about the other thingy we were talking about," Susan said, "before that woman at the next table got so nosy? I thought she was going to drop her fork when you said something about a vagina." Ted shrugged, and put on his *'pardon me for asking'* face when he saw the look on his wife's face.

Susan looked at Jack now. "Speaking of dinner, darling, what's that young woman's name again, the one who works for you and stopped by the table? She was very attractive."

"Linds, Lindsy Evans," Jack replied, barely listening.

"Yes—that was it," she said thoughtfully. "What exactly does she do for you, darling? She's not one of your private eyes, I hope. She's much too cute to be lurking about in dark alleys."

They had by chance run into Lindsy and Randy Wahlrode at dinner that evening. After a few strained pleasantries, they had gone to their own table, which Jack was pleased to see was on the other side of the dining room. After the telephone trace had come back that afternoon, Lindsy and Randy had both suspected Susan of sending the photos and they had been polite yet cool to the Davenports— even more so toward Bev.

"Linds can handle herself," Jack said. "But most of the lurking these days is done on computers in broad daylight," Jack offered. "And she pretty much runs the office. She also makes the best coffee between LA and Frisco."

"Well, I don't mean to complain," Susan went on, "but they both practically ignored me, almost acted like I wasn't there tonight. Did you notice, Teddy?"

"No, dear, not really," Ted said, hedging slightly, not sure that he could explain what he actually had noticed. At first, he had thought how much the man with the Lindsy Evans resembled the cable guy who had been at the house a few days before. The hair was different, and the cable guy wore thick horn-rimmed glasses and had a prominent hooked nose. But they were both extraordinarily large men, which probably accounted for the resemblance. However, he had noticed that the Evans woman definitely had not been ignoring him. He caught her staring down into his lap when he casually glanced up with a ready smile during the introductions, causing him to think he may have spilled something.

"You're just used to being the center of attention, Sue," Jack said with a tight smile. "She's been pretty busy trying to track down the photos I showed you at lunch." He glanced at Bev. He had not shown her the e-mailed photos when he got back to the house that afternoon on the chance that it may spoil the evening, but he wondered if Susan had. When Bev ignored the remark, his gaze drifted back to Susan. "She's got a lot on her mind," he said, having decided not to tell her they knew who had sent the anonymous photos.

"Well, just as long as she doesn't have *you* on her mind, darling. She's a lovely girl, but I hate competition." She had patted his hand patronizingly and wondered what Jack would do if he found out where the photos came from.

Susan cleared her throat, brushed a long strand of hair from her face, her makeup perfect, and moved on. "As I was saying, I think we need to talk about some of the things that are bound to come up from time to time." By default, she had taken on the role of group leader, since the whole arrangement had been her idea from the beginning, and she suspected from some of the looks she'd been getting that the responsibility was causing her to be too academic at times.

"What's this all about then?" Beverly asked. "Things people generally don't talk about in mixed company?"

"Well, dear, I think that's a good start, to agree on a few things," Susan answered. "We can't just all hop in bed together, as delightful as that sounds." She grinned modestly, doing her best to ease the tension.

"I still vote for vagina," Ted spoke up dryly, his expression deadpan, recalling when he'd said as much at dinner the woman who had been eavesdropping at the next table had nearly choked on her minestrone.

Susan looked nonplussed and glanced around the room for support, settling on Jack, who was sitting across from her. "I suppose it really doesn't matter. Jack, darling, what do you think?"

Jack was preoccupied with his own thoughts and could not shake the awkward feeling that had been dogging him all evening as he sipped his coffee and the room grew suddenly quiet. He had been listening, if only halfheartedly, and looked up to find everyone staring at him.

"Well, actually, I think talking about all of this is a little awkward in the first place," he began, his voice measured. He wanted to smile at the thoughts he knew they all must be harboring, but knew it could be misunderstood for something else. What he was really having trouble with was imagining his wife with Ted and everything that went with it. It was almost as disturbing as some of the thoughts he'd had about Susan since lunch that afternoon.

"And not very romantic, either," Susan agreed, glancing at Ted, who just shrugged his broad shoulders again. Then, turning her attention to Beverly, Susan said, "How about you, darling? Any ideas?"

Beverly was also uncomfortable and tried to keep it from showing, but knew that Susan was just trying to keep things moving along before it all collapsed in on them. "I'm not sure I know why we have to talk about it like this," she said a bit stiffly. "It seems a little silly, like we were kids playing spin the bottle and afraid of being caught."

"Good point, darling," Susan agreed, still struggling with her self-imposed leadership role and not sure of what to do next. "It's just that ..."

"It's really all the same when you think about it," Ted interrupted.

Susan glared at him again and thought with all the wine at dinner he might be a little tipsy after all. "I think we're all feeling a bit awkward about now," she said and turned her attention back to the others when Ted ignored the scolding look she was beaming his way. "I just thought it might help to break the ice a little, you know, to talk about it, about different things ..." She paused, glancing around the room, as if to reassure everyone, including herself. "I think the really hard part will be taking off all our clothes for the first time. I've tried to think of different ways to warm things up, to get us moving along this evening ..."

"We could put some music on and dance," Ted offered. "I've

heard that's how some of these parties get stared. There's always strip poker," he added, more confidently this time. "That could be fun … interesting, anyway."

There was a collective sigh and Susan took a deep breath, her smile stiff. "That sounds a little bourgeois for what we're talking about, darling. I'm sure we'll all look back on tonight after we get to know each other a little better, more intimately, and have a good laugh." She chuckled at the thought and made a funny face. But no one joined in. She remembered feeling this way after one of her movies had been a flop. It wasn't a good feeling.

"Well, if nothing else, I guess we could just turn off all the lights and go for it," Susan finally said, her frustration obvious.

"Or leave them all on," Ted tacked on, his dry sense of humor coming through. He glanced around for approval; however, no one was paying any attention to him. He was about to shrug again, but decided not to bother this time.

Susan said, "Then maybe it's time for all of us to change into something more comfortable and get to know each other better a little better. Does everyone agree?"

They all suspected that "comfortable" was a euphemism for getting naked—and no one moved. All eyes were downcast, except Ted who took a quick look around to see if he was missing something. He wasn't, and he joined them in bowing his head. He felt like he was in church instead of waiting to get naked.

An awkward silence settled over them. They knew the entire evening would have fallen apart hours ago had it not been for Susan, and they waited for something to happen, not knowing exactly what that would be.

"All right, my darlings," Susan said, breaking the awkward silence in an authoritative tone, their reluctance obvious. "There's still the matter of the ground rules we were discussing at dinner before that woman next to us practically had a heart attack."

"The guy with her was smiling," Ted offered, his grin broad.

Jack, who seldom missed the small things that often foretold the difference between war and peace, had also noticed the smile.

"I think we all agree that it's important that we have some rules," Susan said, then paused again when there was no reply. "Anybody want to start? Any ideas?" The silence hung like a heavy fog thick enough to cut with a knife. "Anyone—?"

She waited. "Oh come on, people, we need some cooperation here. I can't think of everything," Susan said. Ted looked like he was about to say something, but thought better of it when he caught his wife glaring daggers at him. A silent pout settled into his square face.

Susan scanned the others, but there were no volunteers. Jack had gone back to staring into his coffee cup, and Beverly wore the same serious expression she'd had all through dinner.

"Okay, my darlings, then I'll have to start," Susan offered, but her familiar cheeriness was beginning to sound a bit strained by now. "I think we've agreed that in order for our little arrangement to work, we'll only get together if there're at least three of us. Two boys and a girl, or two girls and a boy. Better still, all four of us at the same time, which I personally think is the best way. But no couples on their own, unless it's your wife or husband, of course. In which case, that doesn't count."

Beverly looked up now. "I thought the original idea was that if we all agreed to something—whatever it was—it was okay," she interjected, recalling part of an earlier conversation they'd had at dinner, her voice calm and steady. Jack looked at her now as she continued. "I think the important thing is that we're open and honest with each other. No secrets, no holding back, no worrying about what your partner may or may not think, if this is going to work. Most of all, we need to respect each other's feelings and talk about any problems that might come up."

"Sounds pretty clinical," Jack said. "What kind of problems are you expecting? We all know why we're here, what we're doing. It just seems that we're not sure how to go about it ... yet."

"How about having sex with someone else while your husband or your wife is in the room," Beverly replied rather sharply.

"I thought we agreed that's the only way we'd do it," Ted chimed in. "No pairing off or meeting up somewhere. At least three of us or not at all."

"Of course, darling," Susan agreed. She thought it was one of the more intelligent things he'd said all night. "I think what Bev means is that if there is any jealousy or other negative feelings that come up, we'll all try to help each other through them, or this isn't going to work very well. We might just as well go home right now."

"But we're already home," Ted said, his customary deadpan all over his face.

Susan rolled her eyes to the ceiling, dismissing his juvenile humor, and said, "Then we're all agreed? We only have … um, relations," she cleared her throat for emphasis, "when we're all together or at least a threesome?"

A muttered agreement went around the room, and Susan said with a smile, "I'm sure we'll get better at this as we go along. So, since we all agree, what do you say we get out of our clothes and go about this in a civilized manner? Actually, just talking about it is making it a little hard for me to breathe," she said, fanning herself lightly with her hand, a grin of anticipation curling up in her face now that the formalities were behind them.

Beverly cringed, her anxiety clearly showing. "Excuse me, but I don't think I can just sit around like that—I mean naked—trying to act normal, Susan." She loved the woman and knew she was just trying to organize an impossible situation, but the thought was unsettling just the same.

"Of course not, darling. Not that it wouldn't be interesting, just not very mysterious. And there is such a thing as modesty. That's why I stopped on the way home this afternoon and did a little shopping for all of us. I found the loveliest robes for our special times together. They're very sexy, especially if you don't wear anything under them." Her grin turned lecherous. "Which is actually the whole idea, of course."

Susan did not wait for an answer before she went on cheerily, as if she was speaking to a kindergarten class. "Now, I suggest that we all get undressed and meet back here, s'il vous plaît. Girls in the master bedroom, boys in the guest room, just for the first time until we get to know each other a little better. After that, whatever makes you feel good."

"What, then?" asked Ted.

Susan had not taken him into her confidence when she had planned the evening for reasons of her own. "Then, my darlings, it's off to the hot tub," she said sweetly, not bothering to scold him. "I turned it on high the minute we got home."

Twenty Seven

"Robes are on the bed!" Ted's booming voice rang out from the bathroom. "Help yourself, bud!"

Jack could hear him through the partially open door. He stood beside the bed where two robes that looked rather feminine were neatly laid out. Feeling foolish, he kicked out of his loafers and worked at the buttons on his shirt, tossing it on a chair when he finished. He did the same with his chinos and stood there self-consciously in a pair of light-blue boxers. He heard the toilet flush and then water running in the basin. A few seconds later Ted came into the bedroom—*stark-ass naked*.

"If you need to take a leak before we go in with the girls, go ahead," Ted said as he crossed the room to the bed and retrieved one of the new robes. "My God, you can see right through these things. Might as well not have anything on." He held the sheer robe up like a matador's cape. "Guess they're one-size-fits-all." He searched for a label before deciding he was right and slipped it on.

Jack was somewhere between completely surprised and totally stunned. Bev and Susan had both warned him what to expect.

But nothing they'd said prepared him for what he could not help staring at. Ted wasn't as tall as he was by several inches, but weighed about the same, and had the lithe body of a serious swimmer. All that betrayed his age was his graying hair and slightly thickened waistline.

But that wasn't the only difference between the two men.

Heeding his wife's warning earlier in the evening as they dressed for dinner, Ted had been fully expecting what he saw in Jack's face, not that he hadn't been the recipient of similar gawking in locker rooms most of his life. Still, Susan had cautioned him against any show of superiority that might scare Jack off before their cozy new arrangement could even get started.

Ted had always regarded his unusual attribute as unique and followed Jack's gaze to what had been a source of pride for him—and disappointment at times—since he was old enough to know that size really did make a difference.

"So, what do you think, bud? Not bad, huh? A real lady killer." He couldn't help the immodest grin that spread across his square, blocky Pennsylvania-Dutch face, despite Susan's admonition and her prediction that he could ruin things for everyone.

"That's sort of, uh, putting it mildly," Jack replied and tried to look away. But he couldn't take his eyes off the damned thing. Especially, since it was what the bastard was stuffing into his wife—or trying to, God only knew how—and in a few minutes, unless someone declared World War III, was about to again.

The prideful smile Ted was wearing continued to do a slow waltz across his face. If Susan were there, she would be kicking him in the balls right about now.

With his curiosity overpowering him, Jack said, "How … uh … I mean, do you know how …" He could not get all of the words out without sounding even more envious than he already was, but he was doing the best his trampled and crushed ego would allow at the moment.

Ted's expression brightened even more, knowing exactly what he had in mind. "Susan measured once. Can't remember what she said exactly," he hedged when her warning went off in his head again. But his pride was overpowering and he couldn't resist. "As I remember, it was somewhere around eighteen inches—fully loaded." His white teeth flashed through the huge grin his handsome smile had turned into.

He was somewhat short of that now, still Jack checked his eyes for any sign that he might be stretching the truth, but there was nothing except his easy smile looking back at him. And, the evidence was right there in front of him to judge for himself. It also occurred to him that Susan was obviously not nearly as diminutive as she seemed, and that Bev was considerably more capable than he had thought. He was left with the unsettling feeling that he was about to find out the accuracy of both of those conclusions.

Ted did not have to guess what Jack was thinking. "I guess I don't need to tell you that Bev's quite a gal. I'm sure you know that. It took a while, but she did just fine. First time out, too. That's never happened with me before, bud, not even with Sue." Ted caught the strange look that came over Jack as the color drained out of his face.

When he had momentarily recovered and his brain was working again, Jack said, "If you say so—bud." With dark thoughts of revenge clawing at him, he couldn't think of anything else to say. That's what he'd signed up for. He was supposed to be in his "understanding" and "tolerant" mode. *Jesus!* All he had to do now was "get a grip." He didn't know if what he was feeling was hate or envy, and then decided it was a toss-up.

"So, you and Bev … I mean, she was actually able to …" After a moment, he felt his color start to return, but his heart was still playing zippity doo dah in all four chambers.

"Oh, yeah, pal," he said proudly. "Loved it, too." Ted saw his color begin to deepen and wondered if he was pressing his younger, taller, better-looking competitor too hard. For a minute, it looked like he might be sick. "You're a lucky guy, Jack, to have a gal like her. She's not at all like Sue, you know, a much bigger girl, except for—well, you know what they say about little women." He couldn't help the superior grin that had curled up into his face on its own and gave Jack a friendly wife-sharing wink. "But I've always had this thing for big girls. You too, I guess. Sue's so little, but she's ... well, you'll find out about Sue pretty quick." Ted cinched his robe around him, the transparent material thinly veiling the one huge advantage he had over Jack.

"By the way, you don't mind a little man-to-man talk like this when the girls aren't around, do you, pal? Susan would consider it vulgar. She's pretty prim and proper that way. Although I'll bet they do the same to us guys when we're not around. But, like I said, it's nice to have another guy to talk to once in a while, man-to-man."

Jack forced himself out of the killing mode his trampled ego had been sucking him into all day. "No, it's—it's okay," he said, taking in a breath of air. "Wouldn't have it any other way, ol' buddy. We're just talking about our wives, here." His smile was thin and unfriendly, but it was all he could manage. "Maybe I can return the favor when I get to know Susan better." He wasn't sure if the empty challenge sounded like a threat, or even if it was, but the trim former Olympian didn't seem to take it that way. He knew he was blaming Ted for the mess his life was in, and that it wasn't fair. And it certainly wasn't Susan's fault. Maybe it wasn't even Bev's fault. Basic logic told him there was only one person left.

The answer saddened him even more.

"Well, tonight's the big night, pal," Ted said. "Susan's always had this thing for other men. You'll find out soon enough. And she's talked about you and Bev."

Jack did not know whether to thank him for the heads-up or let it go. "She said there's something I've been—I guess neglecting is the right word—with Bev."

Ted's grin broadened. "I was surprised when Bev told me about that." He hesitated to give the big ex-cop marital advice, but he brought it up, practically asked for it. "All you had to do is ask her about things like that, Jack. You know, what she likes, what makes her feel good?"

Jack raised an eyebrow, something he learned from Bev. "For some reason, I figured after being married for a while, I knew about all of that."

"I don't know, pal. But she says it drives her crazy. And you didn't seem to be all that interested, according to her."

"Why wouldn't she say something, for God's sake? I don't remember even discussing it, that. We …" He was about to tell Ted that they had explored different things, but decided it was none of his goddamned business what they did in bed.

"There're a few things I guess a gal just expects you to know, like what makes her happy—turns her on."

Jack wondered what else he had neglected to ask her about over the years and if it was too late to change things between them, but his hopes sunk with the thought. No wonder they were on the verge of divorce.

"You know, Jack, if you ask a beautiful woman a question like that, you just might get a pretty good answer," Ted advised in a fatherly tone, his smile broader than before, the one that Susan would kill him for if she were there to see it. "And a little variety is good for the soul, right?"

Jack's fists balled. His *tolerance* and *understanding* were starting to fade again, along with his stupid ego and a huge chunk of his own stupidity along with them.

Twenty Eight

wo of the robes Susan had purchased that afternoon were
in the master bedroom, one neatly draped on either side of
the big king-size bed that took up a full third of the large room, the
thin silk as white as newly driven snow.

Susan had already begun to undress. "You can fold your things
over the chair there in the corner, darling, so they don't wrinkle."
Then she giggled. "My goodness, if we keep this up I'll have to get
you some closet space." She slipped her jeans over her narrow hips
and then pulled her cashmere sweater off over her head, careful not
to muss her hair. She wiggled out her thong next and unfastened the
full-figured bra it took to contain her large breasts, allowing them
to settle untethered onto her chest. When Susan was completely
naked, she turned to face her friend, hands on her shapely hips
and a mischievous smile on her face. "Well, darling, what do you
think?" They had been shopping before and down to their bras in
the dressing room, but had never been completely nude before and
Susan watched her closely for her reaction.

Surprised at how tiny Susan was with her clothes off, Beverly gazed with curious approval at her perfect figure. She had shapely legs, with tight cheeks below her slim curvy waistline, and a flat tummy. Her breast, while large for her petite frame, were supple and sloped sensuously with nipples the size of plump sun-ripened raisins surrounded by large pink areolas that had begun to pucker the minute she took her bra off. She noticed how they quivered seductively with the slightest movement of her body, and resisted the urge to reach out and touch them to see if they were as soft as they appeared. Then Bev's gaze shifted to the thick auburn triangle nestled at the apex of her thighs.

Susan saw the inquisitive expression in her face. "It was the testosterone shots, darling," she said, reading her mind. Her thong had compressed the thick mat of pubic hair and she lightly fluffed it up with her fingertips, making bushier and appear even larger. "It was getting a bit thin, and the shots did wonders. Unfortunately, it doesn't just work down there. I had to stop taking the damned things when I started growing a mustache." She grinned at her friend. "I don't understand why the kids today shave it all off. I mean, I can understand a bikini cut—but totally, for goodness' sake? I hope you don't do that, darling. It's so juvenile, don't you think? Like you're pretending you haven't even started your period yet. And Ted likes it nice and fluffy. Thinks it's terribly sexy."

Susan slipped into one of the robes she had laid out for them and pulled the belt around her slender waist. At room temperature, her nipples were already firm and doing their best to break through the thin fabric.

Even with Beverly's approval written all over her, Susan coyly asked, "You haven't said a word, darling. Do you like?" Her hands were on her hips as she cocked one shapely leg like a Victoria's Secret model, striking a perfect ballerina pose. She tilted her head coquettishly, her long strawberry-blonde hair cascading over her bare shoulders, breathing an enticing fire into her already seductive image.

"Let me catch my breath, girl. My God, I had no idea. I—I guess I just never thought about it—you, like this. You're absolutely lovely." Beverly knew she was gawking, but couldn't help it. Seeing Susan completely nude for the first time and knowing why they were there and what they were about to do, was affecting her in a strange way. "I—I never realized—that is …" Her voice faded and she struggled with the sensual thoughts that had leapt into her mind; more, how easily they had come to her.

Susan's expression brightened as she beamed a huge smile back at her before coming down from her tiptoes. "We've just never been naked before, darling." Then she added, "Your turn. I've been dying for a peek at that big butt of yours for ages. And the boobies. I've wondered what your boobies are like, darling, if they stand up. I know they're real."

"Watch your *big* mouth, darling, when you're talking about my butt," Beverly mocked her. Then, because it was her turn, she took a deep breath and began to disrobe while Susan watched her intently with more than casual interest. She kicked out of her sandals and pulled the light sweater she was wearing over her head before slipping out of the Liz Claiborne jeans she had worn for the occasion, folding both neatly over the chair. She slowly removed her lacy white bra and panties that were in sharp contrast to her all-over tan. When she had finished and was completely nude, she turned to face Susan, feeling like a peeled onion under her piercing gaze.

Susan's slate-gray eyes twinkled as she slowly took in every inch of Beverly's shapely body, lingering here and there to study the parts she had never seen before; her full breasts, taught and perky, the sexy pooch of her tummy, the wide child-bearing hips and solid upper thighs. She was pleased with the dense knap of a triangle that arced across her lower belly and as black as midnight.

When Susan silently twirled an index finger in the air, Beverly hesitated at first, feeling like the entrée at a lesbians' convention, then slowly began to turn in place. Susan's hot gaze played over the feminine slope of her shoulders, only the faint ghost of a bikini line showing beneath her perfect tan. As Beverly did a slow pirouette, Susan searched the firm cheeks of her buttocks and the backs of her thighs for any signs of cellulite, but found her body smooth and supple. She finally had an image to go with some of the wicked thoughts she'd had almost from the time they'd first met. A satisfied smile twitched at the corners of her mouth as she stepped back to take in the full length of the younger woman.

"My God, darling, you are simple gorgeous. Every bit of you," she said, almost under her breath, her eyes glued. Then, unable to control herself, she moved in closer for a better look at the little tattoo she noticed peeking out from between her thighs, the one Ted had told her about the night of the party.

"How quaint, darling, your little tattoo. Is it a little pussycat. Let Susan see." Beverly obliged, cocking her right leg for a better view. It was just as Ted had described it—a tiny black-and-white pussycat staring up into the dark abyss of its larger namesake. "How clever, dear," she murmured.

Susan lightly traced the outline of the tattoo with her fingertips before moving to graze in the silky manse above, causing Beverly to twitch. "How in the world did you think of something so creative? Especially there, darling. "I'll bet you didn't have to tip the tattoo guy."

Beverly awkwardly retrieved her robe and slipped it on to escape what she saw lurking in Susan's eyes and thought she felt in her caress. The revealing fabric clung to her, leaving little to the imagination. Susan began to struggle with the vision of Beverly and Ted making love. She was more to his size. She imagined they fit perfectly together.

"I can see why Ted's attracted to you, dear." She stepped closer for a friendly hug that lasted long enough to mean something else, and she felt Beverly stiffen under her touch. Susan gazed into her sloe eyes and, not seeing the rejection she might have expected, rose up on her tiptoes and kissed her full lips for the very first time.

Beverly wasn't sure why she was having difficulty organizing her thoughts, except that it had everything to do with Susan's phone call that afternoon. The resulting anxiety was beginning to catch up with her, taking its toll. When Susan opened her mouth, her tongue cautiously searching, Bev was surprised at the warm tingly feeling it caused her to have and pressed her body into hers. Susan could feel Beverly's tension flowing out of her, melting under her exploring fingers. Beverly did not stiffen this time and slowly moved her hips in rhythm to her probing.

The fantasies spinning through Susan's mind were making breathing difficult until she finally abandoned all the inhibitions that had been holding her back, and knelt down. After several impossibly long moments, the younger woman shuddered, her hips arching. But before she could finish, Bev coaxed Susan up until they were facing each other, their bodies pressed tightly together. They kissed, deeply this time, biting, tasting, taught, erect nipples rubbing.

Then Susan broke away. "Lie back, darling." She maneuvered Beverly back onto the bed and came down over her. Breathing erratically and beginning to tremble herself, Susan paused before she turned around, each holding the other's gaze intensely. But there was no mistake.

They both saw the truth of their desire in the other's eyes.

Twenty Nine

"And what do we have here? A private party?"

Interrupted by the sound of Ted's deep baritone voice, the two women parted in surprise and sat back on the bed—Susan sporting a wicked grin, Beverly cloaked in embarrassment. The two women pulled on their robes, but were unable to hide what was showing on their face.

"I thought we had rules about this sort of thing." Ted was standing in the doorway, Jack just behind.

"Nothing is private tonight, darling," Susan said gaily, unintimidated, her grin broad and beaming as she took Beverly by the hand and led her toward the door. Her robe hung loosely from her slender shoulders and she cinched in the belt tighter, making it even more transparent. She stopped when she reached Ted to embrace him, kissing him wetly, passing Beverley's essence. "Oh, my—!" Susan cooed and wiggled her hips into him, his excitement unmistakable. "This is going to be fun."

Ted licked his lips, Beverly's Chanel and musk intoxicating, pulled Susan into him and kissed her again. After a moment, she stepped back moved to stand in front of Jack's solid six-foot frame.

"Oh my, darling," she said, seeing him practically naked for the first time, his square shoulders, the broad chest. Her eyes lingered approvingly below his waist. "Aren't you the gorgeous one tonight … just like your wife," she said impishly. She pressed herself against Jack and kissed him, exploring, just as she had with Ted.

When there was no reaction, Susan reached up to put her arms around his neck and pressed herself hard against him, moving her narrow hips slowly from side to side. After a moment, Jack's hands slipped under her arms, cupping the sides of her heavy breasts for the first time.

Until that moment, feeling her slim naked body through the thin silk of her robe, he had not realized how tiny Susan was. Then, Jack saw that Bev was already curled up into Ted's arm, pressing herself hard against him. She was as tall as he was, and their bodies fit into each other perfectly, touching everywhere. Her arms were tightly curled around his neck as they kissed. He began to grind his hips into her, her own—trapping the hugeness between them— moving with his motion.

Susan turned, following Jack's gaze, and saw the look on his face. She took him by the hand and led him to the door where she gave Ted a sharp smack on the butt that bore the sting of revenge. "Come on, you two, break it up. We can't stand here in the doorway all night. There's a lovely hot tub waiting for us."

When Beverly and Ted parted, his arousal jutted obscenely before him, the sight wilting any amorous thoughts Jack may have had a few minutes before.

He did not have to imagine what was next. He just didn't know how Bev was going to do it.

The Ménage à Trois, Plus One

Thirty

The secluded patio was concealed behind a high, thick hedge of fragrant night-blooming jasmine that ensured total and complete privacy. The large sunken spa at its center was surrounded by a tropical garden of exotic plants that filled the enclave with a pungent fragrance that hung heavily in the night air like burning incense. The crimson glow of the spa's submerged lights resembled an erupting volcano, exhaling towering clouds of steam upward through the boiling waters into the cool of the night.

Wild thoughts had been dashing through Susan's mind all day, churning there like a miniature tornado. The intimacy she had just shared with Beverly had been intense and natural, heightening her desire rather than dampening it. And by the time the two couples had shed their robes and entered the hot tub, each of them was filled with anticipation.

It was after one o'clock in the morning by the time they gingerly settled into the steamy water—the temperature a tingling 104 degrees—that rapidly relaxed every muscle in their taught bodies without dimming the excitement that had been building in them since early afternoon.

For Susan, who was beginning to feel a bit exhausted from all of the tension, everything had gone perfectly so far in the short time she'd had to prepare. Ted was in rare form and had not seriously screwed up anything—yet. And Jack was all-over delicious, exactly as she had expected. There was still a part of him, however, that had not yet shown itself, leaving her curious. But she fully intended to put it to the test tonight.

Beverly, however, had been the biggest surprise of the evening. She was even more gorgeous than she had imagined. So far, Susan thought with satisfaction, the evening was living proof that something very special happened to people when they took off all their clothes; they also shed their inhibitions.

First to enter the spa, Ted had comfortably settled back into one of the wide contoured bench seats; his arms stretched out along the marbled coping as he watched the others gingerly settle into the hot, bubbling water, his silver-covered chest glistening in crimson glow of light from below.

When the others had gingerly settled into the hot water, he said, "You girls were putting on a pretty good show a few minutes ago." He was doing his best to sound casual, even playful. "I think that was pretty sexy, two beautiful girls having a little fun together." Once she got started, Susan had been insatiable in bed the night she had forced his confession out of him, and had welcomed him back with an enthusiasm that had temporarily quelled his passion. But seeing the two women together had titillated him, making him anxious and impatient.

Susan shot Beverly a guilty glance and the knowing smile that went with it. She knew men liked that sort of thing, but still, Bev had surprised her. The water came almost up to Susan's shoulders, but she noticed with more than casual interest how the taller woman's breasts bobbed seductively just above the churning surface. Susan also noticed her downcast gaze.

"No offense, darling, but it's more fun with a beautiful man, don't you think?" she said to Beverly, who was sitting across from her, dispelling any lingering thoughts that they might prefer women to men. Then she shifted her gaze to Jack who was to her left and staring at his wife. Ted sat to her right, and was also looking at Bev with a slack expression.

"I think it would be nice if you girls put on another little show for us, had a little more fun together," Ted urged, his customary boyish grin returning, his features slightly distorted by the shadows cast up through the spa's roiling waters. Susan watched Bev, but there was no change in her. "How about it, Jack? Would you like that, too?" Ted said, without taking his eyes off the women, Bev's full breasts glistening above the surface, Susan's just below. His question hung heavily in the moist air with the same uncertainty that had been dogging each of them all evening.

Jack thought he saw something in Bev's face, a hint of embarrassment possibly, or was it his imagination? The last thing he expected to find a few minutes ago were the two women together like that and it gave him pause to wonder. When he'd asked her, Bev had quickly denied being with another man before Ted. However, he had not thought to include women in the equation, and it now appeared that there was a side to Bev that he did not know.

"I guess that's up to the girls," Jack answered when he realized Ted and Susan had shifted their gaze to him and were waiting for him to answer.

"Well, darling, it's certainly a good way to get things moving along," Susan said happily, rising out of the hot water that came nearly to her waist when she stood up, her upper body aglow, steam rising off it in the chill of the early morning air as if she were on fire. With the makings of a smile on her face, her breasts bobbed seductively in a low arc as she moved, flashes of amber and red glistening off her as she crossed the spa and nestled down next to Beverly, giving her a peck on the cheek.

When there was no response, Susan whispered in her ear, "You're so tense, darling." She nibbled at the crook of her neck, tasting the tang of perfume, her hand touching her privately below the surface. Susan had bundled her long strawberry-blond hair on top of her head, securing it in place with several rhinestone-encrusted combs, making her appear taller, her skin so white it seemed to glow in the dark.

Beverly flinched when Susan touched her. "Sorry …" she said, her voice small, just above a whisper.

"Now-now, darling, don't be nervous. And there's nothing to be sorry about," the older woman purred in her ear just as softly, her tone as reassuring as her words. Beverly managed a strained grimace that served as a smile. "Put your arms around Susan, darling. Give her a big hug and take a deep breath. You'll be fine." Her other hand caressed one soft breast. "Tonight is the hardest part. And cheer up, darling. We're supposed to be having fun, remember?"

Beverly focused on what only a short time ago was the unthinkable for her, and forced herself to relax. With their bodies touching, tingling where their flesh came together, Susan kissed her, wetly; their mouths open, tongues uniting, her fingers playing firmly but gently over Bev's hard nipples.

The two men watched them in silence as they settled back onto the submerged contour of the seat, Susan's head resting lightly on Beverly's shoulder, her unseen hand exploring beneath the bubbly surface.

Several long moments passed, then Ted stood up, his excitement preceding him like an outsized divining rod. "All right, ladies, that was very nice. Now it's our turn," he said. Over Susan's mild protest, he took Beverly by the hand and brought her back to his side of the spa where he sat down facing her. She automatically straddled him, his passion rising up between them all the way into her cleavage.

Jack watched as his wife curled her arms around Ted's thick neck, her breasts flattened hard against his chest as she began to suck the breath out of him. With her knees tucked high under his arms, she slowly began to rotate herself against him. After a moment, Ted grasped her by the hips and raised her lower body high out of the water, maneuvering himself into position. Beverly slowly began to come down over him with a visible shudder and a throaty groan that grew louder the farther she went. It seemed to take forever until her knees were tucked under his arms and she was once again seated heavily in his lap. After a moment, Ted began to move beneath her, holding her firmly in place when she pushed at his shoulders and cried out. The sharp, gasping sounds she was making echoed across the darkened patio and pounded through Jack with the force of a trip-hammer.

Then Ted stopped. They both remained motionless for several long moments—Beverly panting for air, her breath ratcheting, Ted intense and flushed. The fiery glow of the spa lights dully illuminated them, casting erotic shadows among the swirling clouds of steam until Beverly began to rotate her hips, slowly at first, then with increasing urgency until her back arched and she thrust her lower body hard against him with a deep grunt that was laced with both pleasure and pain.

As Jack watched them, he was consumed by the emotions that were flooding over him like his worst nightmare, making it hard for him to breathe. He knew what Ted was doing to her from the unfamiliar sounds pouring out of her, sounds he had never heard before, and the hungry way she was thrusting her hips into him. He had neglected the same thing all these years out of some misguided sense of propriety. And what he could not see below the frothy surface of the water was easily made up for in his tortured imagination and indelibly etched in his memory.

"Easy does it, big fella." Jack jumped. It was Susan whispering in his ear. She had slipped unnoticed onto the bench beside him just as Beverly cried out again and saw the desolate look it caused to come over him. Watching them across the spa had greatly aroused her. But there was also an uneasy feeling that she had not expected. She had never seen Ted with another woman, but she had tried to imagine it, however the actual reality was proving more traumatic than she anticipated. She wondered if it wasn't the green-eyed monster eating away at her. She knew, of course, that Ted's age had nothing to do with his ability to thrill any woman who was brave enough to try him. What she was watching was unquestionably erotic, and she felt as though her entire body was on fire, and as if her blood was about to boil.

Susan put an arm around Jack's broad shoulders, holding him, one large breast sensually pressing into the side of his chest. "I know this is hard for you, darling, seeing them together for the first time," she whispered, not wanting to interrupt what was going on just a few feet away. It looked as though Beverly had just finished and was starting all over again, while Ted was still deep in the throws. "I'm a little breathless myself." She smiled impishly at him. "Just take a deep breath. You'll be fine, darling. We all will. Just relax a little. Let Susan help." She kissed him affectionately, her hand slipping below the surface, disappointed at what she found, but not really surprised. "Are you okay, Jack?" she asked quietly, gently stroking, but to no avail. He was dense and thick as a bedpost, but lacking strength.

"How are you doing with all this?" Jack asked, teeth clenched, his gaze riveted on the breathless undulating couple across from them. Ted looked as though he might pass out. "You've seen them before?" Just then, Ted made a strange noise and bucked violently.

Susan's breath caught at the familiar sound of Ted's climax gushing out of him, and waited until they settled back into the rhythm they'd been sharing for the past fifteen minutes. "No, it's the first time for me too, darling." She was also watching Bev, since she'd made a few of her own unnerving sounds and had never seen such a look on her before. "They're just having a good time, darling, like two happy people making love." She smiled into his jade-green eyes, seeing the dark shadows of doubt that were definitely clouding his vision. Susan smiled sweetly. "That's why we're here, to make each other happy. To love each other." She firmly squeezed the dense, flaccid thing in her hand, but there was no change.

Jack resisted looking at them, doing his best to tune out the unnerving sounds his wife was beginning to make again. He saw the reassuring smile Susan was wearing now. "I'm okay," he said but knew she could tell that he wasn't. "Tolerance, understanding, and getting a grip, remember?" he said, quoting her advice. If he had not come tonight, he knew the three of them would still be here without him, and he had Susan to thank for that. He shook off the dark, troublesome thoughts and tried to concentrate on her.

Susan glanced at Bev and her husband, who looked like they were about to consume each other, while she gave Jack a second submerged tug. When there was still no response, Susan knew her work was cut out for her. "I hope this isn't because of me, darling."

"Don't even go there, Sue." He knew the ego-bruising trip Ted must have put her through with what turned out to be his temporary impotence. "By the way, I haven't told you that I never realized how beautiful you are," he said, not just to bolster her ego but because it was true. "We haven't had a chance ... but I'm not really surprised, just impressed. I've always been curious about ..." he grinned guiltily, "... about your breasts."

"Bev told you I had a boob job?"

"I sort of suspected, anyway," he smiled. "As for the rest, well, I guess I just wasn't looking."

"We just never got naked together before." She grinned back with renewed confidence as the shadow of doubt lifted from her attractive face. "But thank you for saying so, just the same. I'm glad you find everything to your liking, darling." She gave him a lingering kiss, the tip of her tongue teasing him, sweet on his palate.

The flavor of her lipstick and her soft body pressing against his were causing a faint stirring in him. Then Susan released what had been steadily growing in her hand and whispered in his ear as she rose up out the hot water. "Come with me, darling, we need to leave these two lovebirds alone. I hope the old boy survives by the time that gorgeous wife of yours is finished with him."

"What about the rules?" Jack said, wanting to go, but also wanting to stay.

"Screw the rules, darling," Susan said, her naked body cloaked in a cloud of steam in the cool night air. Her large nipples softened by the hot water, consumed the end of each of her cascading breasts. She tugged at his arm. When his lower body cleared the surface, she happily saw the improvement she had been hoping for. It was enough to please any girl.

Susan smiled to herself. Her job was not going to be as hard as she thought, after all.

Thiry One

They stood in the dim light of the living room as she finished toweling him off, starting with his feet and working her way up his hunky six-foot frame. When she finished, Susan dabbed at the light dusting of dark hair on his chest and then around his broad shoulders until she had him reasonably dry. On her way up, she had come face-to-face with his thick arousal, but decided against the distraction and moved on.

When she finished and they had kissed lustfully, Jack began to reciprocate, starting on her back at the shoulders, moving down over the curve of her spine before dabbing at the firm cheeks of her buttocks, running the towel between her toned thighs. When he finished, he turned her around and began to work on her sloping breasts, raising first one and then the other to pat her dry. He continued down the flat of her stomach, taking his time with the damp mop of pubic hair until it too was dry and fluffy. When she shifted her weight, he went between her legs, touching her lightly with the soft towel, and then on an impulse bent to kiss her there, lightly teasing in all the right places.

"Oh, Jesus, Jack … stop that!" Susan shuddered, an urgent hand going to the back of his head, but then the other pushing him away just as quickly. "I adore that, darling. But I swear you've got me so excited I'll collapse right here on the floor if you don't stop it this minute."

When Jack rose up, Susan was already panting softly. Her entire body had taken on a pinkish glow from the heated spa, soft and alluring. "That was very nice, darling. You definitely know what a girl likes," she said, staring up into his hooded eyes.

"You're pretty sexy yourself," Jack said, snuggling into her, his flesh crawling, liking how small she was, the way she fit perfectly into him as if she belonged there.

"Of course, darling, especially when some big hunk is trying to drive me crazy," she panted back, shifting her narrow hips into him. He held her even tighter, but did not reply. After a moment, she said, "So tell me, darling, do you still like my boobies now that you've seen them and had a little sample? Bev said you did."

Jack smiled his approval and took a step back to take in the full extent of her, the swell of her large breasts, nipples turned hard now. She had let her hair down and the long silky curls cascaded around her face like a halo. Her skin was the color of pink ivory, her muscle tone that of a ballerina. She radiated a sensual vitality that made it hard to look away.

"You look ma'velous, da'ling—all of you," he quipped with his best Latin accent, and wondered if Ted had completely lost his mind or just going blind with old age. It would be impossible for him to live with Susan and not try to get her pregnant every chance he got—if that was possible.

"Oh, Rickie! He was such a darling man," Susan swooned. "And so sexy." She snuggled her hips into him as if he were a consolation prize.

"You knew him?" However, he wasn't surprised and touched the heavy contour of one of her breast where it settled onto her chest, unable to keep his hands off her. He couldn't resist lightly tweaking one sensitive nipple, instantly arousing it to the size of a maraschino cherry.

"Oh—!" she cried, her breath catching, and slapped at his hand. "As well as he'd let me. I tried more than once to convince him that I should be in one of his movies. But he was married to that lovely girl. I forget her name. Georgiana something or other. Loretta Young's younger sister. But he just wasn't interested. Bev tells me you knew a lot of Hollywood people in your cop days."

"A few," Jack said. But in truth, it was more than that. The people he had met in the entertainment business when he wore a badge were the backbone of his very successful PI business, but this was hardly the time to reminisce. "Did you ever make a movie with him?"

"Rickie—? No, darling." She sighed. "But I'll bet I could have talked him into it if he'd given me half a chance." She smiled confidently. "Especially if you could deliver. And believe me, darling, I've delivered plenty in my day. But there's an old saying in the movie business: 'There's no substitute for talent.'"

Jack smiled at the hidden promise that also turned up in her twinkling eyes. "Do you have any idea how many men there've been in your life, Sue?" He tried to play with her other nipple now, which had already hardened in sympathy with the other one, but she moved the offending hand into her cleavage and held it there for safekeeping.

"No, but I hope I'm about to add another very handsome trophy to whatever the number is, darling," she purred without hesitation and donned a seductive smile to back it up. "But I really have no idea. I never kept score. We did very little sleeping though. I know that much." Then her expression turned lecherous, and she wiggled her fingers at him, calling him into her again. "Come here, my darling. Susan has something wonderful for you. I've been having some naughty fantasies about you lately." She cupped his handsome face in her hands, moistened her full lips as she pressed her body against his, feeling his arousal, and tilted her head slightly before licking his lips with the tip of her wet tongue.

"Umm—" His voice was heavy, rattling deep in his throat. "I can't imagine what that would be."

Her eyes hooded much the same as a king cobra being challenged by a foolish mongoose. "Let Susan give you a hint, darling."

It wasn't what she whispered in his ear that surprised him. It was the way she described it.

Thiry Two

*B*everly was lying comfortably in the contour of the submerged bench of the hot tub, her head propped against the wall with the hot foamy water spilling over her. When Ted eagerly settled over her, she winced at his abruptness and pushed him back.

"Teddy …?" Her eyes were slitted, her nails biting into his shoulders emphasizing her discomfort.

Ted shifted his weight, then pushed again until she pulled back a second time. "Stop that! You're hurting me." She raised her knees and then adjusted to the change it caused. "Mmm …" she groaned as he settled more easily into her, scooted down a bit, tested the new position, and then nodded her approval. "That's better … much better." The hot water was soothing, lubricating, causing her skin to tingle. When it felt like he nudged her sternum, she flinched and bit her lower lip with the sensation.

"You okay, baby girl?" He moved more firmly.

"Ahh—" she groaned. "Slow … eeer."

"Oh, G—God, Ted!" she moaned when there was no longer

251

any space between them and he had completely engulfed her. He stopped, but only for a moment, then began again.

Bev took in a gulping breath of steamy, moisture-laden air and opened her eyes. "Give me a minute, baby—" A small shudder went through her. After another breath, she shifted her weight, easing the pressure on her neck and back.

When she nodded, Ted slowly pulled back to begin again.

Jack moved in closer until their bodies were lightly touching, her breast dusting low on his chest as they kissed open mouthed, probing and tasting. His excitement eagerly reached out to her as he moved to kiss the slender curve in her neck, taking in her warm feminine scent. He sucked at the lobe of her ear, causing her to shudder slightly. Then he hefted her heavy breasts in both hands and moved from one nipple to the other, drawing each deep into his mouth, coaxing small sounds of delight from her as he nibbled at them. After a long moment, with her arousal intensified, her hands went to the back of his head, coaxing him downward. Jack kissed his way to the flat of her stomach, lingering briefly at a tiny diamond stud in her navel. As he knelt in front of her, he felt the forward surge of her body, her hips jutting when he found the place she wanted him to be.

"I thought this made you lightheaded." He glanced up to see her peering down at him through her ample cleavage.

"Just shush-up down there and do your job, darling," she groaned. Her eyes hooded now, both hands pushing at the back of his head this time. When he resumed, Susan moaned as if she were in pain. "Oh God, darling, yes … umm … right there … Oh, my goodness … Aahhh …!"

Moments later Susan shuddered convulsively, clutching him hard against her until Jack thought she would collapse. When the spasms passed, she pulled him up and kissed him wetly, her own essence serving to heighten the aftermath. As they embraced, he forced himself between her thighs and slowly rotated his hips, coaxing a tiny squeal from her as she went up on her tiptoes panting hotly in his ear.

"Now, darling," she groaned hoarsely, her hips matching his.

"But I thought you just …"

"That was just to get ready, darling, for …" Her voice had gone husky with the first orgasm that had prepared her for the next more promising one that was already threatening, causing her to break out all over in a light sweat. "I need you to do me now, Jack … Right now—" Her whispery voice was deep and urgent, slurred with passion.

He looked at her curiously. "Do what?" he whispered back with a mischievous grin, his tongue pressing deeply into her ear.

Susan shuddered again, shaking him off. "You know very well what I mean. *It*—" she croaked at him and pulled him into her even closer, pressing her fleshy breast hard against his chest.

"*It* could mean a lot of things. Which *it* are you talking about?" He was all but holding her up now and enjoying the love game. His voice was low, his hips pushing firmly into her, and then withdrawing in slow succession.

"Oh, Jack Edwards, you stop teasing me this minute before I faint right here in your arms," she squealed, holding on to him for dear life. For some reason, she was glad that they were alone for their first time. She didn't want Ted to see her like this. She was off-balance, weakened by the preparatory climax she'd just had and growing weaker by the minute. Then her teeth flashed as she tried to bite him.

Expecting retaliation, Jack deftly pulled back just in time. He was making her aggressive. It was a side of her he had never seen before; one that he liked very much.

"Then why don't you tell me what you want? Can't you say *it*? If that's what you're talking about." He was well over a foot taller and looked down on her as if he were holding a China doll.

"Of course I can say *it*. But that's so awful," she squeaked at him in a small voice. "Besides, you know exactly what I mean." A profound shiver demanding satisfaction ricocheted through her again. She was near the end of her rope, holding back against what she felt building in her, and trying to focus on him before she went completely to pieces.

Jack pulled back again, with a half smile this time. "Well, then, I don't think we should do anything *awful*," he said and tried to disengage from her. With an all-out effort, Susan clamped her thighs tightly together, refusing to give him up.

"Oh, you terrible man. Don't you dare stop now!" she squealed at him again, but much louder this time.

"Then you're going to have to say *it*! Tell me what you want to do!" he demanded with slightly more authority.

"No—!" she squawked hoarsely. "I won't say that word. It's horrible. Just do it to me!"

"Not until you say it! Do what?" he demanded just as stubbornly.

"I will not! You—you big bully!" she sputtered at him harshly, feeling her edge sharpen instead of slipping away. The look of defiance that came over her was unmistakable, her lips curled, eyes narrowing, her brow knitted.

"Say it, damn it!" he retaliated, jabbing his hips into her, becoming more anxious now, her stubbornness fueling his own inner fire.

"Uhh …!" she grunted with delight at the stab he gave her. "Never!" she hissed once she had recovered, then pushed back just as hard.

"Say it! What you want me to do, or else I'm out of here!" He held her tightly by the shoulders, easily overpowering her, and glared into the large gray eyes that were flashing hotly with all the lust and pure stubbornness of a beautiful woman who was used to having her own way.

"You can't make me! Ever!" Her furious eyes narrowed, lips

clamped in a stubborn scowl, ready to strike again at any part of him that came into biting range.

"Say it before I turn you over my knee and spank that pink little ass of yours," he threatened.

"You wouldn't dare—" she growled. But her eyes opened wider with the delicious possibility.

"Just try me, little girl. You won't be able to sit down for a week."

"And you can go straight to hell, Jack Edwards!" she scowled, the words reverberating in her throat, but twitched somewhere else with the thought.

They were both breathing heavily, a pause hung between them that seemed to go on forever, until Jack decided they were both at the edge and that it was time.

His features softened "Please ..." he said more softly, relaxing his grip on her as he bent to kiss the tip of her nose. "For me—?"

Susan was breathing heavily and her arms tightened around his neck; afraid he might get away or that she would fall if he did. She stared deeply into the greenest eyes she had ever seen with a mixture of anger, frustration, and acute desire, all hallmarks of the love she was beginning to feel for him. He had grown hard and strong and what he was pressing into her was affecting her in a crazy way. When she finally spoke, it was with a small feminine voice yet dripping with lust. She expertly hooded her eyes, and pooched out her lower lip like a spoiled child, making her even more enticing.

"Jack, darling, I want you to do me with that beautiful thingy of yours," she said breathlessly. "But please don't make me say that word, darling. And do hurry. I'm so hot I don't think I can last much longer and I hate to come alone."

Then the little-girl look she was wearing vanished just as easily as it had come on, and the casehardened Hollywood actress took over as she glared up at him. "There, you bastard! Is that what you wanted to hear?"

Admiringly, Jack grinned down at her feeling the effects of the sex game they were playing, but his sense of humor still rampant. "Close enough for government work," he conceded, then added blithely, "Exactly what is a thingy?"

"Don't you dare start with me again, damn you!" She snarled the warning at him through clenched teeth, yet dripping with passion. "Just do me, and stop all this silly talk."

She had broken out in light sweat and the sight of her was also working its magic on him as he scooped her up into his arms. Pressed against his chest, her naked body was hot and damp to the touch, intoxicating him. "You almost said the F-word," he said, smiling down, easily hefting her 105 pounds. "I love it when you talk dirty, by the way."

"Of course I almost did, darling," she said in a small voice that was perfectly in control and meant to be a purr, but the way she was breathing came out more like a muffled growl. "I'm hardly a prude. Still, I have my reputation to think of."

He smiled at his next thought. "And where would you like to ruin this reputation of yours?"

She gave him an unladylike snort this time just as Jack lightly kissed her. "If you're finished with all of this nonsense, darling, over there on the couch under the lamp. I need to see what you're going to do to me with that lovely thingy of yours."

Thirty Three

Susan clung to him as he held her in his arms; her fingers laced behind his neck, toes pointed and her shapely legs slowly swishing with anticipation, her heavy breast swaying provocatively with the effort. She wanted to provide the best possible view for their audience who had entered the room a few minutes ago in the midst of their love spat. She had been facing the patio door when Ted and Beverly quietly slipped in across the room and were now cuddling in the shadows to watch them on the antique sofa by the fireplace. He had been perfectly agreeable to their new arrangement when she had explained it to him. But now she noticed the troubled expression, his face drawn and sullen, and wondered if the first seeds of doubt had finally begun to take hold of him.

Jack carried her to the couch and started to settle her head and shoulders under the shaded light of the small table lamp when she stopped him. "The other end, darling. Turn around," she said, hoarsely. Jack turned, laying her out at the opposite end and bent over her when she had settled back onto the cushions.

"Now that we know where—" he kissed the upturned tip of

her nose again, never suspecting the expert rhinoplasty that had created it, "—do you know how you want to do this?" He had no idea what she liked, or did not like, but he'd bet there wasn't much in the latter category.

Susan cooched back into the soft cushions with her feet under the small lamp that provided the only light in the room. She impishly raised her right leg, hooking the heel over the back of the sofa, and draped the other over the outer edge of the cushions, exposing everything in between. She could feel his eyes burning into the part of her he had never seen before and waited for him to take his fill before she daintily patted her chest, coaxing him down.

Jack was surprised at how big and yet and yet how dainty the woman was as he splayed out over the top of her. Susan reached down to guide him, pleased with his strength. When he began, she crossed her legs over his back and began to match the slow undulating motion of his hips. Watching Ted and Bev in the hot tub had deeply excited her. And the titillating foreplay she and Jack had just engaged in had stoked the fires of desire in her to the point that she was almost immediately engulfed by a short but intense climax that she knew was barely noticeable.

After several minutes, Jack stopped and tried to set up, but she looked up at him, holding him by the arms. "What is it, darling?"

"I hope you don't take this the wrong way, Sue, but ..." He felt her tense slightly. "It's not you. I guess it's actually Ted. He's a pretty hard act to follow. I don't think either one of us is getting very much out of this."

Susan heard the faint chuckle that wafted from across the room. She briefly thought of scolding Ted right there, but decided against the distraction. "Does that mean you can tell I'm not a virgin, darling?"

Jack grinned at her ubiquitous good humor under the circumstance. "Something like that, kid." He looked down into the sex-induced smile she was wearing, never guessing that she had just experienced the female version of *premature ejaculation*, only without the masculine consequences that went with it. The difference was she could do it again within a few minutes, something she had been diligently working toward when he had stopped.

"There's a reason for that, darling, and it's partially your fault. When you threatened to paddle my pink little butt a few minutes ago, it made me very excited," she said with a half grin. "Between that and the good hormones the doctor says I have, you've probably left me a bit gushy." Her voice became a catlike purr. "Then, of course, there's Teddy to consider." She tugged at his shoulders until he settled down over her again and she flexed the special muscles women have deep inside of them. "Better, darling?" she cooed, bearing down as if she were in labor and hoping she didn't fart with the effort.

He could feel the gripping effect she was having, but there really wasn't that much difference. "Let's try something," he suggested and brought her legs together under him, placing his own on the outside of hers until she was snuggly gathered under his large frame. They both immediately noticed the improvement. "Now, do that little thing in there you just did a minute ago."

She did, and he tested it several times. "Oh, darling, that's very nice," Susan exclaimed, feeling a definite tingle as she squirmed under his weight and clamped down even more, holding him tightly.

Jack gazed at her, her breasts spilling seductively off to either side of her slender chest, the bow of her hips a small but perfect saddle, her long silky hair framing her face, and felt the surge it caused in him. "Much better," he said, settling in completely and then starting on her again.

Several minutes later, Susan made a strange noise and dug her nails into his back. He flexed his shoulder muscles and nibbled at one of her earlobes. She groaned, her body quivering. He moved slowly but powerfully with increasing effort. Her thighs gripped him tightly until at the end he rose up on stiffened arms and burst inside of her.

Susan groaned when her own orgasm threatened, and then broke out in a shudder that racked through her body. She crossed her ankles in a stranglehold on what she had trapped inside, her hips arching, demanding more, her strong arms holding him to her, and then exhaled all of the air she had sucked into her lungs before limply sinking back into the cushions in near exhaustion.

When Jack finished, he remained splayed out over the top of her until the last shudder had left him. "Dear, sweet, heavenly, Jesus," he groaned out of breath into the damp hair covering the side of her face. It had been too long since he had felt this way.

The compliment slithered through the swirl of emotion that had already anesthetized Susan, further clouding her mind. In appreciation, she lightly bit the side of his sweaty neck, savoring the salty flavor mixed with the faint hint of cologne. Then she bit down even harder, leaving her brand on him.

Neither of them noticed the smothered sounds that came floating from across the dimly lit room.

The incoherent, slobbery sounds that had come languishing out of Susan set Ted's teeth on edge. He had seen the look on her face before, but never when she was with another man. Watching them together was curiously affecting him, causing his breathing to slow, becoming shallow and labored. Surprisingly, the unsettling feeling had also aroused him, but did little to quell the dull pain that went with it.

When Beverly stirred and snuggled further into the crook of his shoulder, he became aware of her warm, scented presence once again, wrenching him back from the darkness that had begun to consume him. His heartbeat picked up when she responded as he kissed her pouty lips. He touched the nape of her neck and then ran his hand inside of her robe, over the round of her belly before nestling below. She grasped him firmly in both hands and began to massage him. After a moment, Ted convulsed awkwardly several times and then erupted in series of long, intense spasms.

Thirty Four

Perspiring heavily, Susan and Jack settled back. Still trying to catch her breath, Susan felt as though she should say something, but her heart was still beating ninety miles an hour and she needed to calm down first. Jack had not been a disappointment, given the intensity of the experience, and she learned long ago that sex was mostly in the mind. And she had trained hers well over the years.

When Jack finally raised his bulk, Susan took in a deep breath before kissing him, her long hair pasted to her temples, her heat lingering and sticky. "Thank you, my darling," she said smiling sweetly up at him when she was finally able to speak without her voice cracking. "That was wonderful. I hope it was for you too."

Only Susan noticed the low groan that echoed out of the gloom as Jack gazed down on her. Her lips were swollen and pouty, her face flushed and awash in a glow only sexual satisfaction can produce, and it pleased him to think that he had been the one to put it there. Perhaps he could compete after all.

"Actually, I felt a bit lost at first," he said tactfully. "I know you're used to Ted."

Susan blinked her sleepy gray eyes at him, a mischievous smile crinkling up in the corners. "Don't be silly, darling," she said and gave him a peck on the cheek just to show she meant it. "You were marvelous. Believe me, I should know. And thank you for being so patient with me." She almost added "the last time," but didn't want to explain that there had been two before that. There was no need to show off. Bragging rights would come later when she and Bev compared notes. "I told you it's not size that counts."

Nonetheless, even with his little trick it had taken her longer than with Ted. But then, the difference between them was enormous. Even so, she decided, it was well worth the wait. She thought of the disappointment had he not been able to bring her along the last time and she'd had to fake it. Then she laughed to herself, making a mental note to make an appointment with the cute little Jewish doctor in Beverley Hills who liked to flirt with her once she had donned one of his flimsy little gowns and settled into the stirrups.

Susan absolutely adored the effect she had on men. However, it had never made her feel powerful, just lucky.

"Don't start with the 'size doesn't count' business again," Jack said playfully. "I know women don't believe that any more than men do." It was flippant of him, but he figured that over the course of the last several hours he had earned the right to joke about such things.

"Just the same, darling, it was wonderful." She was still slightly out of breath from the experience, and heard the belabored *harrumph* from the other side of the room. She would definitely remind herself to have Ted's balls on the half shell when this was over. Nevertheless, she knew the male ego needed coddling from time to time if you planned to sleep with them again. And, in Jack's case, she definitely had plans to do just that—and then some.

Jack, on the other hand, had expected feelings of guilt, even remorse, after being with Susan, but the demon had yet to show its ugly head. The thought jogged his memory. "I wonder how Bev and Ted are doing."

Susan's panting had eased, and she had settled into a more normal breathing pattern as she demurely wiggled out from under him and propped her chin up on an elbow facing into the room. "Why not ask them, darling? They've been sitting right over there watching us."

Surprised, Jack squinted into the gloom, and a wave of embarrassment overtook him when he saw them cloaked in shadows on the other sofa. When it passed, he awkwardly moved to the other end of the couch and crossed his legs, trying to conceal his embarrassment.

Susan had modestly curled onto her side, her knees tucked up to her chest, and smiled after shooting Jack an amusing glance. What he was trying to hide was all any girl could hope for after what they had just done. She shifted her gaze back to Beverly and called out to her across the room. "Bev, darling, are you ready to change partners? Jack has something very special for you," she cooed sweetly, her satisfaction obvious, her smile dripping with confidence.

Bev glanced up at Ted, almost hoping to see some form of objection in his face. But she knew it was time to put the rest of Susan's polyamorous scheme to the test, and was concerned at what Jack was about to discover about her. She had not had sex with him since she started seeing Ted and knew that the changes he had made in her would not only be a surprise for him, but also an enormous disappointment.

And Bev had no idea how he would react.

Thrity Five

Ransome Wahlrode III, the ex-federal DEA agent, sat at his partner's desk at ISI adjusting the dials on an array of the latest electronic monitoring equipment spread out before him. Lindsy Evans was at his elbow.

Randy shifted his considerable weight to relieve the dull pain in his back. He had taken a stiletto between the shoulder blades on the last joint-agency drug bust he had worked on with Jack Edwards in Hollywood. The six-inch blade had narrowly missed his spine, which would have put him in a wheelchair the rest of his life. While the injury was not life threatening, it was serious enough to force his early retirement from the DEA. Within a year, Jack had put in his twenty and the two ex-cops had opened Investigative Services, Inc., the new detective agency they had talked about starting for years.

It was nearly three o'clock in the morning, and they were listening to a live feed coming in over some very expensive equipment designed to pull in high-quality audio and video signals from one of their state-of-the-art high-tech microdot transmitters. The clear-channel signal was rerouted from nearly two hundred miles above the earth via a private satellite service, even though the source of the broadcast was just a few blocks from the office.

"Do you really think this has something to do with the photos?" Lindsy said in a hushed voice, not taking her eyes off the squiggly lines of the oscilloscope as if the sensitive electronic devise might detect her voice. They had both been surprised at what they had just heard come over the speakers.

"I'm still not sure who sent them," Randy said and checked his watch. It was long past office hour and the place was locked down tight. They had just heard the Davenport woman, whom they had met for the first time earlier that evening, ask someone if they were "ready to change partners." So far, however, the showstopper of the evening had been an earlier exchange between her and Jack during some sort of sex game they were playing. It was just after that she had asked him in no uncertain terms to do something of a very personal nature to her. And, apparently, he had done a pretty good job of it, if all of the grunting and groaning and various other erotic sounds that followed had anything to do with it. There had been a lengthy silence following a final spurt of excitement and several more uncouth noises, then nothing but heavy breathing.

To Randy's relief, the crisis they had been working on most of the day was not as serious as they had first thought. While he wasn't shocked by what they had been listening to for the past hour, it tickled him to think that Jack and Bev were participating in such a scurrilous and undignified activity as wife swapping.

But when Jack stopped by the office on his way back from lunch with the Davenport woman that afternoon to cancel the surveillance on her place, Randy suspected that he had left out a few of the more interesting details. Some of which, he guessed, they were currently listening to. He now suspected that a vengeful Susan Davenport had seduced Jack in retaliation for her husband's transgressions with Bev the night of the yacht club party.

What he did not understand is what Bev saw in the older man

in the first place, whom he had met that evening for the second time. He had always thought Beverly was a hottie, who had caused him to have a few thoughts of his own that he wasn't exactly proud of since she was his partner's wife. However, where human nature was concerned, it just proved the old adage: You never knew what to expect when it came down to sex, money, or booze. The three cardinal sins had probably caused more trouble in the world than all of the other sins you could commit with your clothes on put together.

"It still doesn't make any sense for Ted Davenport to have sent the photos," Lindsy said after a moment. "But I'm not sure why she would send them either."

"Well, the photos definitely go to motive, since they show that her hubby is obviously mousing around with Bev," Randy said. "But something's not jibing here for me either. I'm not so sure Jack didn't leave a few things out this afternoon when he came by on his way home from town to cancel the assignment. Otherwise, why would he be there tonight?"

"Jack's a good-looking guy," Lindsy countered. "And maybe she's just interested in a younger man, and all she needed was an excuse to go after him. Besides, we can't really be sure what's going on over there from just the audio."

He gave her a hard look. "I think '*I need you to do me right now, darling,*' is a pretty good indication of what's going on," he said candidly. "At least she's not a garbage mouth. And if that's not good enough for you, what about all the noises, the grunting and groaning, that went on?" When she just shrugged, he added, "If I had to guess from where I planted the bugs the other day, the four of them are in the family room, probably naked, and just worked up a pretty good sweat."

Lindsy's brow raised in thought. "Then you think Bev and Davenport are like ... there too?"

"The last thing we heard was Sarah Bernhardt asking Bev Darling, if she was ready to change partners."

"Right, she did say that," Linds remembered, now that he mentioned it.

"What do you think Bev sees in the old guy, anyway?" Randy was preoccupied adjusting one of the dials on the sensitive satellite receiver and was not looking directly at her when she shrugged her shoulders again.

Lindsy had given him a funny look to go with it, and guessed he hadn't noticed what happened when they had by chance run into Jack and Bev and the Davenports at Windows that evening and stopped by their table. She recalled how Ted Davenport had given her a start when he caught her staring at him, almost as if he were accustomed to it, and knew what she was thinking—certainly what she was staring at.

From a woman's point of view, not only did Ted Davenport have the healthy look of an athlete, but he was quite attractive. Then, of course, she had discovered something else about him that was hard to miss and was surprised that Randy hadn't noticed it also. She was beginning to think that she might be a better detective than he was. But to be fair, most men did not stare at another man's crotch. At least she was sure Randy didn't.

"I suppose it could have something to do with the bulge I noticed … in his pants," Lindsy said, casually enough to imply that she might have had a few carnal thoughts of her own along with the observation. Randy's gaze instantly flicked from the bank of electronics to her. She knitted her brow and pursed her lips in a helpless gesture. "It was hard not to notice," she said in defense.

"Hard—?" he growled at her.

"That's accurate, but probably a poor choice of words." Linds shrugged, and hesitated to even bring up her next thought, but it was definitely part of the puzzle they had been trying to put together most of the day until Jack had summarily cancelled the whole thing without so much as an explanation.

"We are talking about Davenport's crotch, right?" He had been preoccupied and wondered if he might have missed something.

By way of comparison, Lindsy was almost as tall as Beverly, weighed about the same, but was probably ten years younger and could understand that what she had noticed about Ted Davenport tonight might have also made Bev curious. She gave Randy an innocent look. "You have to admit he's good-looking. Cute for his age, actually. Bev mentioned once that he works out every day. I think he was the swimming coach over at Berkeley."

Randy flushed. "Good-looking swim coach notwithstanding, you were actually staring at the old guy's crotch?"

Lindsy cocked her head less defensively this time, but didn't budge, and was trying hard to control the smile that was lurking just out of sight. "Are you trying to tell me you didn't notice the set of knockers on his wife?"

Randy thought for a minute, realized he was busted, and gave up. "Okay, I noticed," he admitted finally. "Pretty good bazooms on her. So what's that got to do with you staring at her husband's crotch, never mind that he's probably old enough be your grandfather's elder brother?"

"So what's that mean? If he were a few years younger, it would be okay? What kind of male chauvinist have you turned into lately?" When he did not argue the point and just stared at her, she added, "Women notice guys too, Ran. That's just the way it is. Besides, how could you miss something like that? I mean something *that* big. Unless he had a sock in his jock, it's enough to make any girl curious ... even a little lightheaded when you think about it," she tacked on for good measure as a little payback for his funky attitude.

Lindsy eyed him, preparing to defend herself again, but the possessive look he had taken on a minute ago disappeared and nothing else took its place. "All I'm saying is that it's possible that Jack hasn't been taking care of business at home lately for whatever reason and, well ... so maybe Bev got to looking around and noticed too."

He kept the blank look on his face, using it as a shield, but he could tell she was already reading his mind. "Good point," he said, then dismissed the whole thing and went back to adjusting one of the machines.

They continued listening, but there was nothing more except silence, with the exception of what sounded like a long sigh that was definitely female.

"When did you bug the place, by the way? And how come we're listening to all of this if Jack called it off, told you to wrap it up? It sounds a little personal to me." She was using reverse talk on him, and actually thought it was very personal indeed.

"Because, he only said to pull the video, nothing about the audio. But all I have to do is push a button here to flick it on too. What do you say …?" He grinned at her mischievously.

Her color deepened. "Don't you dare, Randy. I mean, my God—!" she said, still afraid that he might. She was already feeling like a voyeur just listening to the audio feed.

He was bent over the speaker grill, not wanting to miss what might come out next. "You know something's going on with Jack as well as I do, the way he's been acting lately. As for when, it was a couple of days ago. He said that there was something going on he needed to know about." Randy shifted his heavy shoulders to ease the crick in his neck. He had no intention of activating the microscopic video cameras in the bugs he had planted, but had decided on his own to go ahead with the audio to be safe—just in case. Rule number one in this business was: You could never have too much evidence.

Lindsy frowned at him, disapproval written all over her. Randy glanced up and gave her a deadpan look. "Is a *thingy* what I think it is? I've never heard that one before."

It was her turn to glare. "Then you're saying you think Jack knew there was something going on between Bev and Davenport and then decided to join in for some reason? Maybe that's why he didn't want the video?"

"Could be embarrassing if he had some idea what they were up to. May have something to do with the photos, too."

Lindsy pulled her eyes off the machine to look at him, the beginnings of a mischievous smile curling up at the corners of her mouth. "At least they had their clothes on at the party."

"Who knows? If that's the case, he may have thought seeing them naked tonight might give you a case of the vapors," he wisecracked.

She blinked at him, not nearly the prude he thought her to be. "So, let's assume he knew how personal it was. What we're doing here isn't exactly legal since it also involves the Davenports, provided they found out about it and filed a complaint," she said more seriously.

"I really don't think anyone's going to complain from what we've heard tonight."

"How did you get in the house without them knowing it? I hope you didn't burglarize the place. Not to mention illegally recording them, even if it is a group sex party."

"No need to burgle the place. You are looking at Handsome Ransome, your friendly cable guy, in disguise of course—rental van, magnetic door signing, the whole enchilada. In fact, some guy waved me down wanting me to fix his TV when I was leaving." He grinned at her and saw that she was grinning back, and shaking her head at the same time. "And just to set the record straight, it wouldn't surprise me if Jack didn't deliberately mention cancelling the audio feed on purpose. He's pretty thorough when it comes to taking care of business, but he's got a side to him."

Lindsy rolled her eyes. "Good Lord, Ran, he had to know you'd be curious." Nevertheless, she knew he was right, and sighed with a measure of relief. "Then you're going to tell him about the tape, right?"

"I wouldn't dream of bringing up something so indelicate. I'm just going to leave it right here on his desk, properly tagged like any other piece of evidence. Maybe with a sticky note expressing our appreciation for the evening's entertainment, not to mention the very interesting sound effects. I think I'll add a PS to see if he ever found out what a 'thingy' is."

Randy flipped the switch that turned off the external speakers, leaving the machine to continue automatically on its own. It was voice activated and would start and stop at the slightest sound. He did not need to hear anymore. This was definitely not a case of blackmail or a threat to Jack or ISI, and whoever was doing what to whom, Jack seemed to have a handle on it. He just wasn't sure if he should be happy for him or not. There was no doubt that the former movie queen was a knockout—he'd rarely seen a set of jugs like that—even if her hair was a little too long for her age.

It still puzzled him what Bev saw in the elder Davenport. He had always thought she could probably have any guy she set her cap for. And it appeared that she wanted some ex-jock who was old enough to be her father. One of the reasons could be what Linds had noticed about him at the restaurant tonight. He had always thought that Jack and Bev were meant for each other, the perfect couple. But now, he wondered about that even, and their marriage.

Randy shook off the troubling thoughts and scribbled a quick sticky note of gratitude, pasted it to one of the machines, grabbed Lindsy by the hand, and tugged her toward the door. She knew the look on his face and blushed.

"Ah yes, my little chickadee," he said out of the corner of his mouth in his best W. C. Fields imitation that he sometimes used on her when he wanted something special. "It's time to go home, my dear. Yes, indeed."

Thirty Six

Ted nodded his approval and gave Beverly a patronizing pat on the rump, sending her on her way. Susan got up at the same time, not bothering with her robe—she would just have to take it off again—and lightly brushed one of the younger woman's breasts with a seductive moony-eyes smile as they passed each other in the middle of the room. When Bev reached the other side, she sat next to Jack who was staring at her, contemplating the differences between the two women.

Susan kissed Ted affectionately when she reached the other side and haughtily pushed him onto his back and straddled him, forcing a low groan from him. Then she lowered herself and made a satisfying sound of her own. With Venus hard against Mars, she bent over his prostrate form and dragged her erect nipples across his silvery chest, slowly rotated her hips, her eyes closed with the fullness of him. She didn't have to think about what she was doing with Ted; all she had to do was let it happen. With her upper body parallel to his, the view from across the room was dim yet graphic, leaving little to the imagination.

A feeling of déjà vu crept over Beverly, and she tilted lampshade as Susan's hips rose and fell with increasing urgency. Jack put an arm around her, gathering her in against him and whispered in her ear. "Why not take your robe off, kid?"

Beverly put a finger to her lips; her gaze transfixed across the room, but did not pull away. "Just a minute. I—I want to see this, how she ... My God, I had no idea—" Her whispered words tapered off, leaving only the awe and wonder that had been obvious in her voice. She knew exactly what Susan was feeling at that exact moment. The experience was seared in her memory as if she had been branded with a red-hot poker.

Several minutes later, Susan squealed breathlessly and collapsed heavily over her husband.

Beverly's breathing had picked up as she slipped out of her robe and nestled back into the curve of Jack's shoulder. He kissed her softly. Trembling slightly from the erotic scene they had been watching across the room, she leaned back onto the cushions and beckoned him down over her.

There was very little sensation when he began, yet her unnoticed orgasm was almost immediate—a small, disappointing jolt of excitement rather than the rush of passion she expected.

Jack continued for several minutes until he realized the effort was useless and finally sat up. "This isn't working very well, kid," he whispered. "Roll over on your hands and knees for me."

Beverly let go of what she was trying to coax into something more, turned her back to him, and lowered her head and shoulders onto the cushions.

As Jack positioned himself, he suddenly tensed— then froze solid.

His mind twisted with thoughts of betrayal as a rush of

uncontrollable emotions flooded over him. He instantly felt sick to his stomach, followed by a deep sadness that tore at his insides like a claw hammer as he stumbled to his feet and headed for the bedroom where he had left his clothes.

The
Pilates Class

Thirty Seven

There were fourteen women of various ages and two gay guys enrolled in the Pilates class. The older women tended to cover up everything between their neck and the pink sneakers they favored. The younger set, however, was less conservative. Several of them displayed the upper portion their posteriors from time to time, some of which were artfully decorated with colorful tattoos just above the fault line. By far the most imaginative of these belonged to a nubile blonde in her late teens who sported a bright-red arrow pointing down into the abyss with a boy's name inscribed above it indicating that "Johnny" was the proud owner the territory below. It caused others to wonder what happened if "Johnny" took a flyer.

Two of the women in the class, however, fell somewhere between the extremes in both age and style. Today, Susan Davenport was flamboyant in bright-red spandex tights that clung to her pert sexy figure like a second skin, showing every nook and cranny, leaving little to the imagination—which was just the way she wanted it. For a top, she had donned a skimpy lime-green cotton tee with a cut away hemline that hiked well up onto her midriff and struggled to contain her large breasts.

Beverly Edwards was more subtle in her approach. She wore black Lycra shorts that fit loosely around her shapely Irish-German thighs and provided an occasional flash of the thong she favored in the name of freedom during their floor exercises. She had cut the neck and sleeves out of a faded oversized football jersey for a top that mostly concealed her sports bra and caused many of the bodybuilders in the gym to stare at her in awe. The overall result was a healthy, casual look that emphasized her undeniable sexuality.

At the break, Susan used her terrycloth wristband to dab at the perspiration on her brow as they sat facing each other cross-legged on the polished hardwood floor where they had just completed their warm-up routine. The two women had not spoken of the unfortunate incident of a few nights ago, and Susan had been dying of curiosity.

"So, darling, need I ask how things have been going at your house since our little get-together the other night? Has Jack said anything about leaving so abruptly like that?"

Beverly worked at concealing her annoyance at the mention of the fiasco, but fully expected Susan to compare notes and bring it up at the first opportunity. "We've hardly spoken two words to each other. But it had to be because of Ted."

Bev casually returned the hungry glares they were getting from some of the young men through the Plexiglas partition across the room that separated the exercise floor from the workout machines. She shot a disapproving frown their way and turned her attention back to Susan.

"You seemed to be getting along just fine with Jack after that little disagreement you had," Bev said, not wanting to dwell on why Jack had left without so much as a word. She was well aware of how Susan and Jack had taken to each other from the beginning, and recalled that she had felt envious at the time. Their love spat had unnerved her at first until she realized that it was just a game. Susan was a strong-willed woman, but knew how to please a man, to feed their ego, making them feel like they were in charge when they were really doing exactly what she wanted them to do.

"Jack's never done that sort of thing with me," Bev offered, casually, when in fact she found it curious—even disturbing. However, when she thought about it, he had never needed to.

"You mean our little love spat," she grinned. "Well, it was marvelous, darling. Wonderful, in fact. He's such a sweetheart and it was so much fun. Of course, he's so strong and handsome. But Ted's never been forceful like that with me either. I think I probably dominate him a little too much for that." She gave the younger woman a knowing glance. "Then there was that little trick of Jack's that really helped."

"Umm, I noticed. But that's pretty hard to do when you're on all fours," Beverly said defensively, yet there was no need. "That's when he just got up and walked out."

"Well, it certainly helped." Susan smiled thinly. "It still took me a while. But it was number four by that time. Maybe that had something to do with it." Her tiny smile was seductively and she saw Bev's brow hike up.

"Is that some kind of record?" Bev asked, curiously.

"I'm not sure, darling, but it could be. We were setting all kinds of records the other night. I wasn't sure how the other part was going to work, though … the voyeur thingy, with the four of us. But it was lovely. Exciting really, like old times, performing to an audience like that." She demurely patted her hair into place. "In my day they weren't making pornos like they do now, or I might have tried it," she giggled at the less than modest suggestion. "But you were a sight with Teddy in the hot tub. Some of the yummy sounds you were making, darling, I've never heard before."

"It's hard to remember … with him … that part's a blur." She brushed back a tiny flick of embarrassment. In reality, she had no control over what she said with Ted. Her emotions came rushing over her, wiping everything from her mind, her body taking control until it had passed.

Susan clasped her fingers at the nape of her neck, arched her back and began to stretch the kinks out of her shoulders. She barely noticed the gawking admirers across the room suck in their collective breath as her breasts pressed hard against the thin fabric of her T-shirt, almost to the breaking point.

"Well, darling, I think Jack liked it too. At least he seemed to. Are you sure he didn't say something about why he left in such a huff?"

"No, not a word," Beverly said and glared back at the group of young men that had grown larger then just a few minutes ago and the testosterone-laced looks they were sending their way.

Susan followed her gaze and noticed. "Are those naughty boys glaring at us again?" It was a weekly occurrence and she smiled sweetly in their direction, twiddled her fingers at them and saw several in the crowd wave back just as a wicked thought came over her. "Why don't we give the horny little darlings something to go home and masturbate about tonight, darling?"

Beverly's brow instantly knitted and she glanced at her suspiciously, but not surprised by any means. "You mean …?" But she knew what she meant as both hands automatically went to the hem of her cut-off jersey. It was just like her. Susan had always been outrageous.

"Of course, darling. That's exactly what I mean." Her grin was playfully mischievous. "It seems so selfish to keep all the goodies boys like so much to our selves and not give them the tiniest peek, don't you think? They have to be dying of curiosity. Don't ask me why, but they seem to go crazy over a woman's breasts."

"You wouldn't … not really … not here!" Bev challenged, looking around, but Susan had already hooked her fingers under the bottom of her T-shirt and bra.

"I will if you will, darling."

"You wouldn't dare!" Bev gulped with a huge grin, but hooked her fingers under her shirt and bra just in case.

The instant the unspoken agreement flashed between them, the two women were on their knees and facing the peanut gallery across the room. Glancing at each other, they both counted down: "One … two … three!" and simultaneously hiked everything up under their chin, baring their breasts to the hoops and hollers and the instant uproar of applause.

Susan pooched her lips at the applause and shook her slender shoulders, causing her heavy breasts to sway seductively from side to side. Grinning broadly, Bev followed suit. There just wasn't quite as much sway.

It was only a few seconds until the two women turned away from the wolf-whistling crowd—which was prolonged when Susan had some difficulty tucking her right breast back to her halter— acting casual as if nothing had happened.

When Susan finally had everything safely back in place and had smoothed down the front of her skimpy T-shirt, she said, "That should keep the horny little bastards for a while. Anyway, darling, where were we?" She adjusted a twisted bra strap and gave a modest tug to the bottom of her shirt. "Oh yes, Jack, and the reason he left the other night."

Bev thought for a moment, taking herself back to the distasteful memory of that night. "I suppose I need the name of that doctor friend of yours in Beverley Hills, the nip-and-tuck guy."

Susan gave her a curious look and noticed some of the other women in the class, who must have witnessed their display of feminine superiority, staring at them. She tossed off a demure smile in their direction for their trouble. "I know you think he left because of Ted, the changes he makes in a girl, but I'm not so sure that was the reason, darling."

Beverly's eyes narrowed when she noticed the change in Susan's voice that was also showing up in her face now. "After the hot tub, I'm sure Jack felt … well, *lost,* is probably a good word for it. He even said something to that effect before he left in such a huff."

"He may have, darling," Susan said thoughtfully. "But the doctor thingy doesn't last that long with Ted around. He just screws things up all over again." Beverly's brow arched at the pun. "I know, I know," Susan said. "But it's worth it, right?"

Then, resting her chin on a raised knee, Sue struggled with her next thought. "Let me ask you a question, dear," she started slowly, choosing her words. "You've been with Ted a few times, enough to know that, well, what it's like when he—at the end, I mean, when it's over." She saw the blank look on her friend's face. "What I'm trying to say is … actually, darling, he's something like a fire hose going off. Wouldn't you agree? I think it might have something to do with his over-sized testicles." She grinned. "Which sort of goes along with the rest of it, right?" She shifted her tush on the hard floor to get more comfortable. Then a sudden thought caused her to smile. "I'll let you in on a little secret, but you have to swear never to tell a soul."

Beverly looked wounded at her lack of confidence. "Of course! My God, Sue, we're best friends! What?"

The beginnings of an impish grin crossed Susan's face, and she looked around, though there was no one close enough to hear them. "I used to save it, darling, in the fridge—there's so much of it—and use it as a facial. It's marvelous for the complexion. Acts like an astringent to tighten up the skin. You should try it sometime. It's a hormonal thingy, I'm sure." Susan's expression changed back to a grin following her confession. "And the aroma is so yummy when it warms up. My God, it's enough to make you horny, darling." She whispered the last part and glanced around again, but the rest of the class was milling around, chatting, drinking water, and glaring back at the bodybuilders before their next session began.

"Sometimes Ted would come home and I'd jump his bones right there in the living room the minute he walked in the door. He could never figure out why. He accused me of watching too many soap operas. He never suspected it was actually because of the facial. And I never told him." Susan sniggered while Bev gulped in surprise. They both laughed aloud.

"So, what's the point?" Beverly said when they settled down. "Because Jack isn't anything like that."

"Of course, darling, I know that—now." She said casually, savoring the memory of him and feeling slightly possessive. "I hope this isn't too indelicate of me, dear, but you must have noticed that when you've been with Ted—like that, I mean doing sex—you really need to tidy up quite a bit afterward." Her expression sobered slightly once it was out in the open.

A sudden flood of embarrassment gushed over Beverly. "My God, I never thought—"

"Well, it was pretty obvious, even from across the room, darling. But I don't think Ted noticed." Susan hesitated and then said, "I've never seen such a look on anyone before. I wasn't sure if Jack was going to barf all over my Persian rug, you, or kill somebody."

"Or both," Beverly said, shocked at her own incompetence—and stupidity.

The class moved to the canvas-covered portion of the exercise floor where the Pilates instructor began to transform them into human pretzels. Beverly's right leg was folded under her, her knee pointed straight ahead. She was sitting on her right ankle and calf, the bottom of her left foot flat on the canvas, the heel pressed tightly against her upper thigh, knee against her chest. Then, following instructions, after several grueling minutes she grasped her left wrist with the other hand and pulled hard to the right at the same time she twisted her upper torso until her back was at a ninety-degree angle to her hips.

The pain in her left shoulder came on slowly and then rapidly grew in intensity, until she suddenly clutched at what felt like a knife being driven into her upper back. She moaned briefly, her eyes fluttered, then Beverly slithered unconscious onto the floor.

Thirty Eight

everly cautiously slit open one eye and saw that she was lying on a cot in what seemed to be the Pilates instructor's office. She tried to sit up, wincing at the stab of pain in her left shoulder, but Susan and another heavy-set woman from the class held her down. "I wouldn't try to move just yet," the instructor said. She was standing at her desk on hold with the paramedics. "Can you tell us what happened, Bev? Why you fainted?"

Beverly took in the room to get her bearings and tried to relax. "I'm—I'm really not sure. How long was I ...?"

"Just a few minutes, darling." It was Susan at her elbow. "Long enough for us to get you in here and call for an ambulance. She's on the phone with them now. No idea what happened?"

Beverly shook her head. "No, I've had this pain in my shoulder, off and on. I didn't think much about it at first; a pulled muscle or something. Don't call anyone. I—I'll be fine."

The instructor looked at her questioningly and glanced at Susan for her input, but Susan just made a funny face and shrugged. She hung up the phone after cancelling the call and gingerly touched

Beverly's left scapula and then the area around the clavicle. "That hurt, Bev?"

Beverly shook her head and sipped the small cup of water Susan handed her. The Pilates instructor, a trim, handsome woman in her forties with muscles, massaged her shoulder and back more aggressively, watching closely for any signs of discomfort, but there was no reaction. "Well, it doesn't appear to be anything serious. While you were twisting your upper body, you may have pinched a nerve, probably the ganglion around C4 or thereabouts. That could have caused you to pass out. But I recommend you see the sports therapist in town just to make sure, if the pain comes back. Maybe even an X-ray. Just to be safe."

"That's a good idea, darling. Even if it stops hurting. Besides, the sports guy is cute," Susan said rather seductively for the early afternoon hour and then added, "I'd show him my ganglion any day," she chortled, while Beverly and the instructor rolled their eyes to the ceiling, expecting nothing less from the flamboyant ex-movie queen who was just living up to her reputation.

"I heard you two were showing off something else during the break," the instructor said, giving both Beverly and Susan a stern look.

"I think the sports guy has a wife and four kids," the other woman from the class said, somewhat taken aback by Susan's off-color remark and obviously did not know her nearly as well as the other two women did.

Susan gave her a "So what?" look, shrugged her narrow shoulders and donned an innocent face for the Pilates instructor. "We were just sharing the wealth," she said, and watched as she rolled her eyes skyward again, then turned her attention back to her friend. Beverly slowly sat up and after a moment, cautiously got to her feet, testing her balance. She felt fine, but held on to Susan just in case.

"Walk me to the car?"

Thirty Nine

The two women sat in Beverly's SUV in the parking lot in front of the gym. "Sure you're okay to drive, darling?" Susan asked.

"I'm fine." Beverly rubbed the left side of her neck and shoulder, testing it, but there was no discomfort. "I have no idea what that was all about, but after I drop you off I think I'll run home and jump into a hot bath for a good long soak."

Beverly fished out her car keys, and a few minutes later, they pulled up in front of Susan's place. Somehow, it looked different after the other night, in spite of the many times she had been there. But it seemed like everything was different—her whole life had changed almost overnight. She had purposely stopped short of the side gate in case Ted was home. He would want to talk, and she did not feel like coping—even with Ted.

Susan opened her door and started to get out. "Call me if you need anything, darling?"

"Promise," Beverly said and touched Susan's shoulder with a silent *Thank you*. "I'm sorry about the other night, the way things turned out."

"I'd been wanting to ask you about that, but thought it best to wait until we saw each other. Of course, Ted wants us to get together again. He's been after me to call for days."

Beverly smiled thinly, her embarrassment partially returning. "It's a little awkward even talking about it. I'm not sure I can even face him again. Of course, I had no idea until now, when you told me what happened. It's actually mortifying."

"Oh, don't be silly, darling," Susan commiserated dolefully. "But you know how gushy the big galoot is. And I guess it was just more than Jack could handle, on top of seeing the two of you together for the first time. For that matter, I thought he was going to get up leave when we were watching you in the hot tub. That's why I whisked him inside."

"Was there, umm, very …?" The corner of her upper lip curled, disliking the thought.

"Gobs, darling. Trust me," Susan said before she could finish, imagining how she must feel. "You'd just been with him, of course. And we hadn't been that cozy in a long time, so he had to be loaded for bear." She grinned and added, "More than enough for a good facial." Susan noticed an odd expression glaze over Bev's face.

Beverly saw the "big sister" look Susan was giving her that was all mixed up with her perverse sense of humor, and she hoped it wasn't revenge staring back at her. "I assumed it was because of Ted," she said, "but not for the same reason. Anyway, Jack has been sleeping in the guest room. And that's only made things worse."

"Do you care?"

"I don't know. I'm not sure. I thought there was a chance the other night. It felt good at first, comfortable, to be with him. But watching you and Ted … it was so breathtaking."

Susan thought for a moment. They were so much alike in many respects; she knew exactly what she meant. "You seemed to be okay with us too, darling … you and me. I even thought perhaps …" But she hesitated to bring up that part of the evening even though it had been on her mind.

Beverly held her gaze long enough for Susan to understand the seriousness of what she was about to say. "I was surprised, too. You surprised me. I guess it's true that there's a first time for everything."

Susan did something she did not do very often, and gave her friend a guilty smile before reaching over to kiss her on the cheek. "I guess you could tell it wasn't the first time I've thought about you ... about us ..."

Beverly looked away, a slight rush of embarrassment coming over her but a trace of shame that she might have expected, and then turned back. "You said you weren't into that sort of thing."

Susan's eyes pooled with a nod. "And I'm not, darling, not at all. I guess I don't think of you—of us—like that. My God, I've always believed in 'live and let live,' so long as it doesn't hurt anyone else. And we're certainly different, you and I, but we're both very feminine. Don't you agree, darling?"

Bev nodded thoughtfully. "If you don't mind me asking, have there been other women in you life ... like that?"

"God, no ..." The older woman held her gaze, as if to reassure her and shook her head. "No, not like that, darling. I don't know what it is. There's just something about you, from the time we first met." Then suddenly a grin swept over her again, her bubbly personality returning. "That big butt of yours is fabulous. And I wish my boobies stood up like yours. I don't know what to say. I guess I've fallen in love with both you and Jack."

Beverly matched the plaintive look on her face, her own less troubled and wondered why she had only recently come to realize that there was also something special about Susan and Ted. Putting the thought aside for the moment, she said, "Wasn't that the purpose of this whole thing? What we started out to do?" She gently touched Susan's cheek, her fingers tracing the smooth outline of her jaw.

"And for the record, you're pretty well put together yourself, *darling*. But I think I'm a little jealous. Your boobies are bigger than mine."

Susan stifled a grateful giggle. "Is that what you like about me the most, darling, my boobies, now that there are no more secrets between us?"

Beverly recognized her friend's considerable ego was beginning to shine through, and acted as if she had to think about her answer. "Yes, but everything else too, actually," she said at last. "Most of all, I can't get over how tiny you are without your clothes on, except for … well, where it counts, of course. No wonder you had half the men in Hollywood chasing after you."

"Oh, my goodness," Susan gulped in appreciation, "that's so sweet, darling," she said, batting her large grey eyes with an exaggerated sigh, her insecurity completely assuaged. Then she paused with another thought. "I still don't know what I'm going to do with Ted. He's getting cranky, wanting me to call you."

"I don't know," Bev said with a puff of uncertainty. "I'm not sure what's going to happen after the other night." She took Sue's hand in hers and looked to her for help. "Unless …"

Some of the awkwardness went out of Susan with the look. "Unless what, daring? You can tell Susan." However, Beverly's sheepish grin told her it wasn't as serious as she thought.

"I was just thinking, maybe it's you I've been missing these past few days."

Susan raised a wary brow, wondering if she was reading her correctly. "Do we need to talk about this, darling? Just between us girls over lunch?"

Beverly smiled weakly. "Let's see how it goes. I'll call, okay? Maybe tomorrow."

"And what about the four of us? As I said, Ted's been after me, and I certainly won't let him call."

Beverly shrugged. "I don't think Jack will come over again."

"Well, you never thought he'd come the first time either. But that's no reason to ruin it for everyone, darling—whatever the rules are. Maybe he'll be willing to give it another try if he can go first this time," Susan teased with a wink. "In fact, if you're sure you're up for it, what's wrong with tonight? I've got to close up shop later, but I shouldn't be late."

Beverly thought for a moment and then shrugged. "I'm fine, really. I don't know what the fainting business was about. But I haven't been eating very well the last few days. No appetite. It could just be low blood sugar or something simple like that. And I *am* going stir-crazy. I'm not sure how much fun I'll be, but I do need to get out."

Susan knew her well enough to be worried. "You know you can always come over here if you need a place to stay, or just to get away for a while, darling," she offered.

Beverly smiled, but it was not a happy one. "I know, but Jack would just think we were carrying on behind his back if I came over without him. And I can just hear all the gossip if someone found out I stayed over—alone."

"Oh, screw the gossip," Susan said flippantly, long use to dealing with wagging Hollywood tongues and grinned just the same. "Then tonight sounds good?"

"Why not?" Beverly said, finally making up her mind. She wasn't sure how Jack would react if she came alone, but that was his choice. And he knew the rules as well as she did. "Are you and Ted still getting along?"

"He's been a dear. Hell on wheels, actually. All I have to do is look at him sideways or touch him below the neck, and he's all over me." Susan giggled with satisfaction.

"Good for you. At least some good's come out of all this."

"Make it in time for cocktails, darling. And be sure to call me after you tell Jack," Susan said, getting out of the car. Then she glanced back at her friend with a smirky look before closing the door. "Ted will be tickled pink. If Jack doesn't show up, this might

be a good time for us to gang up on him, show him who is boss."
She had already began to think about what she would do if Jack
refused to come back.

"Screw his balls off, you mean?" Beverly said, haughtily.

"Screw him flat, darling." Susan giggled. She loved being
naughty.

The
Second Chance

Fourty

The door chimes at the gray and white Cape Cod on the hill overlooking the bay were programmed to play the eight most famous musical notes ever written, the opening stanza of Ludwig von Beethoven's Fifth Symphony in C minor:

Da-da-da-dahhh! Da-da-da-dahhh!

She'd been listening to the damned thing for the past five minutes and it was beginning to irritate her as she rang the bell again. She did not particularly care for the melody in the first place, nevertheless she had been to the house enough to know there was no Jerome Kern on the contraption, or Gershwin, both of whom she adored. She shaded her eyes and tried to peer through the beveled-glass side windows of the entryway. She had come straight from work after Beverly called to tell her that Jack would not be coming tonight, but there was nothing moving inside, and she began to wonder if he was home. She wasn't sure what to do if he was, except try to talk some sense into that thick skull of his. Then a small grin accompanied an appealing thought that came over her.

There was something else she could do ...

Jack peeked through the drapes in the study and saw Susan Davenport standing on the front porch among the potted plants, impatiently waiting. And after the tenth ring or so, which was beginning to irritate him, it was obvious that she was not going away. Reluctantly, he stepped into the entry and went to the front door, not sure of what was showing in his face, only that it wasn't friendly.

"Susan? Hi—!" he said, putting on a face of mock surprise, purposely blocking the doorway with his hunky frame. "What's up?" Any fool could tell by the look of him and his tone that he was not happy to see her. He was barefoot, in a pair of faded jeans and an Old Navy polo, which also happened to be navy.

"Well, darling, it's about time," she huffed and tried to move past him, but he did not budge. She looked up. "Well—? Are you going to let me in or just stand there all night?" she said impatiently, undeterred by his lack of manners, or his tone, or the marginal scowl he was wearing, but liking the sight of him just the same. "I've been standing out here for ten minutes listening to that damned 'Da-da-da-dahhh' doorbell of yours. And I need a glass of wine and to use the potty."

Before she left work, Susan had taken the rhinestone clips out of her hair, allowing the long curls to fall over her shoulders and frame her face, making her look ten years younger. She was wearing a soft pink, long-sleeve, silk blouse and a beige gabardine skirt that was snug but showed off the reasons she went to Pilates' regularly.

He glanced at her car in the driveway, relieved to see that she was alone. "Susan, I'm really not in the mood—"

"Jack Edwards," she interrupted sharply, "you stop acting like a spoiled child this minute! And let me in the house before I wet my pants. We have to talk." She pushed her way past him in such a huff that Jack was forced to step aside with an obvious sigh of displeasure. She made straight for the elegantly decorated powder room just off the full-size bar done in beautiful cherry wood and leaded-glass cabinetry.

"Where's that drooly dog of yours?"

"Out! And she doesn't know she's a dog, so please don't say that in front of her."

"Good! I don't need her slobbering all over me."

"That's because she likes you. And she doesn't slobber—just drools a little." He stuck out his tongue at her retreating back like a spoiled child.

"Whatever. I'll have Cabernet, darling!" she called out over her shoulder. "And none of the cheap stuff."

Jack stabbed his middle finger in the air just as she disappeared around the corner of the bar.

When Susan settled into one of the comfortable bergère armchairs that flanked the fireplace where Jack had set her wine on the leather-topped lamp table, she took a fortifying sip. He slouched on the sofa across from her, purposely placing the large coffee table between them, waiting for the lecture he knew she was bent on delivering.

"I'm sure you can guess why I'm here, darling," she began by trying to read his mind, as she often did, but it wasn't hard this time. His dark mood and what he must know she was there to discuss were written all over him.

"For some strange reason I'll bet it has everything to do with sex," Jack said, too acerbically for the way he really felt, about Susan anyway. He was irritable and he did not mean to take it out on her, but was surprised he could be civil at all after the last few days.

"Don't be a smarty pants. And how boring would life be without sex, darling?" She smiled and sipped her wine again, the smooth, deep-purple liquid warming her. "Once you've looked after all the little necessities of life," she waved her hand at the expensive formal living room they were in, "there's nothing left except tasty food, good wine and great sex. And if you care at all about your figure, you can't eat and drink all the time. On the other hand, there's no limit to how much sex you can have, darling." She raised her glass in a toast, noticing that the crystal was probably as expensive as the wine. "In fact, from a dietary point of view, the more the better," she smiled sweetly. "I read somewhere that a good orgasm is worth about 160 calories if you do it right."

His brow rose, questioning her, but not really. It was his surprise at her grasp of trivia more than anything else. Susan sipped her wine again, pleased with herself.

"Very tasty," she said and then got right to the point. "While we're on the subject of sex, if you want to kiss and make up, darling, I can be out of my things in a New York minute. I've missed you." She smiled and stared at him invitingly until a small grin creased his otherwise stoic features.

Jack tried to dismiss the naked vision of her that popped into his head and pushed it aside. "So, what can I do for you? I thought you and Ted were seeing Bev at your place tonight." He could not help notice how attractive she was or how she was used to getting her own way all the time, especially with men.

Susan stood up, crossed over to the sofa and practically threw herself at him, kissing him urgently on the mouth. He could feel her breasts pressing into him, liked the flavor of her lipstick, and did not resist. But he wasn't helping either.

Susan finally pulled back to look him in the eye. "I've missed you, darling," she said again, more seriously this time. "Bev said she told you about tonight and that you weren't interested."

Jack suppressed the urge to touch her somewhere personal, knowing what it would lead to, and settled for resting his hand on her exposed thigh where her skirt had hiked up. "I enjoyed the other night ... mostly," he said. "But it just isn't working out for me."

Susan knew he would never mention the reason he had left so abruptly a few nights ago, but she was not ready to give up either. "I really don't think you gave it a chance, darling. Everything was lovely, but this sort of thing takes time, some getting used to, not to mention a bit of finesse when you think about what we're dealing with here. It's like getting married all over again. Once we get past the honeymoon stage, I think we'll all be just fine. We just need a little more practice, is all."

Susan paused for a moment, and then went on. "What happened wasn't really anyone's fault. It's just part of the learning process we're going though. All I'm asking is that you give it another try. We're all new at this." Susan pursed her lips in concession at the look he shot her. "I mean the foursome thingy, darling. I've had the tiniest bit of experience, but certainly not anything like this. Ted and I love you and Bev to pieces, and I haven't been able to stop thinking about you, darling." She grinned broadly this time. "And since I'm supposed to be the resident expert here, I should have known better, maybe even said something to Bev, cautioned her. Ted's always been like a fire hose. The poor dear was mortified when I told her."

He gave her a surprised look. Susan shook her head. "She had no idea what happened—why you left. And you refused to talk about it, according to her."

"Well … it certainly wasn't your fault," Jack said. "I guess it really wasn't anyone's fault." He dismissed any further need to explain. Still, he knew it wasn't an apology she was after. What she wanted was the four of them together—tonight.

Susan pressed her fingers to his lips before he could continue. "All I'm asking is that you give it another try, my darling. That's all." She held his gaze, pouting all the while, and then added, "Please? Do it for me. I can't bear the thought of not seeing you naked again." The grin that was slow in coming, finally went dancing across her pretty face. As her large, sparkling gray eyes held his, she swore she could see the windmills of his mind churning away like mad. It was definitely a good sign.

Jack resisted an impulse to discreetly run his hand up under her skirt and take her panties off—providing she was wearing any and if such a thing could be done discreetly—the hem already well up on her thighs. With considerable difficulty, he settled for changing the subject. "So, how are you and the Hulk getting along these days?"

"I hope you don't think this is gross, darling, but lately we've been screwing like crazy every chance we get, and I'm beginning to get used to it again. I'm not objecting, mind you, but it just makes me miss you all the more. And I think he was just the tiniest bit jealous of you the other night." She hooded her eyes, pooched her lips at him and shrugged her slender shoulders, causing her heavy breast to bobble seductively in spite the constraints of the substantial foundation garment it took to contain them.

She studied him openly for a moment. "You know, my darling, there's somewhat of the dark side to you. I can't quite put my finger on it, but it's even a little scary at times. Maybe it's because you carry that awful gun around with you all the time. But I have to admit, it also makes you seem very mysterious … and sexy. Have you ever—like used it, before?"

"Only if someone tries to shoot me first," he said, giving her a sober look.

She flicked an eyebrow at him and wondered if it was true, or if he was just trying to intimidate her. The thought of how he had made her beg for sex a few nights ago flashed though her mind. "Bev and Ted are probably doing it like crazy this very minute, since I'm already over an hour late. And did I mention that I haven't been able to stop thinking about you since we …?" She perked up now and drew closer to him. "Or that I think I've already fallen in love with you, darling?"

"—And with Bev?" he said, sobering slightly.

She looked surprised, but really wasn't. In fact, she had expected him to say something the first time they were alone. The thought of being with Beverly heightened her excitement. "Does that bother you, Jack?" "Do you think—?"

"—Not really," he said, cutting her off. "It's just, I guess didn't realize how close you two were. It was …"

"Exciting—? Watching us, two women—?"

"After I got past the idea, that you and Bev were that friendly. Have you two done that sort of thing before?"

Susan shook her head and could see the signs of the stress he had been under showing up in his face now. "No, darling. Not that I hadn't thought about it. She's so gorgeous and I just love her to death. But nothing ever happened before. It was a complete surprise for both of us. We were just getting undressed and I posed in the nude for her, showing off. We had never had all of our clothes off before, only down to our bra and panties a few times when we were shopping. Anyway, it just happened. The thought of what we were all doing that night, of what we were about to do, was terribly exciting. It just … well, it just felt so natural, and …"

She did not finish the thought and lightly brushed his lips with her own. Then she laughed and began to pat him down. "You're not wearing that awful gun of yours, are you? Do I need to search you, darling—all over?"

They laughed together, what was left of the tension between them finally melting away. The more he came to know Susan, the more she intrigued him. "There is something else," he said evenly, "while we're at it."

"You don't have to tell me. I'll bet I know," Susan said, anticipating his thoughts, impressed at how good she was getting at that lately. "Ted, right? And that log he carries around in his shorts."

Jack flashed a surprised smile at her now. "You do have a way with words, kid. But you have to admit that log is a pretty hard act to follow."

"Then you can imagine what it's like for us girls. Not that it's all bad, mind you, once you get past the shock. In fact, from a female point of view, it's quite an experience, which I'm sure Bev would be happy to share with you if you'd just talk to her. You have to be dying with curiosity about what it's like for her to be with him, the competition thingy men have. God knows, I would be if it were the other way around." She shrugged and flashed a smile at him. "You might even learn something, darling. Ted has a tendency to make some pretty drastic changes in a girl. But I suggest you stop trying to follow him and just be your own, adorable, sexy self. It worked just fine with me."

"I felt like a kid in his father's galoshes. They just didn't fit!"

"That's your ego kicking in again, darling. But I suspect women have been telling men that size doesn't matter since Adam and Eve. And, in a sense, I suppose it's true. But I know someone as unusual as Ted has a way of spoiling things for those who follow. All I can say is that there's a lot more to making love than the physical part. A lot of it is all the other yummy thingies that go with it." She smiled sweetly again. "So, what about it, handsome? Are you willing to give it another try, especially if you can go first?" she teased.

He stared back at her, his expression noncommittal.

"For me, darling?" She pouted, her lower lip pooching out.

"What did you have in mind?" he asked finally, still not giving in, but his expression softened noticeably.

"I have to tell you, darling, that being with you and all this sex talk has made me a little excited," she said, fanning herself with both hands. When she leaned over and kissed him, her lips parted, the invitation obvious. Then she told him exactly what she wanted him to do and how she wanted him to do it. When Jack grinned, she groped his crotch. Encouraged by what she found, Susan gave him a tug and then began to wiggle out of her panties.

"What about Bev and Ted?" he asked. "And the rules?"

"I'm sure they're busy as little beavers as we speak, darling, and have a head start on us," she said, dusting off any intention of obeying the rules. "Will you do that yummy little thingy of yours to me first, dear? I just love that. It makes me *so* hot. That's actually why I went to the powder room, just in case you came to your senses."

Jack laughed aloud this time. "Are you always so confident when it comes to sex … and men? Getting what you want, when, and how you want it? And what made you think I'd even let you in the door, let alone have sex with you?"

Her face lit up. "Because, darling, you like doing it with me as much as I do with you, and you're falling in love with me, too. I can see it in those beautiful green eyes of yours." She lay back on the big sofa, her skirt hiked up over her flat tummy, knees parted wide, when she suddenly thought about what she had said. "You naughty boy," she hissed. "You've got me talking dirty again." She began to giggle when he bent to kiss her there and peered down at him. "Isn't this fun, darling?"

Jack looked down at her half-naked body, the slightest aroma of fresh lilacs causing a surge in him, and began to pull out of his clothes. As he did, he thought curiously how big she was for such a small woman.

And Ted had nothing to do with what he was talking about.

Fourty One

It was dusk and the sun had slowly begun to settle below the distant horizon. When atmospheric conditions were just right and the huge fiery orb of the sun dipped below the crest of the ocean, a brilliant flash of green known as the "emerald effect" lit up the darkening sky. This evening, however, a dense, puffy line of cumulous clouds sitting at the edge of the visible world prevented the phenomenon.

Ted Davenport was near the end of his daily workout of twenty-five laps. His muscular arms pulled his body through the warm water of the lap pool with ease, each powerful stroke launching him ahead by nearly half a body length with surprising speed. When he reached the deep end of the pool, he expertly tucked under and kicked off with such force that he did not resurface until he was nearly a quarter of the way back to the opposite end.

Braless under a top of thin white crepe with matching slacks, Beverly dressed for the occasion and had been watching Ted for the past fifteen minutes from the poolside lounge where she was nursing her martini. When he reached the shallow end of the pool,

Ted propped his elbows up on the coping and shook the water out of his thick mane of silvery hair. His breathing was steady and even, unlabored by the workout, his face filled with delight as he watched Beverly just a few feet away, the outline of her curvy figure obvious through the sheer fabric of the outfit she was wearing.

"How about a swim, kitten?" he called to her. Not only did she arouse him, but when they were together she also had a way of peeling away the years he sometimes felt were catching up with him.

Bev cradled her chin in her palms, and leaned forward on her knees. "Susan should be home any minute. You weren't planning to stay in the pool, I hope. I just had my hair done," she said, reaching for her glass and took another sip of her martini, the Tangueray helping to settle the slight case of nerves she had developed since leaving the house. Jack was in the guest room when she had called out that she was leaving, but there was no reply.

"No, but we could fool around a little until she gets here." Ted grinned at her. He always swam nude in the secluded pool, enjoying the freedom, and he could feel his excitement strengthening.

"Uh-uh!" She wagged a finger at him, smiling at the same time. "You know the rules, at least three of us or nothing at all."

Ted made an uncouth masculine noise in his throat. He also knew that rules were made to be broken, but let it pass. He had just started his daily workout when she arrived, and they had not had a chance to talk. "So, what's with Jack? He looked pretty upset when he left the other night. Susan said it was because of me, something I did, but didn't go on about it."

"It was more like something *we* did," she said, sharing the blame, but not sure there was any blame to be had. "She really didn't tell you?"

"Nope." He shook his head. "Just some girl talk about it being a delicate matter and she needed to discuss it with you. What happened? Did I do something?"

Beverly thought for a moment but knew that no matter how

delicate her answer, it was bound to embarrass both of them. She sobered with a thought that came to mind and sighed audibly. "No, it wasn't anything you did. It's something that just happened, that's all," she said, but saw that she was being too vague. He wasn't making the connection, and she tried again. "What I mean is, when we were in the hot tub ... when we, er—well, afterward ..." She hesitated again and then decided to just go for it. "I guess you could say there was enough left behind to fertilize the entire first and second string of a women's volleyball team, including the water girl."

They both laughed awkwardly, Ted rather intrigued with the idea. When they settled down, he said, "If you're not coming in, why don't you bring me a drink, puss."

Beverly got up, filled one of the martini glasses from the shaker she had prepared when she arrived nearly an hour ago, and took it to him. Ted took a sip, set the glass down carefully on the edge of the pool, and then with a Tanzanian "Whoo-ha!" snatched her up by the wrist before she could get away and pulled her into the pool on top of him. Beverly shrieked and tried to get away, but it was too late.

"Oh, Ted, my hair!" Anticipating the protest, he had managed to hold her head above water, but her linen outfit became instantly transparent as he gathered her into his arms and hungrily kissed her for the first time in nearly a week. Beverly half-struggled, at first trying to break free, then realized it was useless. He was too strong, and her heart was not in it. After a moment, she settled into him, kissing him back, pressing her body hard against his.

They clung to each other until Ted impatiently tugged at her waistband and pulled her out of the thin linen slacks and panties at the same time. When he had them down to her knees, Beverly gave a wiggle, sending them to the bottom. Ted pulled her into him again, forcing himself between her thighs, pinning her to the wall of the pool. She crossed her arms over her head and pulled off her top, tossing the drenched garment over her shoulder toward the lounge and nearly upsetting the martini shaker. Ted caressed her breasts and suckled at the large nipples, lightly scissoring his teeth across each one, causing a catch in her breathing. After a moment, Beverly pulled free, forced his head up, and kissed him. They fondled and touched, aching and withering in the other's arms as they waited for Susan to come home.

Rules were rules.

Fourty Two

The sky had changed from twilight to the softer shades of darkness by the time they were toweled dry, had donned thick terrycloth robes and were seated on the wicker lounge beside the pool where Ted had replenished their drinks.

"How old are you, Bev?"

She glared at him. "None of your business," she said haughtily, caught off guard by the impromptu question that under other circumstance would have been rude. "Why do you want to know?" But she could see from the awkward smile he was wearing, even through the gloom of early evening, that it was not just curiosity.

"Just thought I'd ask. Wondered if maybe you thought I was robbing the cradle. You could be my daughter, you know."

"Well, I'm not your daughter," she said, and nuzzled her face into the crook of his thick neck. "And if that's another way of saying you're old enough to be my father, you can just knock it off." She bit him on the side of his neck hard enough to leave a love mark. "Anyone who thinks that is just plain jealous."

"You don't feel like—that I'm too old for you?" He absently rubbed the place on his neck where she had left the hicky.

The uncertainty in his voice caused her to look up at him. "Teddy, we've been all through this before. I've already told you, no one has ever made me feel the way you do." She straightened to kiss him reassuringly on the lips.

"Then I think we should wait for Susan in the house," Ted said when they parted, and slipped his hand into the gap of her robe. He had been exercising all the restraint he possessed, but was beginning to lose the battle.

Beverly could feel his tension and put her head back. She liked the way he touched her and was sure it showed. "And exactly where in the house did you have in mind?" she said with a coquettish smile, already knowing the answer.

"How about the bedroom?" he said, his grin honest. He was growing impatient waiting for Susan and since Jack would not be there tonight, he was looking forward to being alone with the two women and had been thinking of all sorts of ways to take advantage of his good fortune. He had never been with two women before at the same time. But wasn't that every man's fantasy come true?

"You know better than that," Beverly teased. His groping was making it hard for her to think clearly. "Once you get me on my back, it's all over." Beverly really meant it would be over for *him*—for a while, at least. And what if Susan showed up then? However, she wasn't sure if Susan might be teasing them, since she was already over an hour late. She began to wonder if she might not show up at all now that she and Ted were playing house again. Then, just as suddenly as the thought had come to her, she decided not to worry about it anymore and clutched the part of him that only a few weeks ago had terrified her.

Ted kissed her lightly at first, and then more intensely, forcing her mouth open as wide as it would go. She liked the way he kissed, going halfway down her throat. She had never been kissed like that. His tongue was so long and thick she had gagged the first several times. But now, she opened her mouth as wide as possible, encouraging him. He slowly played the tip of his tongue across the sensitive uvula at the back of her throat. She bit down on the thick base, sucking hard at the same time, preventing any possible retreat. Her temperature kicked up a notch as he went deeper, until she was forced to push him away to catch her breath. He lapped at the mixture of lipstick and saliva on the outside of her mouth before lightly biting her pouty lower lip, his impatience growing by the minute—and becoming more obvious.

Then, as he nibbled on one of her diamond studs, he whispered in her ear, "I didn't realize you could open your mouth so wide, kitten. Makes me wonder if something else might fit. We've never tried that." His breathing quickened with the erotic vision that popped into his head.

Beverly pushed him back again, far enough this time to look him in the eye. The mischief she saw lurking there left no doubt in her mind what he was thinking, and the hungry grin that came over him confirmed it.

"No way, Jose! It won't fit! That's why we haven't tried it," she said, firmly.

"Where have I heard that one before?" His voice was low, seductive, determined. "How can you tell when we haven't tried?"

"Some things you don't have to try," she said sternly. "You just know by looking at it." There was no doubt in her voice, no room for negotiations.

"But how do you really know unless—" he coaxed softly.

"Because anyone with two brain cells to rub together could tell just by looking, that's how," she said and glanced down at what she was holding in both of her hands that seemed to be growing larger by the minute. He was completely breathtaking and already weeping with anticipation.

"That's what you said about the first time," he argued gently with an unmistakable pout in his voice. "You might like it." But he knew there would be no pushing the issue this time, unless, he thought, unless he could persuade her to try. Then—?

The frown already showing in Beverly's serious expression deepened. Still, her pulse had quickened with the challenge. The thought was as intriguing as the idea, and the way he refused to take no for an answer, how he tried to dominate her, making her want to try. And, when she thought about it, he had been right about the first time, opening up a world she had never dreamed possible before.

"I admit I was wrong about the first time," Beverly said finally. "I didn't think it was possible, that I could ..." She paused, but then went on. "You can't blame me." She glanced down again. "It's still hard to believe ..." Just looking at it made her dizzy.

"But you're glad you did?" He was patronizing, still pressing, trying to convince her.

Beverly could feel her resolve slowly begin to soften and lightly touched his face. "Of course, I am, Teddy. I'm just amazed, that's all. Do you have any idea what a challenge you are for a girl?"

Ted grinned and shrugged his broad shoulders like a draft horse freshly out of its traces. "If you really love me, I think we should at least try ... just to see, to be sure."

"I am sure, and I do lov ..." she broke off and realized she could not say the words he wanted to hear. Ted thrilled her beyond words, but she had not said that to anyone in a long time, even to Jack. "Besides, I think I've already proven that. But there's a limit to everything," Beverly said with a sigh. However, when she considered what he was asking, the possibility piqued her competitive interest. Moreover, as a safeguard, she had a full set of healthy teeth on her side of this argument that she would not hesitate to use should the need arise.

Beverly moved closer and nibbled at the crook of his neck. She felt his hand at the back of her head, urging her downward. She resisted the pressure, moving her lips down his chest at her own pace, refusing to be hurried by his lust. She paused over the nub of one flat nipple, taking it into her mouth then biting it hard enough to show that she was in charge this time.

When Ted recovered from the small act of revenge, she continued her descent. But before she had reached the flat of his stomach, Ted had thrust himself upward to meet her pouty lips. She held him in both hands and examined the thin, even scar that ran the entire circumference where he had been neatly circumcised. Curiously, she made several serious calculations, all of which brought her to the same conclusion as before. Unless she could unhinge her jaws like a hungry python, there was no way she could do what he wanted.

Just as she was about to share this with him, Ted thrust his hips upward again and pushed hard at the back of her head at the same time, forcing several inches into her mouth. Surprised, with her cheek resting high on his chest and her lips stretched to the tearing point, the musky aroma and slightly salty taste was pleasantly familiar. She squeezed hard at the base, causing an additional release. Ted felt the surge in his groin and jutted his pelvis upward.

Fourty Three

"*Woof—!*"

The sharp bark came leaping out of Ted like a clap of thunder. He jerked back so quickly that Beverly did not have time to fully release him, causing her teeth to rake painfully across what he had so painfully crammed into her mouth, nearly unhinging her jaws.

When it was obvious that he intended to go even deeper, Beverly had immediately bitten down hard just behind the glans of the monstrous intruder. When she was free of him, she looked up with a crooked smile of revenge and saw the pain etched in his face. "I told you it wouldn't fit," she said, and wiped the traces of residue from her lips on the sleeve of his robe, pleased to see there was no blood on it—his or hers.

"Sorr—rry," Ted mumbled, a belated grimace coming over him. "Just ... checking."

"Hope I didn't leave any teeth marks," Beverly replied, performing a hasty inspection of the entire circumference, satisfied with the results. Two could play at that game, and she was sure he wouldn't try that one again any time soon.

"It … it was worth it just to see—I think," he said when he was able to manage a grin and a cursory examination on his own for any possible damages, but found only the reddish scrape marks her teeth had left.

"I'll bet I'm not the first girl you've tried to bully like that."

"Maybe, but it's been a while." He was still panting lightly with a mixture of incomplete fulfillment and the painful bite she had just given him.

Beverly kissed him lightly on the lips that were still crooked with surprise. Then she placed her hands at the back of his head and began to force him down into her lap where her robe had fallen open. "Your turn, buster," she purred at him. "I want you to look around for my uterus you jarred loose in there the other day."

Ted grinned and bent to kiss the soft flesh of her belly, his shin nuzzling in the thick, dark mound just below. Then, instead of continuing his descent, he scooped her up into his powerful arms, surprised at the effort it took, wondering what she weighed—but knew he could never ask—and started for the house with her head resting doll-like on his shoulder. Susan would either show up or she wouldn't, and at that moment, he didn't much care which.

They could hardly be expected to wait all night.

Ted had stripped off her robe and laid Beverly out in the center of the big king-size bed in the master bedroom. He turned on the bedside lamp that washed the room in a soft glow that accentuated the sensuous curves of her body. Bev's eyes were mere slits when she clutched at the back of his thick, silvery mane, guiding him to exactly where she wanted him to be.

She felt the promise that was building deep inside of her and had caused a prickly sex flesh to creep over her entire body. Breathlessly, she held back, not wanting it to be over. There was no rush and she tried to relax, to bring herself back from the edge.

Then her eyes suddenly flew open when she felt probing fingers tracing the curve of one of her breast.

It was Susan. She was at the edge of the bed bending over her. When she saw the startled look, Susan held a finger to her lips, her eyes flicking toward Ted at the foot of the bed and then back again in silent caution.

"How long have you been …?" Beverly hissed, but broke off unable to contain her surprise. At the sound of her startled voice, Ted tried to raise his head, but she firmly pushed him back down a little too hard, causing her to wince when he bumped the most sensitive part of her body.

Susan carefully settled full-length onto the bed facing her, propping her chin on an elbow. She was still caressing her breast, rolling the hardened nipple between her fingers, when she licked at the opening of Beverly's ear.

"Ohhh, stop that," Beverly complained in a low whisper and tried to push her away with a raised shoulder. "Not you!" She groaned aloud when Ted tried to look up again. When he settled back and had taken up the steady rhythm of a moment ago, Bev gasped softly at the sensation and raised her hips into him. "Oh God …" she moaned softly.

After a moment when she had quelled the impulse, she turned back to Susan. "I've been holding back, trying to wait for you. Where have you been?"

"Nice waiting, darling," Susan said, without sarcasm, and glanced down the length of her naked body to where Ted was making all sorts of yummy noises. "But why are you holding back?" Susan whispered into her damp ear where she had been kissing and licking her, flicking her tongue in and out of the narrow canal. Then she cupped the base of one breast in both of her hands and squeezed firmly, forming it into a large mound of soft pinkish flesh and sucked on the protruding nipple, milking her, drawing it in and out of her mouth.

When Beverly shivered and pulled her off the swollen nipple, Susan licked at the saliva left behind and said, "I've just had the most delightful time with your husband, that's where I've been, darling. I also have some wonderful news." Her voice was as hushed as a church mouse as she fondled the rigid nipple again, prompting yet another shudder from the prostrate woman it belonged to.

Beverly was beginning to feel the delight and the stress of being worked on from both ends and grimaced when Ted nibbled at something that had become far too sensitive for that. She sank back into the pillows when the pleasure-pain sensation had passed and glanced down at Susan, who had gone back to suckling her.

"Could this wait for just a minute, please?" she protested, huskily. "I'm a little busy right now, just in case you hadn't noticed." Both of her hands were clutched at the back of Ted's head, carefully guiding him, pushing him firmly into her this way and that as she slowly rotated her hips. Then Bev closed her eyes and bit her lower lip when she approached the edge of the climax that was about to consume her. But she had already let go of reality, and the look that screwed up in her face proved it.

With growing envy, Susan watched her squirm, her hands clamped full of Ted's long hair as she forcefully squirmed her lower body into him. She fought down a pang of jealousy, and hoped that the good news she had left standing in the doorway was able to do the same, and that he would not bolt again.

Susan kissed her wetly on the mouth, coaxing even more from her, until Beverly sucked in one last deep breath, let it out in a throaty groan, and arched her back for the final time as a rush of ecstasy ratcheted through her body.

The Good Life

Fourty Four

*T*ed felt the trailing edges of the shudder that had coursed through Beverly before she released her hold on him and had collapsed limp and exhausted back on the bed.

He slowly raised his head and was disappointed at what caught his eye just a few steps away. He could not imagine how Susan had managed to get Jack to come back or what she had done to accomplish it. He was less surprised to see his wife standing beside the bed, peeling out of the outfit she had worn to work that morning.

Susan caught his eye, smiled demurely, and winked. She had already slipped out of her skirt and panties, and when she had removed her blouse, she gave a perky nod toward the bedroom door and the trophy she had brought with her. Ted also noticed the red flush that was awash in Beverly's face, spilling down into her chest and coloring the tops of her slackened breasts. She had turned onto her side, her long legs curled, her chin resting in her palm as she glared at her best friend and her husband.

Beverly's gaze darted between Susan and Jack. She was already practically naked, and he was standing there with a dull look on his face. She did not have to guess what Susan had done to get him back. She and Jack had hardly spoken in days, though she had tried to bring up what happened that night, but he had refused to discuss it. She finally stopped trying and had mentally written him off—again. He had moved into the guest room after that, and she did not care.

"Are you just going to stand there all night, darling?" Susan said to Jack as she moved toward him, her voice lilting, yet unable to completely mask her anticipation. She had already stripped down to just her bra and began to fumble with his trousers. Jack slowly pulled his shirt off as she unfastened his jeans, letting them fall. He was not wearing underwear. The last she had seen his boxers they were under the coffee table at his house. Jack looked uncomfortably exposed and rigid by the time she finished.

Susan turned her back to him, bent forward from the waist, holding her long silky hair off her neck and glanced at him over her shoulder. "Do you mind, darling?" Jack did his best to ignore the angry daggers Beverly was shooting their way and noticed the expectant grin on Susan's face. "Please," she added coyly.

He fumbled with the sturdy three-pronged clasp on her bra for a moment before he had them unhooked and her heavy breasts came loose, her nipples already firm, the brownish areolas beginning to shrivel, yet still large. Stripped naked, she tossed her bra on the bedside chair with the rest of her things and turned back to face him, pressing her petite body into his. She kissed him lightly, one shapely leg bent at the knee in a feminine gesture. After moment, Susan drew back, took him by the hand and led him to the bed where Beverly had been watching them with an aloofness that Jack had come to know well lately.

"Isn't this lovely, my darlings? Being all together again—and naked," Susan said brightly, her chirpy voice tingling with excitement, her hips swaying with a tantalizing bounce as she moved. She looked diminutive standing next to Jack, who towered over her, her breast dancing as they cascaded sensually before her, inviting, tantalizing. She gently nudged him toward the bed.

"We need to make sure we get off on the right foot this time, darling." Her voice had turned soft and reassuring now, yet still projecting the quality of leadership she'd assumed from the beginning. She glanced at Jack and patted the bed beside his wife. He sat stiffly. "Now—I need you both to listen to me." Then she turned to Bev, for whom the coming lecture was actually meant. "Jack and I have just had the most lovely time together, darling. Now it's your turn. I want you two to kiss and make up right this minute." When no one moved she added, "Isn't that so, Teddy?"

"Hmm—ah—yes, yes, of course, my dear." Ted hemmed and hawed briefly, trying to rearrange the possibilities in his mind now that Jack was back, and had not really been paying that much attention. He had, however, been staring lustfully at Beverly who was sprawled naked before him. She had left him greatly excited and he was disappointed that he would not be alone with the two women tonight as anticipated, but not sure it mattered as long as something else didn't go wrong and put an end to it all—again.

No one moved in the deafening silence followed. Ted held his breath for a moment, curious to see what would happen next. Jack was fixated on his wife, her sloping breast, the curve of her raised hip accentuating her slim waist. The scorched expression she was wearing was made even more intimidating by the lipstick smeared around her downturned mouth. The first thought that came into his mind seemed impossible. Beverly glared at him defiantly, her dark eyes turned black as night.

Ted sensed the tension between them. Fearful of what it might lead to said, "Jack, old buddy, good to have you back." His deep baritone voice broke the silence like a foghorn at midnight. He was sitting upright at the foot of the bed now trying to conceal his excitement that Beverly had just taken to new heights. Jack merely blinked a nod in his direction. His eyes darted back to the bed, resentful of what Ted was attempting to hide, yet envious at the pleasure it brought his wife.

Susan gave Jack another nudge toward Beverly who was deeply flushed now, looked as if she were experiencing equal parts of embarrassment and annoyance when she noticed him standing in the doorway, and that he had been watching while Ted rung a deep groaning orgasm out of her.

Grudgingly, Jack settled in closer but not close enough to suit Susan. Using both hands this time, she scooted him over even further. Again, Jack obeyed until their bodies were lightly touching. When Bev just continued to glare at him, he lay down beside her, propping himself up on the opposite elbow, their lips only inches apart. The pungent mixture of her warm breath and Chanel caused a surprising throb in him as he noticed her smudged lipstick again.

Good God! he thought, had she actually tried—? But that was impossible.

Jack glanced at Ted again for the evidence that would corroborate his suspicions. Their eyes met over the battleground of Beverly's naked body and he noticed there were no lipstick smudges on his face, but were clearly visible on what he was doing his best to conceal. Jack's only consolation was the angry welted teeth marks that accompanied them.

Beverly was still glaring at him when Susan spoke to her in a sisterly tone of voice. "Now, darling, Jack has admitted that he overreacted the other night. He's sorry about that, swallowed his pride, and he's come back. Let's put all of that unpleasantness behind us, shall we? We all love each other here, and I think it's time we started showing it."

"I'll vote for that." It was Ted, of course, his ubiquitous, if somewhat juvenile, sense of humor cropping up again. With Beverly's back to him and her long legs tucked up to her chest, he could see the tail of the small tattooed pussycat she had on her inner thigh, its namesake looming dark and pouty just above. With the taste of her lingering at the back of his throat, the brooding thing seemed to beckon to him. Ted forced himself to look away before he gave in to an urge that had suddenly come over him to touch her there. With the tension in the room as thick and heavy as a London fog, he knew it would give her a start and God only knew what else, possibly putting an abrupt end to yet another evening.

This time it would unquestionably be his fault.

And this time Susan would definitely cut his balls off.

"Teddy, you just sit there and behave!" she sniped, sensing they were at a critical turning point in the evening and knowing the mischief he was capable of. She gave him her version of the *stink eye* as a back up, a putrid look she learned from her mother and had used it on him to her great advantage in the past. She knew that Ted's stupidity was occasionally as huge as the totem he was so proud of. After the effort it had taken to get Jack to come back, she certainly did not need him screwing things up—again. When she was cautiously satisfied with the contrite look that belatedly settled over him, she turned back to the younger couple and noticed Beverly was glaring accusatory daggers at her.

"What—?" Susan said innocently.

"Did you have to screw him again to get him back—*darling?* You seemed to like that."

Fourty Five

The sarcasm cracked like a bullwhip. "You can bet your sweet bippy on it, *darling*," she groused back, and tossed off a quick smile toward Jack. "And I did him good, too." This was said as a matter of pride, and given as coolly as she had taken.

"You couldn't get enough of him the other night." Beverly's voice was icy cold and flat, unmistakably patronizing, and totally opposite from the way she had felt earlier that afternoon. "And what about the rules?" she added for good measure.

In truth, Beverly was shocked to see Jack standing in the doorway when she had practically begged him earlier in the day to come with her tonight. His presence had set off a flood of emotion in her, and a strong sense of competition she couldn't account for. For the second time, Susan was able to bend him to her will, and obviously exerted a strong influence over him that she no longer could. It torched a fire in her that she had never felt in all the years they had been married. Then the reason for the sinking feeling she had suddenly broke through her disquiet and became obvious.

Beverly Edwards was jealous.

The green-eyed monster was alive and well.

"I know about the rules, darling. I made them up, if you recall," Susan countered, glaring up and down at her spread out on the bed as if she were the "Queen of fucking Sheba" with Ted curled up at her feet like a diminutive sex-crazed sphinx. "I had to do something to get him to listen to reason."

Jack noticed they were talking about him as if he weren't there. He also noticed the serious scowl that had screwed up in the faces of both women as they fought over him. He toyed with the idea of simply leaving again to eliminate the problem, just walking out as he had before. But the situation tickled him and was starting to get interesting, and he actually wondered if one of them might not leave instead.

Susan took a moment to control her temper before she spoiled everything. She happily realized that Bev's little display of jealousy was proof-positive that she still had feelings for Jack. She knew exactly what the woman was feeling and that the "monster" had just mauled her up one side and down the other.

Susan cleared her throat without trying to hide it and softened her voice as she returned to her self-appointed role of leadership. "All right, let's stop all this nonsense, my darlings. I want you two to kiss and make up," she ordered before Beverly could challenge her again, her voice matronly this time, still in charge, but much more friendly. "And do any of those other lovely thingies you might feel like doing while you're at it." Then her expression softened even more and she wrinkled her nose and wiggled her fingers at them—French manicure perfect—coaxing them even closer.

Jack cautiously watched Bev's eyes narrow when she shifted her gaze and stared at him. He knew the look, and that it would be up to him to break the ice and said, "I came back because of you, kid. I wanted to be with you. So, how about it? Want to play house?" His voice was soft, casual and repentant at the same time.

Bev continued to glare at him. It was her pride again, or whatever it was that brought out the stubbornness in her; her Irish-German heritage, no doubt. However, the longer she glared at him the more she realized that they were all adults and acting as if they didn't know why they were there or what to do next. The thought struck her as so absurd that she couldn't keep the makings of a smile from creeping into her otherwise serious face.

Jack saw it immediately and had his answer. He also noticed that she did not glance at Ted this time for permission as she had the other night when they had changed partners. He was not sure why, but that had fried his ass almost as much as watching them together.

Susan had also caught the look on Beverly's face, and flushing every negative thought she'd just had out of mind, gave Jack an encouraging pat on the butt to urge him on. When he moved closer to Bev, she said, "Oh, that's much better, darling. And now I want you two to give each other a big fat kiss, say you're sorry, and take up where we left off the other night while Teddy and I sit back and enjoy." She giggled, and then added, "Oh my goodness, this is so sexy, all of us together again."

Susan scooted to the foot of the bed and cuddled up against her husband. Jack lightly kissed the tip of Beverly's rather straight Roman nose. Her eyes blinked closed, expecting more. He gave it to her. Her soft lips parted willingly, encouraging him. He fondled her soft breasts, gently teasing the nipples until they were firm as sand pebbles, his fingertips tingling with long familiarity.

Beverly rested her head on his shoulder, ran her hand down the length of his body and cradled his arousal with curiosity. She had always thought of him as above average, but now was sure of it.

Jack rolled her over onto her stomach, gently pulled her up by the hips until she was on all fours, and effortlessly pressed himself into her. He was hard and compelling, and she began to quiver with the effort.

After several long moments, surprised at the depths he was now able to reach, Beverly grimaced and then whimpered softly.

Knowing what had just happened, he bent to kiss the back of her neck and moved his legs to the outside of hers, squeezing her thighs tightly together. Moments later, he felt another familiar shudder overtake her, small but noticeable nonetheless.

Before she could finish, Jack slowly rolled her onto her back, hooked her legs over his shoulders, and began again, this time reaching places he had never been before. His orgasm was sudden and electrifying; Beverly's continuing deep inside of her—feeling like it would last forever.

By the time Beverly and Jack recovered enough to notice, Ted had already collapsed heavily onto his side, drained and spent, half of his body still partially over the top of Susan. Susan raised her head, peering over his bulk and saw the knowing smiles beaming at her from the other side of the bed. She merrily twiddled her fingers at them and grinned back at the pair of happy, sex-glazed faces.

"My goodness, you two look like you did more than just kiss and make up. I told you it would get better once we worked out all the little thingies," she said brightly.

Then, assuming the leadership roll that she had done so well with the past few weeks, Susan began to wiggle out from under her husband, who outweighed her by nearly a hundred pounds. "And now, my darlings, it's time to change partners and start all over again!"

Ted moaned laboriously. He was definitely getting too old for all of this kid stuff.

Jack groaned less noticeably and thought—*Maybe?*

Beverly sighed, very satisfied and contented. All she had to do was show up.

Susan laughed to herself at the happy sight.

Men were such little boys, she thought, and so easy to understand if you just know how to enjoy them.

Life was lovely.